Heavens,

Before she could gather her
over her with insolent thoroughness.

"You're very lovely, but I don't recall asking for your business."

Phoebe gasped at the man's effrontery. Her hands balled into fists, but she strove to control her temper.

So this was the great Gabriel Cutter. The same man who had decided to deny the mail-order brides their rightful passage on his train.

Her anger seethed anew.

"It is *I* who has business with you, Mr. Cutter."

He didn't seem impressed by her statement. Instead, he began circling her, scrutinizing every inch of her frame in a way that reminded her of a hungry lion she'd once seen being fed at the London Zoo.

* * *

The Other Bride

Harlequin Historical #658—May 2003

Praise for Lisa Bingham

"Lisa Bingham breathes life into your wildest fantasies!"
—*Romantic Times*

"Lisa Bingham captures perfectly the spirit of late nineteenth-century America."
—*Affaire de Coeur*

"Her characters are delightful, full of dimension and individuality and make you laugh, cry and leave you sleepless while you try to read just one more page."
—*Affaire de Coeur*

THE OTHER BRIDE

LISA BINGHAM

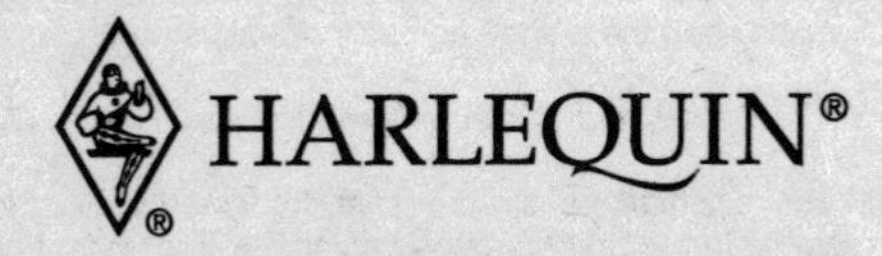

TORONTO • NEW YORK • LONDON
AMSTERDAM • PARIS • SYDNEY • HAMBURG
STOCKHOLM • ATHENS • TOKYO • MILAN • MADRID
PRAGUE • WARSAW • BUDAPEST • AUCKLAND

ISBN 0-373-29258-9

THE OTHER BRIDE

This edition published by arrangement with Harlequin Books S.A.

Visit us at www.eHarlequin.com

Printed in U.S.A.

Available from Harlequin Historicals and LISA BINGHAM

The Other Bride #658

Other works include:

Harlequin American Romance

Nanny Jake #602
The Butler & the Bachelorette #635
The Daddy Hunt #651
Dana and the Calendar Man #662
The Princess & the Frog #692
And Babies Make Ten #784
Man Behind the Voice #835
Twins Times Two! #887

Harlequin Intrigue

When Night Draws Near #540

Prologue

Devon, England
April, 1870

"Louisa! Louisa, where are you?"

The call was distant, urgent, riding on the back of a gusting wind that threatened to obscure the query altogether.

From her hiding place beneath the willows at the edge of the graveyard, Louisa Haversham debated whether or not to respond. The storm would be here any moment. If she waited long enough, the rain would come and the student who had been sent to find her would balk at entering the cemetery, and return to school. Then she would be alone once again.

"Louisa! Mr. Goodfellow and Mrs. Pritchard are looking for you!"

Louisa grimaced. She didn't really care if her absence angered Mr. Goodfellow, the owner of the school, or Mrs. Pritchard, the headmistress. They might scold or keep her from her meals, but they wouldn't dare to exact a punishment harsher than that. Not when her father was their principal benefactor. In her years with the school, Louisa had been anything but a biddable student. She'd been an angry, hurt child when she'd first arrived, and her temper hadn't improved much over the years.

"Lou-i-sa! Your *father* is here!"

Several seconds passed before the meaning of the words permeated her brain. Jumping to her feet, she scrambled in the direction of the school, racing pell-mell through the sodden grass, until she arrived breathless and disheveled at the side door.

Mrs. Pritchard waited for her there, her body quivering in displeasure. "Into the chapel," she snapped. "Your father is waiting."

Louisa hurried to comply, her knees growing weak with anticipation and anxiety. Her father was a rare visitor to Goodfellow's and his sudden appearance didn't bode well. The truth of the matter remained that Oscar Haversham despised Louisa and had despised her from birth. She hadn't been a boy and had therefore proved useless to him.

But the last laugh is on you, Father, a tiny voice within her whispered. Her father, who had married five times in an effort to produce a son, would soon die "without masculine issue." The ravaging effects of consumption would claim him soon enough.

The irony wasn't lost on Louisa, nor could she ignore the tragedy of the situation. She was the only child of one of the wealthiest men in England, yet she'd lived a life of virtual poverty within the walls of Goodfellow's School for Girls. Only at Christmastime was she permitted to return home—a fact that had been more of a burden than a delight. For seven days, she was dressed in clothes and jewelry chosen by her father to impress whatever business associates had been invited to Haversham Hall. She was expected to keep to herself, refrain from speaking, and appear suitably grateful for the scraps of attention he threw her way. Then, as soon as the New Year dawned, she was hustled back to Goodfellow's posthaste.

So why was her father here now?

Hearing the distant sound of voices, Louisa froze. Could she dare to hope that she was about to leave Goodfellow's School for Girls and return home for good? Or was her father on his deathbed? Was he frantic about the inevitable disbursement of his title and the bulk of his business empire passing to a distant male cousin rather than a son?

Louisa wove her fingers tightly together to still a burst of trembling. Her panic grew so intense it nearly choked her. Damn her father for his meddling, for his hard-heartedness. But most of all, damn him for his inability to love her for something she could not change—being a female. If she ever managed to get free of his clutches, she would never allow another human being to have such control over her.

Especially not a man.

Louisa was but a few feet away from the chapel when the door suddenly swung wide, revealing the sour face of Mr. Goodfellow.

"In here, child," he said curtly, clearly holding his tongue to avoid criticizing her in the presence of her father.

Moving on quaking limbs, Louisa crossed the threshold. In an instant, she took in the tall figure of the local magistrate, her dour cousin Rodney, her father in his rolling chair, and an unknown woman in black, her face obscured by a mourning veil.

Louisa's heart thumped in her breast.

What was happening? Why had her father come to Goodfellow's—and why had he brought Cousin Rodney and another woman with him?

As if sensing her thoughts, her father, the eleventh Marquis of Dobbenshire, spoke. "You're to be married by proxy," he rasped, his voice hoarse and quavering like a man of eighty rather than his mere fifty years. "Your husband-to-be, Charles Winslow III, is a business associate of mine in Boston. He was unable to make the crossing—" Haversham paused, struggling for breath "—so he sent word...that you were to be married anyway, with Rodney standing in as the groom." Again he paused, and the pallor of his skin alarmed even Louisa. "At the end of the week, you will board a ship for America. Once there...you'll have a proper church wedding."

Married?

By proxy?

Ice began to seep into her muscles. Her mind worked frantically, trying to grasp the meaning of her father's pronouncement. But with each inescapable tick of the clock, she was able to grasp only one fact.

Her father was a brilliant man. The last time she had seen him, he'd railed at the fact that his wealth, power and title were to be passed on to an "ungrateful cousin" rather than his own flesh and blood.

But by selling his daughter to the highest bidder—and she had no doubts that was exactly what he had done—he could pray that he would soon be supplied with the heir he craved.

A grandson.

Louisa opened her mouth to protest, but all sound choked in her throat before it could even be uttered.

It was clear from the jut of her father's chin that this marriage would occur, one way or another.

Run! an inner voice urged.

But where would she go? How could she ever hope to escape? She was totally at her father's mercy. She had no money of her own and no references that could lead to employment. Furthermore, at the first hint of disobedience, her father would see to it that she was locked up—either here at school or a convent. If she managed to elude him, his money and power would provide the means for her to be found.

Hope faded like smoke rising from a snuffed candle. She would not escape this marriage. She would exchange her prison here for one in America, with a stranger of a husband as her keeper.

Her father made a brusque gesture toward Rodney and the magistrate. "Let's get this...over with."

Numbly, Louisa took her place. In a daze, she heard the magistrate speak.

"Dearly beloved..."

Was there no way out of this? None at all?

But as she scrambled to find a way to derail her father's machinations, her only solace lay in the fact that this marriage by proxy would offer her time.

Time for what? Another solution? And what would that be?

Your new husband won't have seen you, her inner voice whispered again. *Someone could take your place.*

The thought was so sudden, so startling, that Louisa jerked.

Rodney, who had been asked to take her hand, took the movement for an attempt to pull back, and tightened his grip until her bones felt as if they would crack.

Could she do it? Could she find someone who would be willing to marry a stranger and assume her identity in exchange for…

For what?

Her inheritance. Her title.

But who would that woman be? Who would be willing to submit to a loveless marriage? Worse yet, Louisa would have to find someone who had a passing likeness to her in case her father had described her in his correspondence.

"Louisa!"

"Yes?" The word was spoken before Louisa knew what she'd done. Too late, she realized she'd been asked if she would "take Charles Winslow as her husband."

"I now pronounce you husband and wife."

Louisa's thoughts suddenly scattered. Shocked, she realized that the ceremony was over and she had barely heard a single word.

"Sign the papers, Louisa," her father panted. "I want to get out of this…dank air before it finishes me. Then I'm off for an…extended stay in Italy to improve my health."

It was the magistrate who said to Louisa, "I hope you will be happy, Mrs. Winslow."

Winslow. Louisa Haversham Winslow.

The magistrate took her hand. "Don't worry, dear," the man said with a reassuring pat. "I know a woman of your background balks at the informality of a civil ceremony. But as your father has said, once you're reunited with your husband, you'll have a church wedding with all the trimmings."

Reunited? So the magistrate had been led to believe that she had met Charles Winslow.

"Sign the papers, Louisa."

Moving on wooden legs, Louisa crossed to a side table set with a sheaf of documents, an inkwell and a pen.

Dear God, help me. Help me to find a way out of this. Help me to find someone who might be willing to take my place.

When she'd finished, her father eyed her with disdain. Clearly, he still wished she'd been a boy.

He held out an imperious hand to his valet. Immediately, the servant crossed to Louisa, handing her a hinged, wooden box. She opened it and gasped, recognizing several pieces of her mother's jewelry as well as a heavy signet ring with the family coat of arms.

She gasped. The gift was so unexpected. Her mother's jewelry!

"Father, I don't know what to—"

He cut her off.

"I won't have you besmirching the family name with an absence of jewels. I've only provided you with a few items of lesser value. The rest will be given to you or your heirs upon my death." He paused. "*If* I feel you deserve them. I've provided you with a good husband, Louisa. Be grateful."

She clamped her teeth together, wishing she had the courage to speak her mind about her father's "arrangements."

"Charles is a solid business associate. He'll make your life…an easy one." Her father coughed, his whole body jerking with the effort. When he'd managed to catch his breath, he added, "He asks only that you…supply him with a male heir."

Charles wished for an heir? Or did her father?

As if sensing her thoughts, her father's narrowed his eyes and lowered his voice to a chilled sliver of sound. "Take great care as you embark on this life, Louisa. Charles walks in...important circles. As his wife, you must guard every word, every deed. If you prove...an asset to him, I'm sure your life will be a happy one."

Louisa knew her father wasn't overly concerned about her emotional welfare. Instead, he was offering her a none-too-subtle warning to behave.

"Charles has made great concessions on your behalf."

Again Louisa bit her tongue. In her opinion, Charles Winslow had done little more than instruct someone else to take his place.

Her father's voice grew brittle and his gaze flicked in the direction of the magistrate. "He has supplied you with...a wardrobe befitting your role as his wife. Traveling trunks...feminine frippery..."

Lord Haversham held out an imperious hand to the lady who had been waiting in the shadows near the door. "This woman...is also on her way to America, where she will be wed. Charles and I have arranged for her to be your companion."

At that moment, the woman stepped more clearly into the light surrounding the altar. The glow pierced the folds of the veil that draped from her mourning bonnet, and a gasp of surprise lodged in Louisa's throat.

No. It couldn't be. God couldn't have answered this one prayer when he had ignored so many others.

But as the woman lifted the veil and stopped mere feet away, one inescapable fact lodged in Louisa's brain.

She looks like me.

Chapter One

New York
June 1870

Gabriel Cutter caught the line being thrown over the bow of the ship. Tying it to the skiff, he clambered up the rope ladder to the deck and accepted a helping hand.

''Gabriel Cutter?''

''Yes.''

''Follow me, sir.''

Gabriel did as he was told, being careful to keep his hat pulled low and his face averted from a striking pair of redheaded women who were standing nearby. He had no wish to capture the attention of anyone on board. And if he were to be seen, he didn't want anyone to remember him too clearly.

The sailor led Gabriel to the lower cargo decks, then motioned to another figure waiting in the shadows. Without another word, the sailor withdrew.

''Gabe Cutter?'' the second man asked.

Taking a leather folder from his pocket, Gabriel

held his Pinkerton identification card beneath the glow of a lantern.

The man heaved a relieved sigh. "It's good to finally meet you, sir."

Gabriel extended his hand in greeting. "I appreciate the work you've done so far, Roberts." Lloyd Roberts had been one of the Pinkertons assigned to guard the shipment during the crossing.

"I'll be happy to have you take control of the shipment, I can tell you," Roberts said, leading Gabe to a cargo hold, and from there to a stack of crates that had been under constant guard.

"Sir." The acknowledgment came from a second ruddy-faced guard, who stepped from the shadows where he'd been hiding. The fellow was little more than a kid.

Gabriel grimaced. He had requested that the Pinkerton offices give him experienced agents for this assignment. They'd sent him a boy who was barely out of short pants.

Gabe supposed he shouldn't be surprised by the home office's decision. He'd grown used to fighting for every concession he could get. Despite Gabe's abilities as an agent, there were too many men above him who remembered him from the war. It wouldn't matter that Gabe had a sterling reputation with the Pinkerton Agency. The memory of his wartime desertion would outlive any successes he might have had in the succeeding years.

"What's your name?" Gabe asked brusquely.

The boy blinked and shifted uncomfortably beneath Gabriel's narrowed glare.

"P-Peterson, sir. Luke Peterson."

"How long have you been with the Pinkertons?"

Gabriel asked. A brief glance at the boy's grip on his rifle confirmed that he was quaking.

"Th-this is my first job."

Gabriel took a deep, calming breath, then asked, "Do you know what you're doing?"

Peterson blinked, clearly confused by the question. "I—I'm guarding these crates."

"Why?"

The kid sent a pleading glance toward Roberts. "B-because they told me to."

At the frank answer, Gabriel's lips twitched in the beginnings of an unconscious smile, but he quickly controlled the impulse. It wouldn't do for the boy to grow too relaxed around him.

"There may be some hope for you, Luke. Continue to do as you're told and we'll get along together just fine."

The boy offered him a shaky grin. Then he drew to attention as if remembering that the job was a serious one and Gabriel...

Gabriel had a reputation of being a bastard.

Gabriel was fully aware of his reputation. He was a tough taskmaster, demanding infinite obedience from his men. Nevertheless, it wasn't his role as a senior Pinkerton agent that alarmed Luke. Gabe could gauge the moment Peterson remembered everything he'd been told. Bit by bit, the warmth faded from the boy's eyes, to be replaced by a horrified curiosity. Gabriel could almost read Peterson's thoughts.

Was this Gabriel Cutter? Was this the man accused of desertion?

"Any problems?" he asked, turning his attention back to the elder Pinkerton.

''None. I doubt anyone even knows we transported the shipment of gold.''

''Don't be so sure.'' Gabriel's tone had a hard edge to it.

To date, four payroll shipments destined for the Overland Express had been stolen en route to the construction sites in the Oregon Territory. The laborers were growing restless and threatened to revolt if they weren't paid, leading Josiah Burton, the owner of the Overland Settlers Company, to enlist the aid of the Pinkertons in transporting the latest shipment.

''Stay on your toes. There have been four previous robberies. Whoever is responsible will be watching, have no fear.'' Gabriel nodded in the direction of the shipment. ''You'll be relieved of your posts in an hour. I've got rooms reserved for you at the Golden Arms Hotel under the names Walters and Williams, but I'll expect you to be here when the ship docks in the morning. At that time, you'll meet up with the rest of the crew and see to the transfer of the crates. You'll have little more than a few hours to rest and relax tonight, so get some sleep. You'll need it.''

Peterson offered a muffled, ''Yes, sir.''

Roberts merely nodded.

''I'll see you tomorrow afternoon then.''

As he turned to leave, Gabriel motioned for Roberts to follow. Once they were out of earshot, he asked, ''How's the boy?''

''He's young, but he's eager to please and he's capable. He served with the First Pennsylvanian Battalion during the war.''

Peterson couldn't be more than nineteen, yet he was a veteran in a war that had ended more than five years before. The fact didn't surprise Gabriel. There had been so many boys who had run away from home to join the cause—either by serving as drummers or lying about their ages so they could enlist in the infantry.

"Keep your eyes open, Roberts, for your sake and the boy's. He might have served in the war, but his hands are sweating—and we haven't even docked yet. Veteran or not, he's too wet behind the ears for my taste."

Gabriel waited until Roberts had returned to his post. Then, tugging his hat more firmly over his brow, he wound his way through the narrow corridors to the deck again.

The sooner he left the ship, the better.

Gabe had barely climbed to the first class cabins when a door a few yards away suddenly opened.

The figure that emerged was clearly that of an aristocrat.

Immediately, he recognized her as being one of the women who'd been on deck when he'd climbed aboard. She was willow slim, with red-gold hair coiled in an artful arrangement that did nothing to disguise the natural curls that many women would have found "unfashionable." Her indigo silk gown was simple, with stark, tailored lines. Except for a small amount of lace that circled the collar, and an elaborate strip of pleats at the cuffs, her bodice was unadorned with the usual manner of feminine frippery. The lines were tight and form fitting, ending at a skirt festooned with elegant swags of fabric that puffed over a full bustle.

In all, Gabriel wasn't prone to admiring the latest fashions. But as this woman turned, offering her back, Gabe acknowledged for the first time that there was one clear advantage to the exaggerated silhouette. Indeed, as she moved and the bustle twitched, he found himself infinitely aware of the sway of her hips and the tiny circumference of her waist. To his disgust, he felt an immediate masculine reaction.

The thought caused him to draw back and curse his own wayward imagination. Damn it, he was exposed here in the corridor. If the woman were to turn around, she would see him clearly—and such an eventuality could lead to complications he didn't want to envision.

But even as he berated himself for the waywardness of his thoughts, Gabe's eyes slid back to her again.

She was a striking woman, in his opinion—although some might consider her a bit on the plain side with such pale features and that red hair. Moreover, there was a jut to her chin that showed a streak of obstinacy.

Or was it passion?

Gabe took a step forward as if to follow her. But in that same instant, another shape appeared in the doorway—another redhead, this one smaller and more voluptuous. A sister, perhaps? The similarities between the two women were astounding.

"Louisa?" the woman called from the doorway. "Don't you think you'd better take your shawl? It's chilly outside."

"I'll only be a moment, Phoebe." The one named Louisa turned, and Gabriel shrank deeper into the shadows, praying that she wouldn't look in his direction. "I left my drawing book and my shawl on deck. I'll return directly, I promise."

For one more moment, Gabe was able to study the woman wearing sapphires and silk—the elegant contours of her profile, and eyes that were a deep, stormy blue. Then the smaller woman closed the door, and Louisa turned, hurrying toward the companionway in a rustle of skirts.

Not really understanding his own motives, Gabriel followed her. He wanted—no, he *needed* to be near her for a moment longer. And even though caution nagged him to return to his duties, he trailed her as she made her way into the chill evening air.

All too soon the woman found the items. Shrinking into a space created by two stacks of crates, Gabe grew still, knowing that she would return to her cabin as promised.

But to his infinite surprise, the woman didn't immediately go below deck. Instead, she tipped her head up to the stars as if she could feel their scant light upon her cheeks like the warmth of the noonday sun. Then, wrapping the shawl around her, she gripped it tightly to her chest.

"Tomorrow," Gabriel heard her whisper. "Tomorrow, I will be free."

Free? He frowned. Free from the ship? Or something more?

Gabe scowled at his own musings. What had come over him? He didn't have time for any of this. Tomorrow morning, the dummy shipment and the actual payroll would be transferred onto the boxcars bound for California. Before that could happen, he needed to brief his men, review guard schedules, meet with Josiah Burton.

Flipping his collar up around his chin, Gabe shook away the invisible sensual threads that had begun to bind him. He had a job to do, and he was determined to do it well. His name was at stake. His reputation. Moreover, he wasn't the kind of man to keep company with someone of "quality." He'd grown too crass and coarse for anyone from such rarified air—and he was honest enough to know he was the sort of man that mothers warned their daughters about.

But even as he would have retreated toward the rope ladder, he hesitated. A gust of wind brought a hint of sound that sounded suspiciously like…

Weeping.

Gabe would have been the first to admit that the sound of a woman's tears generally tended to drive him in the opposite direction. But there was something about the noise, about the efforts Louisa exerted to keep her emotions private, that caused him to hesitate.

Hairs prickled at the back of his neck and he cautiously searched the darkness. What had happened? Was she in trouble? The woman had altered from joy to sadness so quickly that something must have affected her deeply. A terrifying memory, perhaps?

His jaw clenched.

He knew all too well how flashbacks from the past could arise without warning. He'd become an expert on such matters. Over the years, he had discovered that a hint of spring lilacs could wipe away the intervening years so that he was standing again in the orchard, staring down at the sprawled, battered bodies of his wife and son.

No. He mustn't think about that now. He had to keep his mind on the job, only the job.

But as he took a step backward, he looked at the woman in blue and a wave of protectiveness surged within him. If she were being threatened or intimidated, he would…

What?

What would he do? He didn't know the woman and he had no business interfering in her affairs.

Gabe's hand tightened around the butt of his revolver and he hardened himself to the sounds she made. Blast it all, he was a man who prided himself on finishing a job without interference. If that were true, why had he allowed himself to be so easily distracted now, at a point in his career where one false move could mean the end of everything?

The woman's sobs intensified, but Gabe steeled himself against their appeal for help and steadfastly stared at her back. He had troubles of his own to tend to. He didn't have time to worry about those of a stranger.

And yet…

Damning himself for his weakness, he didn't walk away. He couldn't. Instead, he stepped forward, slowly, quietly.

Although Gabe could never have been accused of rescuing damsels in distress in the past, he reached into a pocket, removing a clean handkerchief. Shaking it free of its folds, he extended it to the woman over her shoulder.

She started, clearly unaware of his approach. But when she would have turned, he took her shoulders in his hands, forcing her to remain with her back to him.

"No. Don't," he said, so quietly that he wondered if she would hear. "Let the interference of a stranger remain just that…the actions of a stranger."

He didn't know where the words came from. His voice was gruff, telling. Kindness had become a foreign emotion to him. For so long he'd been angry at the world and most of the people who inhabited it. And yet at this moment, with this woman, he found his anger slipping away, leaving him bereft, hollow, and infinitely sad.

Long, long ago, in another lifetime, his wife had

hated to be caught crying—and uncomfortable with such womanly emotions, Gabe had been happy to let her vent her grief in private. Now, years later, he didn't think that he could bear to see this woman's cheeks stained with tears. He didn't want to remember her that way. Days from now, months, years, he wanted to recall the way he'd first seen her in the corridor.

Beautiful.

Happy.

The woman sniffed, taking the handkerchief. "Thank you. I don't know what's wrong with me. I'm not normally so…what I mean is I…"

Her hand waved in the air, a bright patch of white from his handkerchief and a darker, eloquent shadow caused by her gloves. Inexplicably, Gabe wished that her hands were bare. He wanted to see the velvety texture of her fingers. From his vantage point behind her, she was little more than a shadow. Only the lighter patch of her hair and a brief glimpse of the skin at the nape of her neck helped to remind him that she was flesh and blood.

Gabe's heart floundered sluggishly in his chest. Years of avoiding even the barest hint of attraction seemed to dissolve, leaving him aching with loneliness. He suddenly felt like a shell of a man. The anger that he had carried with him left a taste on his tongue like ashes.

Dear God, what had this woman done to him? In the space of a few minutes, she had exposed his life for what it was—an endless struggle to forget. Nothing more. Nothing less.

But could it ever be anything more? He'd had his one chance at happiness, and through his own carelessness, his wife and son had died. It was his fault that he hadn't sent them away to safety during the war. He should have forced Emily to leave their farm—or at best, should have ensured she'd had someone with her for protection.

A breeze caught at the tiny curls that had escaped the coils of the woman's hair. The scent of lilies wafted around him, making him ache with sadness.

So delicate…so feminine…

So real.

He shouldn't be here. He shouldn't pollute her presence with his own. She was so clean and fresh, while he…he was a mere shell of a man, one who had brought more than his fair share of shame and pain upon his family.

Even as he tried to remind himself that he wasn't worthy of a woman like this, a yearning began to pulse within him. He wanted to feel the softness of a woman against him, caress the velvety texture of her skin. But he soon realized that the hunger had far less to do with a sexual need than with a hunger for companionship and compassion.

Instantly, he shrank away from the idea. No. Hadn't he learned his lesson already? Could he so easily forget that such indulgences could bring a searing pain along with the pleasure? Could he forget his responsibilities?

He was tired, that was all. He'd already decided that this would be his last job for the Pinkerton Agency. He'd grown increasingly restless within the structure the job required.

But where did he intend to go? What was he looking for that he didn't already have?

Not a woman, surely. He wasn't a man worthy of

a good woman, and he'd already sworn to himself that he would never allow another female into his heart. He owed Emily that much. He might not have been the husband she'd needed during her short life, but he would grieve her properly now that she was gone.

Which was the very reason he needed to return to his duties and forget this woman, this moment.

But just as he would have released her, Louisa shuddered, and in that instant, he knew he had no recourse but to remain for a few minutes longer. If he didn't, he would regret his aloofness for the rest of his life.

"I'm sorry," the woman sobbed again.

Reaching out, he briefly laid his fingers on her arm. "There's no need to explain." He didn't want to know what had upset her. Once he learned the cause of her pain, a bond, no matter how innocent, would be formed between them.

Louisa looked down, then took a shaky breath.

"I don't know why I'm crying. I have everything ahead of me. Everything I've ever wanted." She offered a sound that was half laugh, half sob, and pressed his handkerchief to her mouth. "I guess that the strain of worry has merely worn me down."

Not sure how he should respond, Gabe stated, "You'll be on dry land tomorrow." Despite his matter-of-fact observation, he stroked her hair with his thumb, and one of the tendrils wrapped around his knuckle as if to trap him there.

She nodded. "Yes, but I still have a long journey ahead of me."

"Eventually you'll arrive at your destination."

"I suppose that's true. I'll be glad when I have a home of my own." Her tone was wistful.

A home of her own.

Gabe could understand the woman's longing. There were times when he failed to work long and hard enough to exhaust himself before sleep. On those evenings, he remembered when he'd belonged to something other than himself.

A family.

Dear heaven, why think about that now?

Just as suddenly as he had been swamped with the need to follow this woman, Gabriel now had an overwhelming urge to walk away. In the scant moments they had been together, she had managed to stir emotions that he had buried in the same cold earth that now held his wife and son. If he didn't leave her now…

He tore his hand free from the capricious tendril that would have held him captive.

"Will you be all right here alone?" Although he kept his voice a soft whisper, he couldn't completely conceal his sudden brusqueness.

The woman stiffened in obvious embarrassment. "Yes. Yes, I'm sorry."

She made a move to return his handkerchief, but he quickly said, "No. Keep it. You may have need of it sometime in the future." And he didn't need another reminder of how quickly this woman had infiltrated his defenses.

He hesitated only a moment, feeling that he should do more, offer more. But with a final light touch to her hair—an action that was more caress than dismissal—he retreated into the darkness, stepping behind a stack of crates.

He waited there for long moments, his heart pounding inexplicably, until he finally heard the rustle of silk.

Then she was gone, hurrying below deck, narrowly missing Gabriel's hiding place in her haste.

Berating himself for being ten times a fool, Gabriel made his way to the skiff. He had a job to do, and he'd best be keeping his mind on the matters at hand. He didn't have the time or the energy to worry about a mysterious woman whom he would never see again.

Nevertheless, as he rowed into the shadows, his mind returned irresistibly to the woman in silk and sapphires. What had brought her here to New York? And what kind of freedom awaited her that would make her call out in happiness, then cry as if her heart were broken?

Dawn was still hours away when the woman stretched sinuously, her hand sliding over the cool silk of the sheets.

"I should go," she murmured, lifting an arm to plant a kiss against the spine of her lover.

She wasn't surprised that he hadn't slept long. He was a restless creature—and with everything on his mind, he was bound to have a few sleepless nights. It was just that...

She stifled an inner sigh. What worried her was that he seemed removed and distant, even in the heights of passion—as if she weren't enough for him.

Brushing the thought away, she ran her hand over his taut flesh. Scars crisscrossed his back, but she carefully avoided drawing attention to them. She had learned long ago that to caress them would cause a black mood to descend over his features. At those times, he could be cruel.

"Isn't there a way you could arrange for the brides to take the train West?"

He grew tense and she immediately wished that she'd kept her complaints to herself.

"No." His tone was curt. Cold. "From what I've been told, Gabriel Cutter is adamant. The mail-order brides will have to make other plans. He absolutely refuses to allow the women to make the journey."

She frowned. The gold would be on that train. She could feel it. Gabe Cutter, the trail boss for the Overland Settlers Organization, had decided at the last minute that the mail-order brides would not be allowed to accompany the rest of the group—and his arbitrary decision merely strengthened her suspicions.

Damn that man and his meddling. Since it would prove suspicious for her to travel on her own, she had agreed to pose as one of the brides so that she could journey West with her lover. She'd been left out of so many raids against the Overland Express that she didn't want to miss this one as well.

Her gaze darted around the luxurious hotel suite with its hand-painted frescoes, gilt and antique furnishings.

She loved money and everything it could buy. By becoming this man's mistress, she'd been showered with riches such as she had never imagined. But she feared that her lover was beginning to grow restless—not with her, but with the effort of stealing so many payroll shipments. He had decided that this would be his last raid.

She shivered, knowing that there was more to the enterprise than mere greed. This time, with an old enemy guarding the shipment, the plots had become personal.

Her lover meant to have revenge.

Which was also her greatest fear. If he managed to

punish Gabriel Cutter and ruin the man's reputation, she feared that her lover's darker needs might be met…

And he would suddenly find her superfluous.

No. She wouldn't let that happen.

Biting her lip, she reached for her own clothes, knowing that it was past time she returned to the boardinghouse. Once there, she would begin her role as a mail-order bride anxious to head West.

She could only pray that someone would find a way to get Gabriel Cutter to change his mind and allow the brides to travel with the train as originally promised. She wanted—no, she *needed*—to be there when all of their plans came to fruition. Then her lover would turn to her again, this time in exaltation.

Chapter Two

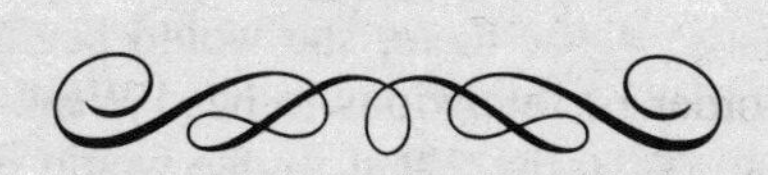

The moment the woman formerly known as Louisa Haversham debarked from the ship, she donned her new identity. Although she was a few inches taller than her former cabinmate, she wore Phoebe Gray's clothes. She'd claimed the other woman's more modest trunks as her own, and had even signed Phoebe's name on the ship's register.

I am Phoebe in word, deed and thought, she repeated over and over to herself. *Now and forever.*

Despite the serious nature of her transformation, "Phoebe's" heart was light as she joined the throng of people at the quayside and arranged for the delivery of her belongings to a local boardinghouse. Once there, she would meet the other mail-order brides destined for the Oregon Territory. Tonight she would sleep in a real bed with real pillows, and tomorrow she would board the train for the West.

Her steps were almost jaunty as she wove through the throngs of passengers eager to make their way into New York proper. She paused only once to turn and wave to her friend and fellow conspirator.

"Louisa" returned the greeting, looking every bit

"the lady" in her silk visiting gown and tiny bonnet, and Phoebe knew her friend's eyes must be snapping with mischief.

In the short time they'd spent together, Louisa had grown to love Phoebe Gray and look upon her as an adopted sister. The woman was impulsive, witty and nearly as headstrong as Louisa. But where Louisa tended to defy authority and carry her grudges like a badge of honor, Phoebe hid her frustrations with laughter, an eccentric imagination and a tendency for retribution.

Physically, Phoebe was very nearly Louisa's twin, and throughout their journey, the two women had often been mistaken as sisters. They were of the same age, slim, fashionably pale, their features regally exotic. Mere inches separated them in height. But while Louisa had curly red-gold hair and eyes that were more blue than gray, Phoebe had deep auburn tresses and eyes that were more gray than blue.

So alike.

And yet so different.

Phoebe smiled ruefully. Her father would be appalled if he could see her now—blithely throwing away her birthright without a second thought and allowing a stranger to take her place. She'd kept only a few reminders of her past—the indigo gown she'd worn the night before, two sets of delicate underthings and two pairs of shoes. The items were hidden deep in one of her trunks, along with a few pieces of her mother's jewelry and the signet ring her father had given her as a wedding present.

She grimaced. She doubted that the heavy piece had been a sentimental endowment. Instead, she was sure that the ring was meant to remind her of the name and title her father intended to pass on to her firstborn son. He would never discover that his daughter had abandoned his legacy until it was too late to rectify the mistake.

Pausing for a moment, she opened the catch to a carpetbag and withdrew the paper where she'd copied the boardinghouse's address. There she would meet the eight mail-order brides who would make the journey by rail. Once in San Francisco, she would wed Neil Ballard—a simple farmer looking for a woman to take care of his house.

"Let go of me! Unhand me, I say!"

"Watch out, miss! Move over!"

At the sound of a scuffle behind her, Phoebe flattened herself against the wall. To her horror, she saw a grizzled old man being hustled down the street by a pair of uniformed policemen.

Phoebe recognized the old man instantly. Poor Mr. Potter. Halfway through the Atlantic crossing, the scruffy octogenarian had been discovered on board as a stowaway. Within minutes, he'd been locked in one of the lower cabins. He'd spent the remainder of the journey there or shackled in chains on the deck of the ship.

"Lass, lass!" the man shouted as he passed her. "Tell them I'm too old to be sent back to England. Help me, please! Don't let them do this to me! I'm good for the fare!"

Startled, Phoebe found herself unable to say anything, so Potter turned his attention to the policemen on either side.

"If they'd only let me have a day or two, I could raise enough to pay for my passage. Tell them that, will you?"

But neither gentleman seemed inclined to listen. Instead, they bundled him into an enclosed wagon with iron bars over the windows. Phoebe could only wave to him as the team jolted into a quick walk and the vehicle lumbered away.

Inexplicably, the glow of the sun seemed slightly tarnished. What would become of Mr. Potter? He'd wanted to go West, and in that respect, Phoebe had felt a kinship with him. That was why she'd taken to sneaking him bits of food whenever she could.

"Out of the way, miss!"

She jumped, noting that she was about to be overrun by a pair of men attempting to load a heavy crate marked Farm Equipment onto a wagon. For a moment she stared at the men, noting the way their faces gleamed with perspiration and their bodies strained to lift the heavy box.

Eager to be on her way, Phoebe crossed the street, avoiding the foot traffic and buggies that tangled the thoroughfare. Although she would have enjoyed lingering on her journey to the hotel, time was of the essence. She needed to meet with the other mail-order brides and ensure that her trunks had been delivered. Then she would make a few purchases to augment those items from her friend's wardrobe that had proved to be too small. She would need sensible shoes and hose, as well as needles, thread and other sewing supplies to alter the hems of those garments that were too short.

Phoebe hailed a hansom cab. Although she was "purse poor" and likely to remain so for some time, she decided that the extravagance would be worth the time saved.

Climbing into the cab, she clutched her carpetbag

in her lap, straining to see as much as she could of the city through the narrow window. But even with the plethora of sights, she found her mind wandering back to the night before.

To the stranger.

The memory had the ability to make her skin tingle. How she wished she had found the courage to turn and face the gentleman who had come to her aid on the deck of the ship. He had been so kind....

And yet there was far more to the encounter than a chance meeting with an unfamiliar man who had offered her comfort. His nearness had thrilled her in a way she had never experienced before. From the moment he had spoken to her, she had been tuned to his nearness, his height, his strength. His muffled voice had been deep and warm, yet had retained a harder edge—like velvet over steel.

If only there had been more time.

If only she'd seen his face.

"Here you are, miss."

The cabby pulled to a halt so abruptly that Phoebe was nearly jolted from her seat.

Her face grew hot. The time had long since come for her to gain control of her wayward thoughts. She was engaged to a farmer in Oregon. She had no business mooning over a stranger she'd encountered during her journey.

Straightening her bonnet, Phoebe jabbed the hatpin through the brim with a bit more force than necessary, then dug into her reticule for the amount she owed the cabby. She would do well to remember who she was. Phoebe Gray, a mild, hardworking Christian woman with a long journey still ahead of her.

Reminded of her new persona, Phoebe thanked the

cabby for his efforts, adding a penny tip from her neat stash of coins. Hefting her satchel, she marched up the sidewalk and twisted the gleaming brass doorknob.

"Come in," a distant voice called from within.

Stepping into the dim interior, she allowed her eyes to become accustomed to the darkness, but even before they did, she absorbed the smells of lemon-scented furniture polish and baking bread.

A plump woman wearing a brown wool day dress, an oversize apron and a lace cap bustled into the room. "Hello, dear. May I help you?"

"Yes. My name is L—" Phoebe's face flamed. Here was her first encounter with a stranger and she'd nearly made the mistake of using her real name. *Never, never, never,* she chided herself. *You are Phoebe now. Phoebe Gray.*

Clearing her throat, she began again. "My name is Phoebe Gray. I was told to meet with—"

Phoebe didn't have a chance to finish. The woman began clucking in concern. Taking the satchel from Phoebe's fingers, she looped her arm through her elbow and drew her irresistibly toward a narrow staircase.

"I'm Mrs. Cates, the proprietor." She clucked again. "My dear, my poor, poor dear. You've arrived at last and just in time to discover that your journey is over before it's begun."

A moment passed before Phoebe caught the full meaning of what the woman was saying.

"Over? What do you mean, over? Did the Overland group leave earlier than planned? Did I miss the train?"

Mrs. Cates wagged her head and her many chins trembled. "No, dear. It's worse than that. Far worse."

Mrs. Cates steadfastly ushered her to the top of the staircase, but once there, Phoebe planted her feet and refused to budge. "Mrs. Cates, please. Tell me what's happened."

The proprietress sighed. "The other girls are in here," she said, gesturing to a small sitting room visible through a pair of double doors. "I'll let them explain everything, poor darlings."

With that, she urged Phoebe forward and into the parlor.

Upon stepping across the threshold, Phoebe found the room cluttered with luggage and women. Like her, some of the girls were still dressed in dusty traveling suits, while others must have been in residence at the boardinghouse long enough to grow comfortable with their surroundings.

A quick count assured Phoebe that there were eight women present. The youngest, a delicate blonde who stared wistfully out the window, looked to be barely more than fifteen. From there, the average age of the women seemed to range from Phoebe's twenty-one to a tall statuesque woman of at least fifty.

"Ladies, here's the last of your group. Miss Phoebe Gray."

The women turned to greet her. But even as they smiled or nodded, it was clear the mood of the group was glum.

"Miss Gray, may I introduce Twila Getts." Mrs. Cates referred to the statuesque older woman with silver-blond hair combed sternly away from a center part. "She'll be marrying a minister in Oregon."

Twila extended a hand and gripped Phoebe's firmly.

Mrs. Cates continued. "These lovely ladies, as you can tell, are twins. Maude and Mable Wilde."

The twins appeared to be in their mid-thirties, with mud-brown hair drawn into identical swirling knots at their napes.

''We were teachers at a private school in London before deciding the educator's life wasn't nearly as keen as we'd hoped it would be.''

The sisters grinned as if sharing a private joke.

''They'll be marrying a pair of twin brothers in the Willamette valley,'' Mrs. Cates offered. She then turned to another pair of women. ''This is Greta Schmidt, from Germany, and Heidi Van Peltzer, from Austria.''

Greta had white-blond hair arranged in two round rolls over her ears. Heidi's hair was only slightly darker and had been wound in plaits around the crown of her head.

''They don't speak English,'' Mrs. Cates whispered—as if by lowering her voice, the announcement would be less shocking. ''They're bound for a dairy farm run by a pair of Scandinavians.''

Mrs. Cates tugged Phoebe in the direction of a swooning couch. A beautiful dark-haired beauty reclined against the tufted velvet. Despite the introductions, she continued to read a book.

''This is Doreen Llewelyn-Bowes.''

Doreen briefly glanced up from her novel. She offered a smile that was somehow lacking in warmth, then returned to the volume of poetry.

Mrs. Cates seemed relieved to be so summarily dismissed. ''This is Edith Diggery,'' she said, her tone bright again. She drew Phoebe toward a delicate blond girl at the window.

''She's an orphan, poor lass,'' Mrs. Cates said under

her breath. "Her father made provisions for her to marry the son of a friend."

Edith offered Phoebe a nervous half smile, and Phoebe's heart ached for the girl. Surely this youngster wasn't ready for the demands of marriage, especially to a stranger.

"And this is Betty Brown."

Betty jumped from her spot on the settee and bounded toward them.

"I'm from Long Island, so I haven't come very far at all, but I'm destined to marry a schoolteacher in Oregon whose name is Harry. Isn't that a rather funny name? Harry? I wrote to him and asked if it was short for something, Harold or Horace, but he wrote back to say, no, it's just Harry. Plain old Harry."

Phoebe immediately warmed to the gregarious girl with the snapping blue eyes.

"It doesn't matter what his name is," Doreen drawled from the swooning couch. "You won't be seeing him anytime soon."

The joy dimmed from Betty's eyes as quickly as it had come. "Oh," she offered forlornly. "That's right."

"What's happened?" Phoebe breathed, almost afraid to discover what calamity could be preventing their journey.

"It's that blasted Overland Settlers Company," Betty said with a sniff. "They've absolutely forbidden us to accompany them on their trip West."

Phoebe felt her stomach lurch. A fuzzy blackness swam in front of her eyes, but with a great strength of will she managed to push it away.

"Help her to the couch, ladies, or she'll swoon!"

Mrs. Cates sang out. Several helping hands moved her to an overstuffed settee near the window.

"Water! Get her some water!"

Before she knew what was happening, a glass was being thrust into her hand. Phoebe took a sip, then gulped greedily when the water tasted cool and fresh—unlike the stale, barreled supplies she'd been forced to drink on the ship.

"I've got smelling salts if you need them," the woman named Twila offered, extending a small vial in Phoebe's direction.

Even a faint whiff of the stuff was enough to clear Phoebe's brain, and she pushed it aside, saying weakly, "No. Thank you."

Phoebe stared at each of the women in turn, her blood turning to ice.

She wouldn't be going West.

None of them would.

"What happened? Why won't we be allowed on the train? Our husbands-to-be have made all the arrangements."

Doreen sighed as if she'd been called upon to explain a difficult concept to a child. "Apparently, it doesn't matter." Doreen's voice adopted a peeved note. "The trail boss hired to take the group West has forbidden us from joining them."

"But why?"

"He refuses to take a group of unaccompanied women on the journey," Maude explained.

Phoebe was still confused. "What do you mean, unaccompanied? We've arranged to travel together."

"She means that we haven't got a male chaperon," Mable explained with a sniff.

Phoebe eyed the glum faces that surrounded her.

"There has to be a mistake. The Overland Company has already accepted payment for our passage, knowing full well that we wouldn't be under the auspices of a male companion. Surely they wouldn't go back on their word regarding their earlier commitment."

Doreen sniffed. "Well, they have, and there's no changing their mind. We've been in touch with the Overland offices, and they refuse to hear our complaint. We've sent letters, notes, telegrams, and they refuse to budge."

"What about the trail boss who made the stipulation? Has anyone talked to him? Can we find a way to change *his* mind?"

Phoebe took heart from the answering silence, and noted the quick spark of hope passing from woman to woman.

"We've written to him, naturally, but we haven't tried to contact him directly," Doreen stated archly. "Personally, I don't think such a course of action would be...appropriate." She looked down her nose at Phoebe and her simple traveling suit. "A woman of proper breeding must draw the line at a face-to-face confrontation. It isn't seemly."

Righting the angle of her bonnet, Phoebe ignored the fear and weariness that tugged at her heels and urged her to sit on solid land and rest, if only for a minute.

She had to leave on that train or everything would be ruined. If she didn't...

If she didn't, too many things could go wrong.

"Propriety be hanged," she muttered, draining the glass of cool water and jumping to her feet. "If that man thinks he can brush us aside like a swarm of bothersome flies, he's about to get a rude awakening."

* * *

In no time at all, Phoebe was striding down the boardwalk again. But this time she was far from alone. In her wake came Maude and Mable, Edith, Twila, Betty, Greta and Heidi. Doreen, who still contended that it wasn't proper to instigate such a confrontation, had stayed behind.

Phoebe glanced down at the tiny scrap of paper Mrs. Cates had given her, then said, "We need to find 65 Fairfield Lane. The location should be fairly close to the station."

The walk to the railway station took much longer than Phoebe had anticipated. The genteel surroundings of the boardinghouse had gradually melted away, and the poorer section of town they entered became more and more tawdry.

Despite her outer bravado, Phoebe felt her skittishness increase. After all, who was she to say that they had nothing to fear from taking matters into their own hands? Only weeks before, she'd had little experience of associating with the masculine gender at all. And here she was, charging through a maze of tangled streets and alleyways as if she knew what she was doing. If any of the women who accompanied her were to discover that her bravado was feigned—

"There's the proper street!" Maude exclaimed.

"The address must be straightaway and to the right," Mable added, pointing in the direction with her walking stick.

Now that their goal was close at hand, Phoebe felt her stomach flip-flop in reaction. She'd volunteered in a moment of passion to speak to the trail boss, but she suddenly realized she had no idea what she intended to say.

Phoebe's worries scattered when Edith suddenly

gasped in horror. Looking up, Phoebe saw a huge, gaily painted placard proclaiming Golden Arms Hotel.

This time it was Phoebe's turn to utter a choked cry. Without thought, she stopped in her tracks so suddenly that the other women crashed into her like dominoes.

"What in heaven's name—" Twila grumbled.

Phoebe gestured to the placard with its brass lettering and a painting of a woman in a shocking state of dishabille.

"No," Phoebe whispered to herself. "It couldn't be."

But a glance at the paper assured her that the address she'd been given as a temporary office for Mr. Cutter was the same as the title emblazoned on the sign.

Phoebe's face grew hot with embarrassment. Surely she wasn't expected to find the man in a *bawdy house.*

Immediately, her irritation ignited into a white-hot anger. The entire situation was intolerable. Intolerable! Due to the edicts of an unknown trail boss who hadn't even displayed enough decency to meet with the mail-order brides, they'd been put in the dire straits confronting them now. They were stranded in a strange city with no funds, no way to quickly communicate with their intended spouses—most of whom lived in areas miles from the nearest telegraph—and no way to make alternate arrangements. To add further insult, in order to voice their appeals, they had been brought here to…

A house of low morals!

Phoebe heard the women behind her begin to shift in discomfort.

"I say," Mable drawled in a droll tone. "We're in a bit of a pickle now, aren't we?"

Phoebe took a deep breath. "No. We're not 'in a pickle,' as you say. That's what they want—or at least what Mr. Cutter wants. He's decided that we are an inconvenience to his expedition. He's thrown us into a dither without so much as a by your leave, and I, for one, don't intend to let him have his way. We've paid for our passage in good faith. Unless he agrees to reimburse us for all expenses—including room and board—then we intend to be on that train. Isn't that right?"

If she'd expected her rallying words to instill her companions with confidence, she was sadly disappointed. The only response she received was Betty saying again, "You don't mean to go in *there,* do you?"

Phoebe brushed at the dust collecting on her skirts, jabbed the hatpin more securely into her bonnet and tugged at the hem of her bodice.

"Yes, I do. I wouldn't put it past the man to be purposely avoiding us by closeting himself in such an establishment. After all, what respectable person houses his offices at a... Well, you know what I mean."

The women nodded.

Phoebe took Twila's hand. "Come with me."

"Me?" Twila grew pale. "Why me?"

"Because you're a widowed woman with a knowledge of such..."

Twila looked frantic. "But Miss Gray..." She leaned close to whisper, "I was widowed before my husband and I...before we could..." She took a deep draft of her smelling salts before continuing. "We were married during the war. He had a two-hour leave. We never…''

The woman was already weaving on her feet, so Phoebe gave up. ''Fine.'' Frantically, she searched around her, finally catching a glimpse of a small park in the distance. ''All of you wait over there. I'll join you again as soon as I speak to the man.''

Reluctantly, the women made their way down the walk, leaving Phoebe to wonder how she'd managed to become embroiled in such a mess.

Anger swept through her as she realized how the careless edicts of one man were responsible for her current dilemma. Emboldened by the emotions bubbling within her, Phoebe strode in the direction of the Golden Arms.

Golden Arms. She should have known something was wrong by the name alone. But she'd thought that…

Never mind what she'd thought. She had to keep her mind on Gabriel Cutter.

As she neared the hotel, Phoebe heard the faint sound of music—not the tinny raucous sort that she had read about in penny novels, but an elegant piano arrangement. She snorted softly to herself, wondering if the proprietors thought that a bit of Mozart would add a note of respectability to the hotel. As far as she was concerned, a full-scale orchestra couldn't hide the fact that this building housed men and women who—

No. Despite the fact that she would be marrying soon, she couldn't even think about it. She wouldn't.

Whispering a prayer under her breath, Phoebe resolutely climbed the stone steps to an ornate door inset with colored, beveled glass. The brass knob turned easily beneath her fingers, and before she quite knew what had happened, Phoebe found herself moving into an elegant foyer. Rich black and white marble floor tiles gleamed at her. The shiny surface reflected the twinkling candles of a chandelier lit even in the middle of the day. To one side, rich maroon draperies were drawn back from the threshold of a reception room, where dapper gentleman spoke in low voices with women in various stages of undress.

Phoebe felt her face flame. She couldn't imagine what would possess a woman to entertain a man wearing little more than her chemise and pantalets.

"May I help you?"

Phoebe jumped. The voice was so soft-spoken and cultured that she was taken aback. A glance at the elegantly dressed woman who had silently appeared at her side did little to settle her nerves.

"I'm looking for Gabriel Cutter," Phoebe blurted, then wished she'd tamed her tongue and had led up to the subject more gradually. "We have business to discuss."

The woman seemed amused by Phoebe's quick reply, but she waved a hand toward a settee positioned against one wall. "Would you care to sit while I get him?"

Phoebe eyed the velvet-tufted sofa. After the difficult day she'd already had, she wanted nothing more than to sit, remove her shoes and rub her aching feet. But she couldn't allow herself to relax until after she'd met with the trail boss.

"No, thank you," she said primly.

The woman smiled and glided away.

Curious glances were being cast her way, but Phoebe refused to reveal her discomfiture at her surroundings. With what she hoped appeared to be a bored casualness, she turned away from the reception room with its scantily clad women and debauched gentlemen and stared instead at the painting hung over the sweeping staircase.

She had been given very few opportunities to study art while at Goodfellow's. Even then, the subject matter had been strictly confined to portraits of sober Elizabethans and bowls of Flemish fruit.

But this…this was lovely. Such vibrant colors, an exotic woodland realm and…

Bit by bit, Phoebe became aware of the prickling of the hairs on her nape. In the same instant, her eyes suddenly registered the content of the artwork in front of her.

Sweet heavens above, she thought in shock as she absorbed the nubile young woman clad in nothing more than a diaphanous silk scarf being ravished by a creature that was half man, half beast.

In shock, her hand encircled her throat, and her gaze leaped to the small brass plaque that read *Rosalind and the Satyr.*

Gasping, Phoebe whirled to escape the startling lasciviousness of the picture. But her shock was compounded when she found herself face-to-face with a man.

And heavens, what a man.

He was tall, with an angularity to his features that was both harsh and intriguing. Eyes the color of cold silver gazed at her with a piercing intensity that made her hands curl around the strings of her reticule. He was forbidding, of that there was no question. Yet even as she would have jumped to the conclusion that he was completely heartless, she hesitated. The shadows lingering in his eyes, the strain around his mouth and the tense set of his jaw bespoke a pain that was at once eloquent and foreboding.

Before she could gather her scattered wits, the man's eyes dropped. His gaze raked over her with insolent thoroughness, making her acutely conscious of her rumpled traveling costume and the ever-present dust that clung to her skin.

"You're very lovely, but I don't recall asking for your business."

Chapter Three

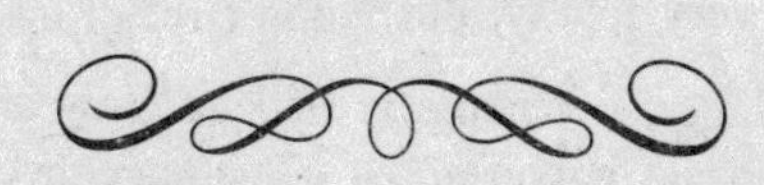

Phoebe gasped at the man's effrontery. Her hands balled into fists, but she strove to control her temper.

So this was the great Gabriel Cutter. The same man who had decided to deny the mail-order brides their rightful passage on his train.

Her anger seethed anew.

"It is *I* who have business with *you,* Mr. Cutter."

He didn't seem impressed by her statement. Instead, he began circling her, scrutinizing every inch of her frame in a way that reminded her of a hungry lion she'd once seen being fed at the London Zoo.

"You're a bit on the scrawny side."

A choked "oh" burst from her lips before she could stop it. "Mr. Cutter," she said indignantly, then quickly lowered her tone to a whisper when she captured the attention of those in the adjoining room. "Mr. Cutter, I would appreciate it if you would step outside so that I could have a word with you."

He stopped, placing his hands on his hips. "There isn't anything outside that can't be said inside."

"I wish to have a *private* conversation."

''I'd be happy to have a cup of coffee with you.'' He gestured to the room beyond the draped arch.

Phoebe felt her face flame at the mere idea. ''Mr. Cutter, I couldn't...I won't...I—I...''

''Then good day to you, ma'am.''

As he offered her a mocking salute, Phoebe resisted the urge to grind her teeth. Of all insufferable, ill-mannered...

''Mr. Cutter, my name is Phoebe Gray and I have come to speak to you about a matter concerning the Overland Settlers Company.''

Cutter folded his arms and regarded her through half-lowered lids. The intense scrutiny had the ability to make the skin on her arms prickle with gooseflesh. ''Ahh. So you're one of the brides.''

The tone he employed made it clear that the news wasn't particularly welcome.

His eyes narrowed. ''What was your name again?''

''Phoebe Gray.''

''*Phoebe* Gray?'' The intensity of his gaze seemed to harden ever so slightly—and if she didn't know better, she would have thought that he'd known she was unused to the name herself.

Before she could think of something to say, Gabe stated tightly, ''The answer is no. It was no last week, no this morning, and it will be no tomorrow when the train leaves the station.''

''Mr. Cutter—''

''*No,* Miss...''

''Gray.''

''No, Miss Gray. No, I will not change my mind. No, I will not allow nine unescorted women to accompany us West. And no, I don't really care that you weren't informed of the change sooner, or that you'll all be stranded in New York. Now, good day to you.''

Phoebe was so stunned, so enraged by Gabriel's pronouncement that it took her a moment to react. By that time, Gabriel Cutter had disappeared down a nearby corridor.

Huffing in indignation, she quickly followed him, discovering that the hallway led past the kitchen and dining areas to a narrow staircase. Sensing the man was heading for his offices, and fearful of losing him, she rushed to intercept him. Gabriel Cutter had just inserted a key in a door and was opening it wide when she burst past him into the room beyond and planted herself squarely in front of him.

''I'm not leaving until we've discussed this thoroughly, Mr. Cutter.''

Again his eyes narrowed. ''As far as I'm concerned, there's nothing to discuss.''

''At the very least you owe us an explanation for your edict.''

''I think 'edict' is putting it a bit strongly. Frankly, someone should have had the sense to point out that it's sheer folly for a gaggle of women to go such a distance unaccompanied. But since no one else bothered to think things through, it was up to me to set things to rights.''

Her hands balled into fists and she wanted to smack him, but she managed to control herself for a few minutes longer.

''Mr. Cutter, I don't remember the Almighty appointing you to be our guardian.''

''No, but two hundred settlers have paid me to ensure their safety.''

''As have we!''

"Which, as I've explained already, was a mistake. I'm sure the Overland Settlers Company will refund your fares—"

"When?"

He shrugged with a carelessness that caused her anger to burn so brightly she feared her hair would catch on fire.

"That's none of my concern."

"Well, it should be!" She was nearly shouting now, and it galled her that this man could have caused her to toss her manners aside and scream at him like a fishwife. Catching herself, she took several gulps of calming air, then began again. "Mr. Cutter—"

"It won't do you any good to argue, Miss Gray. There's nothing you can say that will change my mind."

"But why?" She stamped her foot, then wished she hadn't when she realized this man probably thought all females were hysterical during moments of crisis. Again she took several deep, fortifying breaths and said as sweetly as she should. "At the very least, Mr. Cutter, I think you should explain your reasoning. I hardly think that a group of women could cause much trouble on the train."

Cutter began moving toward her, crowding her, so that she was forced to take a step back, then another and another. Too late, she became aware of her surroundings. Horror rushed through her when she realized that she hadn't stormed into Gabe Cutter's office as she'd supposed, but his bedroom. As her cheeks flooded with heat, she became overtly aware of the small bedstead with its rumpled sheets, a washstand littered with masculine toiletry items and a satchel stacked with neatly folded shirts and union suits.

"Sweet heaven above," she whispered.

"It isn't heaven you should be praying to, Miss Gray," Cutter said, his voice low and dark, his movements taking upon themselves the prowling grace of a cat. "This is exactly why I've forbidden you women to accompany the expedition."

The way he looked at her, the way her body had flushed hot, then cold, left her in no doubt as to what "this" represented. The room became thick with sensual undercurrents. Her breath hitched in her throat and an odd heat settled low in the pit of her stomach.

"Men and women can't coexist without *this* getting in the way."

He was so close to her now that she could barely think. Bit by bit, he'd closed off all avenues of escape except for the bed.

She licked her lips nervously, then wished she hadn't when his gaze centered on that very point. "Nonsense," she retorted, in what she had hoped would be a stern tone. But the word emerged unsure, even to her ears. "Men and women can behave quite civilly and...*this* doesn't have to enter into things at all."

Cutter shook his head as if he were disappointed by her denseness. "You've lived too long in rarified social circles, Miss Gray."

For a moment, her heart seemed to skip a beat. *How did he know?* How had he guessed? Were her years of being in a strict girls' school marked on her somehow?

But he continued on, oblivious to her panic. "It's the same with most women. They're born with blinders, for the most part. They believe that society's dictates can control humanity's baser instincts."

Too late, Phoebe realized that she'd taken several more steps and become pinned in a corner between the wall and the bed.

Gasping for air, she flattened her hands against the plaster as if she could will it to crumble beneath the pressure.

Cutter took another step, his legs pressing into the fullness of her skirts, his head dipping, his own palms resting on the faded wallpaper on either side of her head.

''But no matter what rules you set, human nature will always surface. A man will always want a woman—and despite what she might have been told, a woman will invariably be drawn to the man.''

She felt herself trembling when his head bent.

He's going to kiss you!

No, no, he wouldn't!

But as the space between them disappeared and he came to within a hairsbreadth of touching her, Phoebe was shocked to discover that she wasn't resisting the possibility nearly as hard as she should. There was a part of her that *wanted* to be kissed, that wanted to think she could attract such a man as Gabriel Cutter. A primitive man...a handsome man...a—

A sneaky, conniving, no-good rounder!

Just in time, Phoebe realized that she was about to help Gabriel Cutter prove his argument—and without so much as a whisper of protest.

Anger rushed through her again—anger at him, but even more at herself.

In that last second before his lips touched hers, she moved, bringing up a knee in a way she'd once been told to do by Mrs. Pritchard. Her aim wasn't entirely true, but the surprise of her attack allowed her to push past Gabriel Cutter. In doing so, she snatched at the revolver holstered at his side, then whirled and pulled back the hammer, leveling the gun at him.

"Don't move," she warned fiercely. Biting her lip, she tried to steady the heavy gun, but her hands were trembling so badly that the tip of the revolver wavered. Nevertheless, she closed one eye and sighted down the barrel.

Cutter watched her with patent amusement, and the fact proved galling. How dare he treat her as if she were of no consequence? She was the one with the gun!

Clenching her teeth, she aimed at the bedpost next to him and pulled the trigger.

An explosion rocked the room. The gun kicked back, nearly causing her to lose her balance. Then her eyes widened in horror as she realized that she hadn't shot the bedpost as she had supposed, but had nicked the upper corner of his sleeve.

Her stomach churned sickeningly as she waited for the blood to flow, but as Gabriel pulled the fabric aside to examine his arm, it was clear that the bullet had miraculously left him unharmed.

She was shaking so badly now that she nearly dropped the gun altogether. But when Cutter gazed up at her, his gaze dark and speculative, she knew that he hadn't known her aim was off.

"Next time I'll draw blood," she said, mustering all of the bravado she could. "We're going West with you, Mr. Cutter," she insisted.

"Not without a male escort."

The man was infuriating, positively infuriating!

Phoebe was about to argue with him further when she had a sudden thought.

A male.

Any male? Any male at all?

Her eyes narrowed. ''What if we can find a male escort who is willing to accompany us tomorrow?''

He snorted in a way that made it clear he thought such an event unlikely. ''*If* you can find a man to traipse halfway across the country with a passel of giggling mail-order brides before nine tomorrow morning, then you're welcome to join us.''

Her heart pounded in her chest—this time with excitement. ''I have your word on that?''

''You have my word.''

''Do I need your promise in writing, Mr. Cutter?''

A little muscle at the side of his jaw flickered. ''My word is binding, Miss Gray.''

''Good.''

Without further explanation, she tugged at the strings of her reticule and dropped the revolver inside.

''I'm sure you have other guns, Mr. Cutter. As for this one, I intend to keep it until the end of our journey, to remind you that we aren't nearly as helpless as you think.''

And with that parting shot, she whirled and marched out of the room, not stopping until she was once again in the hot afternoon sunshine. She had the matter of an escort to arrange.

By this time tomorrow, she would be on her way West.

Hurrying away from the Golden Arms as quickly as her feet would take her, Phoebe found the other brides waiting for her at the park. Judging by their hangdog expressions, it was clear they had prepared themselves for bad news.

''Well?'' Mable breathed when Phoebe was nearly upon them.

''He'll let us go if we supply a male escort.''

The women visibly wilted in disappointment.

''Then we're in the same pickle we were in a few minutes ago,'' Betty mourned.

Phoebe couldn't prevent the smile that tugged at her lips. ''Not quite. I think I know where we can find the perfect candidate.''

The women looked doubtful.

''Where?'' Edith finally asked.

''Prison.''

Twila gasped.

The others looked horrified.

''I don't think we can break a man out of prison just to accompany us West,'' Betty said, blinking in confusion.

Phoebe smiled. ''We won't have to stage an escape, you little goose. We just have to gather together a few coins to pay for the man's passage from England.''

''Won't Mr. Cutter object to a former prisoner serving as our escort?''

''I have his word that he will allow us to join the company as long as we have a male in tow—*any* male.'' She patted her reticule. ''I, for one, intend to see to it that he honors his word.''

Needing action to take his mind off Louisa—not, not Louisa, Phoebe Gray—Gabe returned to the makeshift office he'd made of his hotel room. Despite its tawdry reputation, the Golden Arms had large rooms, the modern amenities and enough privacy to let him get his job done.

Slamming the door behind him, he instinctively

squelched his reaction to the memory of Phoebe and leaned over a table spread with maps. But he couldn't focus.

How long had it been since he'd felt anything in the company of a woman? It had been years since the death of his beloved wife, Emily.

Not that he hadn't tried to experience even the faintest stir of emotions. Knowing that he wasn't the kind of man to "taint" a Sunday school teacher or a minister's daughter, he'd found himself at the Golden Arms more times than he could count. But he'd found soon enough that he couldn't will his body to respond. Emily's death had been a blow to him, emotionally and spiritually. All of his tender emotions and sensual instincts had died the moment he'd found the body of his wife and small son in the orchard behind their house.

From that day to the present, Gabe had lived a life of torment. Plunged into an abyss of grief, he had not rejoined his unit for more than six months after his family's deaths. His actions had branded him "yellow" and "untrustworthy" to his fellow officers, but he hadn't cared. Once he'd returned to battle, he'd lived each succeeding day on the brink of disaster, purposely volunteering for one dangerous assignment after another. But the Fates had not granted his death wish.

In an effort to exorcise his memories, he'd drowned himself in his work as a Pinkerton. But never in all that time had his heart pounded with anything akin to real emotion.

Until now. In a single confrontation with a hellcat woman intent on journeying cross-country with a passel of mail-order brides, the tender scars on his heart had been torn wide open.

Growling in self-disgust, Gabe vowed that he would not betray Emily's memory by becoming involved with another woman. He owed his late wife that much, at least.

And he couldn't afford to drop his guard for a beautiful woman. Especially one who was now using a different name. He'd have to ask one of his men to watch the boardinghouse and follow her if she left the establishment.

Forcing himself to concentrate, Gabe traced his planned route West on the map. Unbeknownst to the passengers, the excursion was not all it appeared to be. Gabe had been hired to organize a group of men to escort a clandestine payroll shipment destined for the western offices of the Overland Express Railroad. The shipment would be made under the watchful eye of Victor Elliot, a high-ranking employee for the railroad.

The addition of Elliot to Gabe's team still rankled. The arrival of an Overland Express representative was an open slur against Gabe's trustworthiness, but he hadn't bothered to argue. Gabe knew he wouldn't have been offered the prestigious job at all if Josiah Burton hadn't been an old friend. The assignment was a chance for Gabe to make a name for himself as something other than a deserter. Cracking the case would mean national news exposure.

But if anything happened to the shipment, Gabe also knew that he would be held personally accountable.

The door to his room opened and Gabe peered up at the portly shape outlined by the afternoon sun streaming into the corridor.

Victor Elliot.

Gabe scowled. Although he understood the concerns of Overland Express and their wish to have a member of the company on the railway journey, that didn't mean that Gabe had to like the man.

"The shipment is safely stowed away until it can be loaded onto the train?" Elliot inquired.

Gabe nodded and returned his attention to the maps. Although he'd memorized the route, he traced the lines again and again as if he could imprint the contours of the land on his brain.

"I've got a concern about the men who accompanied the gold from England," Victor continued, with open irritation at Gabe's aloofness. "One of them is little more than a boy."

"I'll be sure to register your complaint at the same time I offer mine," Gabe said tightly.

"You picked them."

"No," Gabe retorted, "I picked most of the local men. The Pinkerton Agency hired the two men who accompanied the funds from England."

"Then fire them."

Gabe looked up then, his eyes narrowing. "On what grounds?"

"They're both green as grass, man! I doubt they could guard their own mothers, let alone a valuable shipment of gold."

"They won't be doing it alone."

"They shouldn't be doing it at all!"

Gabe weighed Victor's concerns against his own, then shook his head. "It's too late. Hiring two new guards would provide a security breach, and we can't afford to go shorthanded."

"But—"

"The matter is finished."

Victor visibly seethed, but Gabe ignored him. Scooping his hat from the bed, he decided it was time to make the rounds and check on security matters himself. Then he would need to make his way into the city to meet with Josiah Burton in the main office.

Maybe by keeping his mind on the details of the job, he would push the mysterious Phoebe Gray from his thoughts once and for all.

Chapter Four

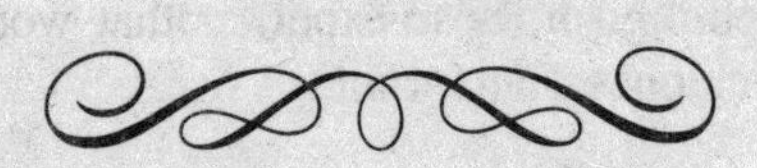

"You're going to do what?" Doreen Llewelyn-Bowes blurted when the women outlined their plan to obtain a male escort. "Have you all lost your minds?"

Phoebe was beginning to grow tired of Doreen. The other women had barely returned to the boardinghouse and gathered together their emergency funds before she'd begun a litany of complaints—they'd taken too long, the weather was too hot, New York was too noisy. When Mable and Maude explained the plan to hire Bertram Potter to escort them West, Doreen had stared at them with as much horror as if they'd announced they planned to strip naked and dance in the streets.

"I really don't know what you find confusing about the plan, Doreen," Phoebe said. "We need a man—any man—who would be willing to travel West with us in the morning."

"B-but you said this Potter person was in jail!"

"Merely a formality. He hasn't committed a crime. Not really. He merely...played stowaway. I heard the captain say that he would forget the charges if Bertram could find a way to raise the necessary funds. If not, they'll send him back to England.''

''So let them.''

''He's our only chance, Doreen,'' Twila said impatiently.

Without another word, Phoebe dumped the bonnetful of coins they had collected onto an overstuffed settee. Allowing for those expenses that would arrive during their journey, the women had contributed any money they felt they could spare. Now, gathered in the sitting room, they feverishly counted their stash.

''Do we have enough?'' Edith breathed.

''If I've figured the correct exchange for dollars into pounds, we're...'' Phoebe quickly counted, then bit her lip. ''We're five dollars short.''

Five dollars. She found it ironic that only weeks earlier she had boarded a ship as the daughter of the Marquis of Dobbenshire. If only the title had come with tangible wealth rather than letters of credit.

En masse, the women turned to look at Doreen.

Betty proclaimed indignantly, ''You haven't contributed yet.''

Doreen sniffed. ''That's because it's a horrible idea. It won't work.''

''You'll contribute or we'll go without you,'' Mable said. She clasped the handle of her walking stick in a way that warned she wasn't so ladylike that she wouldn't consider using it.

Doreen huffed again, folding her arms tightly beneath her breasts. But her stance had lost some of its bravado. ''I don't have five dollars to spare.''

''Give what you have,'' Phoebe said softly, ''and I'll find a way to get the rest.''

It was clear that Doreen didn't believe Phoebe's assertion, but she finally sighed with great theatrical emphasis. Bending, she lifted her skirts to remove a small coin purse stitched to the inside of a petticoat. Removing two large dollar coins, she tossed them on the pile.

"I expect my money back when this preposterous idea fails to work," she proclaimed. "If Gabriel Cutter frowns on women joining his group, he won't let a felon board that train." Then, turning on her heel, she left the room in a swish of skirts.

"We still need three dollars," Mable said, counting the money, then counting it again.

Phoebe mentally reviewed the valuables she'd sewn into her spare corset—a few pieces of her mother's jewelry and the signet ring her father had given her as a wedding present. The items were precious to her, worth far more in sentimental value than they could ever obtain on the market. But she was at a crossroads. She had no money to speak of, merely the smallest amount she had thought necessary for the journey. Even her friend "Louisa" could be of little help to her until she arrived in Boston and was able to exchange the letters of credit for cash.

So Phoebe would have to sell something.

Spying her dusty satchel still lying on the floor next to the door, Phoebe said, "Can someone show me to my room? I'll just freshen up a bit, then we'll find Mr. Potter and obtain his release."

"But how?" Edith whispered.

Phoebe squeezed her hand in reassurance. "I've got a few valuables socked away for an emergency." She grimaced good-naturedly. "I just hadn't thought I'd be dipping into them before I managed to leave New York."

Phoebe's heart thumped against her ribs as she pondered the audacity of what she was about to do. After taking stock of the treasures she'd hidden in her trunk, she knew there was only one item of value that she would ever be able to sell.

The Dobbenshire signet ring.

By selling the piece, she would be severing the last tangible link with her father. And although she had convinced herself that such an action would be an easy enough matter to accomplish, she was discovering that the thought of forfeiting the ring filled her with a small amount of sadness.

True, her father had never loved her. She'd been an inconvenience to him and a burden—and he'd never lost the opportunity to remind her of that fact.

But he was her father. Didn't that title alone demand a certain amount of respect?

Shaking free of that thought, she collected her things and followed the other women down the hall to her room, knowing that if she didn't sell the ring quickly, she might well lose her resolve.

Gabriel waited until he was sure he hadn't been followed before making his way into the ''rarified'' area of town frequented by the wealthy.

Checking quickly to ensure that he'd garnered no attention, he slipped into the lobby of the Biltmore Hotel and quickly made his way to a back set of stairs used by the staff. Tugging his hat more firmly over his brow to avoid giving anyone a clear look at his face, Gabriel wound his way through the narrow corridors to the presidential suite. He knocked once, paused, then scratched the gleaming wood three times.

For one beat of silence, there was no response. Then the door creaked open a slit.

Gabriel waited, knowing that he was being studied. This time a far more experienced pair of Pinkertons completed the inspection. He'd trained the two men himself during the past three years.

"All clear, sir?" a voice whispered.

"Clear."

The space widened only enough to allow Gabriel to slip into the darkened room. Then, with a thump, the door closed and the lock was driven firmly into place.

Gabriel waited, hearing the rasp of a match. A bright flare of light revealed two men dressed like London dandies in creased trousers, silk shirts and brocade vests. With a wry smile, Gabriel noted that the elegant attire contrasted sharply with the ammunition belts draped across their chests.

"Green and Miles." Gabe nodded to the men.

Isaac Green spat a stream of tobacco into a spittoon on the floor. The shot was made with amazing accuracy, revealing just how long the men had been cooped up in the opulent hotel suite.

"You can call me Sally and pin a bonnet on my head as long as you tell me we can get out of this stinking hotel." In as long as Gabriel had known him, Isaac had never been fond of being closeted indoors.

"The crossing was smooth?"

Abner Miles didn't even pretend to misconstrue the meaning of Gabriel's question. They all knew he wasn't speaking of the weather they'd encountered while sailing from London to New York.

"No problems, cap'n. I don't think a soul on board cared if we finished the trip alive for all the attention they gave us. Not much has changed since we've arrived here. No one has given us a second glance."

"Let's hope it stays that way." Gabriel examined the trunks and crates stacked in the corner.

Here was where the real payroll shipment was hidden—amid boxes labeled Farm Equipment and battered steamer trunks bearing the names Miles or Green.

From the moment the Overland Express's payroll gold had been removed from an English vault, Gabe had gone to great lengths to ensure no one would ever know that Roberts and Peterson, the two new Pinkerton agents, guarded little more than crates filled with lead bars. At the same time, on a separate ship, Miles and Green had been unobtrusively making the same journey with their trunks of gold.

Satisfied that the seals on the containers were still intact, Gabriel surveyed the men again. He'd asked them to blend in with the other genteel travelers at the Biltmore, and judging by their attire, the men had followed his instructions to the letter.

"The two of you will need to see to the transfer of the gold before nine tomorrow morning. I'll send the usual agents dressed as stevedores to give you a hand, but I'll only be able to watch from afar."

"No problem, cap'n," Green said.

Miles nodded, then asked, "The rest of tomorrow's instructions are as planned?"

Both of them stared at Gabe intently, knowing the trust he'd placed in them.

"Everything else goes as planned," Gabe confirmed. He studied the men again, noting the ease with which they held their weapons. Despite the duo's casual stances, Gabriel had no doubts that they could shoot and reload faster than the average man. Their senses were highly tuned to each nuance of sound outside the hotel room. They could sense trouble like a deer smelling a hunter. Such skills had kept them alive during the war and made them invaluable to Gabriel now.

''See to it that you change your clothes before you arrive at the station,'' Gabriel said. ''The moment you join the group of settlers on the train, I want the two of you to look like dirt-poor farmers who have finally managed to scrape together a few dimes for your passage.''

It was clear that both men were eager to abandon their current mode of dress for the more comfortable gear usually worn on the job.

''Once on the train, we won't speak unless necessary,'' Gabe continued. ''You'll have two men at your disposal—Garrison and Withers—to spell you off every twelve hours. Use them as runners if you need anything from me. Any questions?''

They shook their heads.

''Until tomorrow.''

Gabriel turned to leave, but paused when both men saluted.

He knew the gesture was automatic. After all, Miles and Green had served beneath him during the war. They'd grown accustomed to taking orders. But after charges of desertion had been brought against Gabriel, more than one man in his old regiment had turned against him.

He wanted to say something. He wanted to challenge the men for believing in him when so many didn't. But he knew the pair hadn't meant to remind him of things he wished to leave forgotten.

''Good luck, gentlemen,'' was all he said. Then Gabriel retreated into the corridor.

The afternoon heat was beginning to mount when Gabe exited the Biltmore and pulled a pocket watch from his vest.

Nearly twenty-four hours remained before the journey West would begin.

Sighing, Gabe resisted the urge to rub away the tension gripping his neck muscles. Instead, he paused outside, leaning his shoulder against the marble facade of the hotel. Hoping to catch a hint of a breeze, he took the hat from his head and wiped his brow with his arm.

Replacing his hat, Gabe looked up, then froze. The man he'd sent to follow Phoebe was mere yards away, sitting on an iron bench with careful nonchalance. What catastrophe had caused the Pinkerton to abandon his orders in order to find Gabe?

''O'Mara,'' Gabe said quietly as he approached.

''Cap'n.''

''What's happened that you were sent to find me?''

The Pinkerton seemed confused. ''Beg pardon? I followed the woman here.'' The Pinkerton pointed to a jewelry shop across the road. ''She's gone in there.''

The fact that Phoebe had felt it necessary to visit a posh jewelers did nothing to calm Gabe's suspicions. Why would a woman dress like a pauper to meet with him, then indulge in a whim for pretty baubles mere hours later?

''Go on home, O'Mara. I'll take care of things from here.''

''You're sure?''

Gabe nodded. ''Perhaps it's time Miss Gray and I had an in-depth talk.''

* * *

As the door snapped shut behind her, Phoebe bit her lip in disappointment. She had instructed the hansom cab to bring her to the ''most expensive jewelry store in New York City.'' But after gathering her courage and entering the establishment, she had been treated no better than a beggar.

Twenty dollars! That was all they were willing to offer her for the signet ring. Granted, twenty dollars would help her buy the things she needed, but the amount was a tenth of what she had been expecting. She'd been so angered by the patronizing tone of the clerk that she'd stormed from the shop with the ring still clutched in her palm.

What was she going to do? She needed money. Desperately. Quickly.

Stepping out of the way of the passers-by, Phoebe vainly tried to brush as much of the dust as possible from her skirts and bodice, sure that there must be another jeweler nearby where she could try again. But with her gloves as soiled as her dress, her efforts were less than satisfactory.

''Problems?''

Phoebe jumped when a deep, husky voice murmured the word in her ear. For a moment, her heart leaped and she was sure that it was the stranger from the boat. But when she turned, it was to find Gabriel Cutter standing at her shoulder.

Her stomach flip-flopped and her mouth grew suddenly dry. ''Mr. Cutter,'' she said weakly. Then, with more strength, she added, ''Has no one told you that it isn't polite to startle a person on a crowded thoroughfare?''

His expression remained neutral, but she thought she caught a glint of humor in his steel-gray eyes. ''I would imagine it's impolite to startle a person at any time or in any location.''

Phoebe pressed her lips together, refusing to rise to the bait offered by the lift of his brows. It was clear that he found her amusing and wished to rile her. But she would not argue with the man. She wouldn't. With her luck, she would make him angry and he would find a way to renege on his agreement.

The thought caused her to frown. ''Have you been following me?''

His dark brows lifted even more. This time his gray eyes darkened with something akin to suspicion. ''Why would I possibly want to follow you, Miss Gray?''

''Perhaps you should tell me,'' she insisted archly. Something about his look made her uncomfortable. So much so that her shoulder muscles grew tight with the effort it took not to run away.

''For your information,'' Gabe said, ''I had an appointment in the area. Imagine my surprise when I emerged on the street to find you here.''

He plucked a stray piece of fluff from her shoulder, and she stiffened. The action was innocent. So why did that tiny point of contact send a flurry of gooseflesh down her spine?

''Perhaps,'' Gabe continued, ''I should accuse *you* of following *me.*''

This time, as he watched her from beneath hooded eyes, she gasped indignantly.

''You can't possibly think that I would...that I could be...that I would *want* to...'' The idea that he could think she'd meant to spy on him caused her to sputter in consternation. ''I—I can assure you, Mr. Cutter, that from the depths of my being—from the very marrow of my bones!—there is nothing on earth that could ever, *ever,* persuade me to follow you *anywhere!*"

He looked far from cowed by her response. But what alarmed her most was that he didn't seem entirely convinced by her protestations.

"Then why are you here rather than preparing for your imminent journey?"

She didn't like his tone, didn't like it at all. Obviously, the man doubted that the women would manage to have their bags packed by sunrise, let alone have a male escort in tow.

"For your information, I had some shopping to do."

He flicked a glance at the exclusive neighborhood where she had chosen to do her errands.

"And just what were you looking for here? A diamond stickpin? That should prove helpful."

She felt her face grow warm. Damning her penchant for blushing, she hastened to exclaim, "For your information, I need some sturdy shoes and a few...personal items." Then, realizing that he would never believe such a thing given the expensive shops that surrounded her, she added, "The cab driver must have misunderstood my directions."

"Ahh, then you'll be needing another ride to a more sensible area of town."

"Yes. Yes, I suppose so."

When she tried to brush past him to hail another cab, he took her wrist and stopped her.

"There's no need to waste your money on a carriage. I've got my horse right over here."

"B-but your meeting!"

"It's finished. And since I'm not due at the railway

yard for a few more hours, I may as well help you with your shopping.''

Once again, Phoebe began stammering in protest, but the words fell on deaf ears. Gabriel pulled her irresistibly toward a large roan gelding tied to an iron hitching ring.

''Oh, no. No, I really couldn't,'' she gasped.

The animal was huge! And with each step, it became more and more clear that Gabriel meant for her to ride atop the beast's back.

She'd never ridden a horse before. On those infrequent occasions when she had been allowed to travel from the school, she had always used a carriage. Even with Gabriel holding her, she didn't think that she could stay atop the brutish animal. And by heaven, she couldn't allow the man to hold her, either!

''Is something the matter?''

She dug her heels into the ground, refusing to budge another inch. ''I really can't accept your kind offer, Mr. Cutter.''

''Why not?''

''It wouldn't be proper.''

''In what way would it be *im*proper?''

She lifted her chin to a prudish level. ''I hardly know you well enough to allow you to take such liberties, Mr. Cutter.''

''Liberties? From my point of view I would hardly describe a ride through the streets of New York as 'taking liberties.'''

''Which is why we will have to agree to disagree on this point. I can't and shan't impose upon your goodwill in such a manner.''

''I hardly think you're imposing on anything if I'm the one who made the suggestion.''

Before she knew what he meant to do, he grasped her by the waist and lifted her sideways onto the gelding.

"Do you wish to remain sidesaddle or would you rather sit astride?"

Phoebe's mouth opened and closed like a fish, but no sound emerged. Never in her life had she been so terrified. She felt as if she were twenty feet up, staring down, down at the rock-strewn ground. If she were to fall, she would surely be killed.

"Sidesaddle," she finally managed to whisper, worried that Gabriel might take it into his head to help her sit astride by rearranging her skirts and lifting one leg over the pommel. Her face flamed at the mere idea.

She was so intent on gripping the pommel that she barely noted the way he swung into place behind her. It wasn't until Gabe wrapped an arm around her waist and pulled her against him that she suddenly realized the danger of her position—and this time it had nothing to do with the horse.

How had she managed to land herself in this predicament? Of all the people she could have encountered in New York City, why had she the misfortune of meeting up with this man yet again?

"Are you sure you haven't been following me?" she said, confronting him face-to-face.

The instant she turned, she wished she'd kept quiet. He was much nearer than she had imagined. She could see the deep creases on either side of his mouth and the bits of silver that flecked the gray of his eyes. This close, his features gave the appearance of being hewn from a block of marble, the sharp angles and blunt edges giving him the fierce countenance of a battle-hardened warrior.

And yet...the way he met her gaze, the way his eyes dropped to focus on her lips, created an intimacy that was at odds with his appearance.

"I'm not following you, Phoebe. Although perhaps I should."

"Why?" The word was a bare puff of sound.

"Because you're dangerous."

She couldn't help laughing. "Me? How can you possibly have come to that conclusion?"

"You have a way of infecting a man's brain so that he can't think of anything but you."

The words were uttered so softly that Phoebe's mouth parted and she blinked at him in disbelief, sure that she'd misunderstood.

He couldn't possibly be speaking of her. She wasn't the sort of woman to inspire a second glance, let alone "infect a man's brain...."

Long moments passed before she managed to whisper, "I think that you must be pulling my leg, Mr. Cutter." The moment she uttered the phrase, she wished she hadn't. How often had the faculty of Goodfellow's scolded her for her informality?

But if Gabe was struck by the commonness of her speech, he gave no indication. Instead, his gaze had dropped to her skirts. She blushed, realizing that she'd given him ideas that he shouldn't entertain.

"Where are you taking me, Mr. Cutter?" she asked imperiously.

"You stated that you needed shoes."

"Yes, but I have a good many things to do today and I'm sure that you don't want to trail after me."

"As I stated, I have a few hours to waste."

Blast the man! Why couldn't he realize that she might not *want* his company?

"Mr. Cutter, I don't wish to be rude, but there are a good many things that I need to do that are of a...personal nature."

"Such as?"

Phoebe didn't know if the man was being purposely obtuse or if he really did have the manners of a goat.

"Stop the horse, please."

"But we aren't there yet."

"Stop this horse at once, or I will jump down in the middle of the street!"

Given the fact that she was clinging to Gabriel with a white-knuckled grip, her demand lost some of its effectiveness. Nevertheless, with a slight touch of the reins against the horse's neck, Gabriel turned the animal down a side street and stopped in the shade of an alley.

"Very well, Miss Gray. What is it that you feel a burning need to say standing still that you can't say while we are in motion?"

For long moments she studied the man, wondering if she could trust him. Heaven only knew that she hadn't had much luck with the rougher sex. Her father had ignored her, and her intended husband hadn't bothered to show up for his own wedding. What made her think that this man would help her?

She studied the hard angles of his cheek and jaw. A shadow was already beginning to appear, giving testament to a heavy beard. The sight should have given him a scruffy appearance, but only served to cause her breath to hitch in her throat in a manner she had never experienced before.

Her gaze slipped to his lips. She had almost kissed him earlier that day. What would happen if he were to try again? Would she allow him to succeed so that she could feel those lips against hers?

The mere thought was enough to bring a sizzling heat to her cheeks.

You mustn't think such things!

"Well? Do you mean to sit here all day?"

Ignoring Gabe's pithy tone, she reached into the watch pocket of her skirt. She could think of no reason to keep her true errand from the man. She had to find a way to exchange her father's ring for coin. Why shouldn't she ask Gabriel's help? As an American, he wouldn't recognize the significance of the crest. He might wonder why she wished to sell it, but the fact that she was willing to marry a stranger was proof enough of her impoverished circumstances. What did it matter that she intended to sell a family heirloom?

Feeling instinctively that she could trust in the man's discretion, she held the ring out for his inspection. "I wish to sell this to someone who will give me a fair price."

She saw his eyes narrow in interest. Briefly, his fingers brushed hers as he took the signet ring and held it up for a better look. Intently, he studied the ornate design of lilies swirling around a griffin with an upraised paw.

A whistle escaped from his lips. "Very impressive."

"It's solid gold, with sapphires and rubies set into the band."

Cutter twisted the ring to look at the jewels. "So this is why you were loitering outside that jewelry shop."

"Yes."

His eyes narrowed. ''Where did you get it? Did you steal it?''

''No! It once belonged to my father.''

''Does he know you have it?''

She offered Gabriel what she hoped was a withering stare. ''My father had it refashioned as a gift for me before I left England.'' She snatched the ring away from him. ''Now, if you will kindly take me back to the jewelers, I would be grateful.''

He clucked to the horse, and again she grabbed at Gabe's waist to keep from becoming unseated.

''I've got a better idea,'' he said as they entered the crowded thoroughfare. ''But you'll need to hang on tight. We've got a bit of a ride ahead of us and only a short time to make it before the shop closes for the afternoon meal.''

Chapter Five

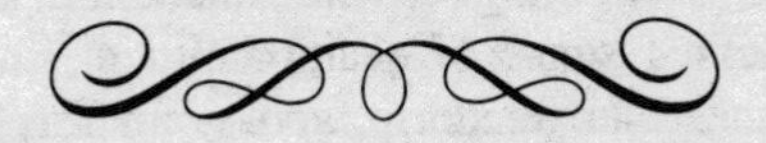

"Where are you taking me?"

"To a friend of mine who's in the business of buying things."

She frowned. "Is this friend a legitimate salesman?"

Gabe laughed, the sound seeming slightly rusty as it emerged from his throat. "As legitimate as a priest."

"Will he give me a fair price?"

"I assure you, if anyone will give you what it's worth, Adam will."

Within minutes, Phoebe had completely lost her bearings. Gabe led the horse in and out of narrow streets and alleyways, until finally, he stopped in front of a modest shop with a simple sign that read Jewelry Fashioned and Repaired.

Gabe slid from the saddle and tied the reins to a wooden hitching rail. As he did so, Phoebe found herself staring at the ripple of muscles that played across his back. Despite his shirt and vest, it was easy to see that he was a powerful man. A formidable man.

So why didn't she run? Why didn't she slide out of

the saddle herself and escape the strange effect he had on her body and her emotions?

"Is anything wrong?"

He had glanced at her over his shoulder, but Phoebe had been so intent on the taut stretch of his shirt that she hadn't looked away until it was too late.

Her cheeks grew hot, but she avoided meeting his gaze by concentrating on her surroundings instead. With a sinking sense of disappointment, she discovered that these surroundings were not nearly so fine as those of the jewelry shop she'd left only minutes earlier.

"Are you sure this is the place to bring my ring?"

"Quite sure."

He reached up to help her dismount, and all thoughts of the ring fled from her brain as she stared at his hands.

Strong hands. Blunt. Long-fingered. They were the hands of an artist or a poet, not those of a travel-weary trail boss.

Her breath hitched in her throat and her heart pounded as those fingers slid around her waist, taking her weight. He lowered her to the ground much more slowly than necessary, allowing her body to brush against him, her feet to rest between his own in the dust. Even then he didn't immediately release her. Instead, his head lowered and he whispered, "You can trust me."

The words seemed to travel from her ear to her heart in an effervescent flurry, chilling her, then warming her.

Trust him? How could she trust any man who had only to touch her to make her thoughts scatter to the four winds? Before leaving the convent, she had vowed that no man would ever control her again. Married or free, she would be her own mistress. Never again would she be brought to a point where she felt trapped or at the mercy of another human being. If and when she lost her heart, it would be because she offered it willingly.

So why was she trembling? Why did this man have the ability to swamp her common sense and tempt her to surrender her problems to him, come what may?

"You're sure about this?"

For long moments she was confused about the meaning of Gabe's question. Sure? Sure about what? About allowing him to hold her? About being tempted to surrender to the emotions he inspired? About his offer to help her sell her father's ring?

No. Don't trust him. He is a man. Eventually, he will betray you. As soon as your usefulness to him is finished, he will abandon you, just like your father.

Mentally shaking herself, Phoebe pushed resolutely against his chest. Summoning all the firmness she could master, she said, "I am quite sure that I wish to sell my ring."

Her tone held a warning—one Gabe clearly understood, because he stepped away, his eyes growing fathomless again. "Then let's get about the business of selling the bauble so that you can get on with your shopping."

Phoebe dug her heels into the dirt. "No. I wish to go inside alone."

She had expected an argument, but Gabe offered a curt nod. "Fine. Ask for Adam, then tell him I sent you. You'll get a bit more that way."

Hurrying to the door, Phoebe could only pray that

the man would offer her more than twenty dollars. She was swiftly running out of time.

Less than twenty minutes later, Phoebe emerged from the jewelry shop, her face alight with joy. Pausing, she raised up tiptoe, searching the boardwalk until she saw Gabe sitting on a bench across the street.

Smiling, she waved at him as if he were the dearest of friends.

As he watched, Gabe had no doubts that she'd been given a fair price. Adam was a good man. He and his family had been in the jewelry business for generations. They prided themselves on their artistry and the reputation for honesty that they had developed over the intervening years. It was Adam who had fashioned Emily's wedding band—a gold circlet of intertwined flowers that even now Gabe wore on a chain around his neck. Adam had been one of the few friends to remain true after the rumors of Gabe's desertion had begun to circulate among his acquaintances.

The sight of Phoebe hurrying toward him caused Gabe to inwardly wince. She was so beautiful and so frank. Every emotion she experienced was patently displayed on her features.

Surely with a face like that, she couldn't possibly be a threat. If she'd had any designs on the gold, wouldn't he have read that knowledge in her eyes?

Damn it, he should be on guard. For reasons unbeknownst to him, she was traveling under a name different than the one she had used on the ship. Nor did her current mode of dress or her willingness to sell a family heirloom fit the picture of the woman wearing sapphires and silk who had journeyed first class from England.

Nevertheless, there was something about her that weakened his resolve to remain aloof. Only one other woman had ever been able to instill such an emotion in him.

Gabe instinctively reached for the chain at his neck and felt for the intricate gold band beneath his shirt. Emotionally, he steeled himself.

Phoebe's ability to arouse him was dangerous to more than his job. He had his own equilibrium to think about. Phoebe was not Emily and she never could be. And he had sworn upon Emily's grave that he would never allow himself to feel so deeply about another person again.

So why, after reminding himself of such a fact over and over again, did he find himself drawn to Phoebe Gray?

And why did he think he could tempt the Fates by surrendering to the power of her smile?

Standing, Gabe intercepted her halfway across the narrow street. Before Phoebe could even speak, he muttered harshly, "We've got to get back. I've just remembered an appointment."

The light dimmed from her eyes, quickly replaced by a glint of pride. In an instant, Gabe knew that he had destroyed the fragile trust that she had begun to feel with him.

"Yes, of course," she said stiffly. "In fact, since I have shopping to do, you may as well run along, Mr. Cutter. I wouldn't want to detain you a moment longer."

He opened his mouth to inform her that he wasn't about to leave her in an unfamiliar part of town with a purse full of cash, but she added forcefully, "I can take care of myself, Mr. Cutter."

Gabe hesitated, but the jut of her chin and the embarrassed tint to her cheeks made it clear that she wouldn't have accepted his help at that moment even if she were lying injured in the street.

''Good day to you, ma'am,'' he said, with a touch of his finger to his hat.

She didn't bother to reply. She merely huffed and offered him her back as she marched toward the line of shops in the next block.

The sky outside Phoebe's window was still black when she woke the next morning. Moving hurriedly in the darkness, she dressed in the new cotton skirt, shirtwaist and basque that she had purchased only the day before. With dark stockings and sensible shoes that laced above her ankles, she felt appropriately attired and completely respectable. Today Mr. Cutter couldn't possibly mistake her for a woman of easy virtue.

As if to further underscore the point, she combed her hair away from a savage part and secured it in a thick plaited knot at her nape, then donned leather gloves and an oversize bonnet to shield herself from the sun's glare.

Gazing at her reflection, Phoebe scarcely recognized herself.

This wasn't the same person who had spent a lifetime immured behind the moldering walls of the charity school. The girl who had railed for years against her father's indifference. The woman who had been married by proxy to a stranger.

Where had she found the courage to switch her life's course with that of another? And why did she feel as if the events had been starkly etched on her features?

She tipped her face to the lamplight. Could others see the confidence that thrummed within her? Could they sense her renewed sense of purpose?

Her fingers skimmed over the contours of her face, then lingered on the bow of her lower lip.

If her challenges were written there so clearly to her own eyes, was it also obvious to others that she'd nearly been kissed?

When she met her own gaze in the mirror, Phoebe was startled by the hunger she found radiating from her eyes.

What was wrong with her?

Drat and bother, she mustn't allow the man to have so much power over her. She would avoid him like the plague during the journey.

And if she were forced to speak to him, she would take whatever steps were necessary to ensure that she was in total control of the exchange.

As the women neared the station, Phoebe feared that a confrontation with Gabriel Cutter might come much sooner than she had anticipated.

Bertram Potter was drunk. Indeed, the man had passed out on the floor of the omnibus the women had hired to take them to the station house.

Sighing, Phoebe knew that none of them would be lucky enough to escape a confrontation with Gabe once he caught sight of their chaperon. And the only hope they had of delaying his anger would be to delay the introductions until after Mr. Potter had been given time enough to grow sober again.

Although the sky had just begun to pinken with the

sun's rays, the roads leading to the rail yard were clogged with traffic. Poking her head out of the window, Phoebe checked to see that the wagon carrying their belongings still followed. Then she sat back against the hard leather of her seat.

Bertram Potter offered a phlegmy cough, lifted his head and eyed the women blearily. ''Are we there yet, dearies?'' Then he collapsed against the floorboards again and renewed his slumber.

Phoebe winced, wondering how the man could have fallen to this low state in the space of a few hours. This morning he had been a bit groggy but presentable. Then somehow, before leaving the boardinghouse, he'd managed to sink into the very depths of dissolution.

''He seemed so happy when we all went to our rooms last night,'' Twila remarked.

If the truth were told, Bertram had been ecstatic about their proposal.

''It seems Mr. Potter decided to celebrate his change of fortunes,'' Maude offered wryly.

''Although I've no idea how he managed to celebrate so *completely* since breakfast,'' Mable added.

Phoebe's nose wrinkled. ''I've a feeling that Mrs. Cates is missing a few bottles of her elderberry wine.''

''What are we going to do?'' Betty moaned from the seat beside Phoebe.

''As soon as we arrive, escort him to the washroom in the railway station,'' Phoebe said, patting the package on her lap. ''Have him change into the clothes we bought him yesterday. Then give him a good combing and a shave.''

Twila gasped. ''We can't do that! It wouldn't be seemly.''

"Well, it's obvious that Mr. Bertram won't be able to do it himself. And I don't think we can afford to leave him as he is."

"We might get him to look respectable," Betty muttered under her breath, "but it will help matters immensely if he's conscious."

Sighing, Phoebe realized she was right.

"You worry about Mr. Potter and I'll worry about Mr. Cutter." Phoebe lifted her chin and clutched her reticule more tightly. The hard, heavy shape of the revolver hidden in its folds gave her a small measure of comfort. "If I have to, I'll distract the man."

Betty's eyes widened. "How?"

How? She had no idea. Biting her lip, Phoebe wondered again how she had become the unnamed leader of this motley group. "I'll do whatever I have to do," she said bravely.

"Will you use…feminine wiles?"

Phoebe's stomach tightened at the mere suggestion. In truth, she'd been thinking about pointing the revolver at the man again. Judging by the wide-eyed expressions of the other women, it was obvious they thought she might have more success with a bit of flirtation.

Phoebe shook her head. "Oh, no. I couldn't attempt a—"

"Seduction?" Twila suggested slyly.

Edith's eyes widened.

Betty gaped.

"It wouldn't work, I tell you," Phoebe insisted. "That man can't be seduced."

"Nonsense," Mable said with a wave of her hand. "There isn't a male alive who can't be seduced in one way or another."

"But—"

"It's not as if you have to bed the man," Maude said, causing the other women to gasp, then giggle in embarrassed fascination. "You merely have to...*dally* with him until the train is about to leave and it's too late for him to deny us passage."

Phoebe felt an embarrassed heat climbing into her cheeks. "I will not...cannot..."

"You aren't married yet," Twila stated, as if that were the only objection Phoebe might have. "It's a game, that's all."

"Then let someone else play it!"

The women turned to Doreen, but she fended off their attention. "I can't set things right." She patted her hair in obvious regret. "Mr. Cutter is already familiar with Phoebe. It would look suspicious if anyone else tried to waylay him."

"She's right," Twila agreed. "No one else can do it."

"Then we'd best spruce you up a bit. You won't be getting the man's attention that way," Mable said, frowning.

Her sister sniffed in agreement.

Glancing down, Phoebe studied her new traveling suit with its severe lines and understated pattern. "What's wrong with the way I look?"

"Not a thing if you're a missionary on her way to do work with the heathens," Maude said with a smile.

"But you aren't exactly dressed for enticement," Doreen added with a disdainful glance.

Phoebe's gaze bounced from woman to woman. "Once and for all, I couldn't possibly...I merely meant that I would..."

Twila patted her hand. "No one expects you to do

anything...compromising. But we need to buy ourselves some time, and nothing distracts a man more than a pretty woman."

Betty tugged at the strings of her reticule. "I have some violet water."

"And I've got a ribbon for your hair!" Edith volunteered.

"But—" Phoebe held a hand to her bonnet, which hid the neat twist of braids at her nape. Before she could voice her objections, the other women had gathered around her. Soon she found her hair more elaborately coiffed with a host of pilfered hairpins and the borrowed ribbon. Her own sturdy bonnet had been exchanged for Betty's tiny, flower-bedecked hat. The buttons of her basque had been loosened and a delicate lace scarf had been tucked in the opening and pinned into place. But she drew the line when Mable insisted she change into a red taffeta petticoat and lift the edge of her hem aside with one of Maude's brass skirt hooks.

"No, absolutely not!" Phoebe gasped, still stinging from the afternoon before, when she'd been mistaken for a woman of easy virtue. She might be willing to waylay Mr. Cutter, but that didn't mean she meant to toy with him as if she were a strumpet. She would talk, argue, banter or cajole, but she wouldn't...

Wouldn't what?

Flirt with the man? Kiss him?

No. Absolutely not. She wasn't that kind of woman. Besides which, the man was dangerous. He had the ability to upset her equilibrium with the slightest glance. It would be foolhardy to tempt fate with anything more than a cool demeanor.

But even as she insisted such a thing to herself, she

mourned the fact that she couldn't be more brazen—like one of the characters in the penny romances she'd smuggled into school.

That was it! She would pretend to be someone else. Rather than being a lonely girl with a charity school upbringing, she would be...*Lorraine of Lagerfield? Jessymyn and her Tragic Love?*

Or *Solome of Sussex?*

Yes, that was the one.

Taking a deep, calming breath, she envisioned one of her favorite heroines—a woman who had dared the wrath of King Richard III in order to save her beloved brother from certain death. She was the perfect choice—beautiful, seductive and entrancing, able to lure a man into bending to her will.

"What is she doing?" Edith whispered.

"I think she's praying," Twila murmured.

Phoebe refused to open her eyes. "I'm preparing myself for the part. I'm transforming myself into a siren."

"A what?" Edith whispered again.

"Shh!"

The omnibus lurched to a halt, nearly throwing the women to the floor and bringing an end to Phoebe's preparations before they could really begin. But after righting her bonnet, she opened her eyes. Summoning all of the haughtiness she could muster, she took a deep, calming breath, then made her way through the tangle of feet and baggage toward the rear door.

For several minutes Phoebe watched Gabe as he oversaw the loading of the train. Staying in the shadows, she decided that she would wait as long as possible before beginning her campaign to delay him. After all, there was no sense in disrupting his routine until he became aware of the women's arrival.

Unfortunately, by cooling her heels, she was given too much time to study the man. Even without having been introduced to him the day before, she would have known that he was in charge. Everything about him displayed a silent mantle of authority, from the strength of purpose in his stride to the proud jut of his chin. And when he swung into the saddle to oversee the loading of a wagonful of crates, the effect was enough to cause her knees to tremble.

Why was she so flummoxed by this man?

As if sensing her thoughts, Gabe looked up. Their gazes locked for a split second, then he returned to his work. But she didn't fool herself by thinking he would continue to ignore her. He would seek out the women soon enough, and when he did, she'd best be prepared to act her part.

"Is something wrong, Miss Gray?"

She stiffened, realizing that Gabe had managed to approach her without her being aware of his movements. Drat it all, she'd been staring at the man only moments before. Why hadn't she kept her eyes on him?

"You appear worried, Miss Gray," he said when she didn't acknowledge him. "Could it possibly be that you and the other women were unable to find a chaperon?"

He was so smug, so certain of their failure that Phoebe couldn't help but offer him a smile of triumph. "Not at all, Mr. Cutter. Things have fallen smoothly into place."

"And may I ask who the lucky man is?"

"Mr. Bertram Potter."

Out of the corner of her eye, she noticed Maude and Mable half supporting, half dragging the elderly man toward the main waiting room of the station. Turning in the opposite direction, Phoebe took a step, praying that she had piqued the interest of Mr. Cutter enough to cause him to follow her.

His expression remained hard and implacable, and she was sure that she'd failed. But to her infinite relief, she felt his hand circle her elbow and turn her to face him. Over his shoulder, she met the twins' frantic glances.

"This Mr. Potter. Is he of legal age?"

Phoebe forced herself to offer a careless laugh. "Did you really think we would employ a child?"

"The thought did cross my mind when I realized I hadn't made a stipulation that your escort should be mature enough to handle the responsibility."

"You needn't worry on that score. Mr. Potter is old enough to satisfy even your most stringent age qualifications."

He frowned. "He isn't decrepit, is he?"

To her relief, she saw Maude and Mable closing the last few yards of boardwalk leading to the main door.

"Decrepit? No. He is of a comfortable age, but not so advanced in years that you would fear he couldn't make the journey."

Gabe continued to watch her with open suspicion. "Why do I feel that I'll be less than satisfied with the arrangements you've made?"

"I would assume it's because you find yourself in a position of having to honor your bargain."

"Perhaps I should meet this chaperon—as well as the rest of the brides."

This time he was the one to turn, and she grasped

his arm before he could see the twins staggering into the station house, with Mr. Potter supported between them.

"Mr. Cutter, please," she murmured again, employing as much urgency as she could muster. "I need to speak with you."

Gabe's lips thinned. "If there's something about your chaperon that you know I'll object to..."

She started, thinking he'd seen Mr. Potter and meant to argue. But a quick glance over his shoulder assured her that Maude and Mable had disappeared from sight.

When Gabriel turned to see what kept capturing her attention, she took a step closer, coming so near to him that her skirts brushed the tops of his boots.

"Please. I must speak with you—and not about our chaperon."

He lifted one of his brows, but his lips retained their stern line.

"He's a very respectable man, I can assure you. He's a good man, a kind, honest man."

Well, perhaps not so honest. He *had* tried to make the journey from England without paying his fare.

Wanting to put as much space as possible between Gabe, the brides and Mr. Potter, Phoebe moved in the opposite direction, all but pulling Gabe after her.

"No, what I have to say is of a more...personal nature."

His eyes grew hard as steel and she shivered, her resolution crumbling before she was able to shore it up again. Just as he had yesterday, he was distancing himself from her—making her plans of seduction even more difficult.

Chapter Six

"Five minutes, Miss Gray," Gabriel said, shaking free of her grip with apparent ease. Obviously irritated by her request for a private conversation, he strode over the heavily rutted road and made his way to a battered building displaying a sign that read Overland Freight Offices.

With each step, Phoebe's tension grew. How could she possibly keep him here for an extended amount of time?

Gabriel threw open the door, surprising a balding man who was hunched over a desk, scribbling figures in a ledger.

"Get out," Gabriel said without preamble.

Jumping to his feet, the fellow stared at Phoebe, his mouth gaping. "Yes, *sir!*"

Phoebe could feel her face flaming. Of all the gall! Hadn't Gabriel Cutter humiliated her enough? Did he really need to draw attention to the fact that the two of them required a bit of privacy? It seemed unlikely that the man would believe they had come only to talk.

But you haven't come merely to talk. You've come for seduction as well.

Phoebe shivered at the audacity of her own thoughts.

''All right, Miss Gray, how can I help you?'' Gabriel said as he propped his hip on the edge of the desk.

Miss Gray. Had it only been yesterday that they'd been on a first-name basis?

''I—I wished to thank you for being so...decent as to allow us to take the train as planned.''

He scowled, obviously annoyed that she'd demanded he leave his tasks for such an innocuous remark, so she scrambled to add, ''But that's not why I needed to meet with you privately.''

''Oh, really.''

Think of something...quick!

''It's about the jeweler you took me to yesterday.''

''Yes.''

''He offered me a fair price—indeed, a handsome price.''

''I'm glad he could help. Now, if that's all...''

Mr. Cutter stood, but she quickly said, ''No, that's not all!''

When he regarded her questioningly, she scrambled to remember her original intent on getting this man alone. But try as she might, she couldn't seem to still her whirling thoughts. Gabriel had a way of driving all sense of reason from her brain and leaving her addled as an idiot.

''I hope that you didn't apply any undue influence on your friend to offer me more money than was fair.''

''Since I didn't speak to Adam and had no idea you intended to sell anything until meeting you on the street, I hardly think that's possible.'' Gabriel swept his hat from his head, laid it on the desk, then raked his fingers through the dark, windswept strands. A part of her noted that his hair was too long to be fashionable. He needed a woman to cut it for him.

Stop it!

''Oh, yes. Yes, that's true,'' she said hurriedly, hoping her cheeks hadn't grown pink with her own embarrassing thoughts. ''I—I didn't think.''

Seduce him. Seduce him!

But how?

''Even if I'd known ahead of time that you wished to sell your ring, I wouldn't have done anything to help. After all, I've been against having you women come from the very beginning.''

''And yet you took me to see your friend,'' she couldn't help pointing out.

''A momentary lapse of judgment.'' He took a step toward her, his eyes growing dark, and she fought the urge to turn and run out the door. He had the look of a panther stalking its prey.

''You seem to have that effect on me, Phoebe.''

''I—I do?'' she whispered, scarcely able to catch her breath.

''Yes. You do. When I'm near you, I tend to forget my job, my goals and my best intentions.''

The admission sounded as if it had been physically pulled from his body. He continued to advance toward her, studying her with an intimacy that should have been reserved for a lover, not a mere stranger. It took every ounce of will she possessed to remain still. Nevertheless, her heart began to pound and her knees threatened to buckle.

''I take it that you bought this dress with part of your money?''

''Yes.''

''It's very pretty, but still not quite what I would have expected of you.''

''Oh?''

He shook his head, slowly circling her, studying her as if she were a statue in a museum.

''No. The color doesn't suit you.''

She tightened her lips in pique. ''Brown is a very practical color for traveling.''

''Perhaps. But I would dress you in...blue. Dark blue. Indigo. And silk.''

Unease curled within her as she thought of the beautiful silk gown she had hidden in the bottom of her trunk.

He reached out, his finger touching her hair, slipping beneath the loose tresses to caress the shape of her ear.

Phoebe bit her lip, wondering how the small point of contact could cause such a potent reaction. Her body flooded with heat and a trembling gripped her from head to toe.

''If it were up to me, I would have Adam supply you with sapphires to be worn here....'' He fingered the sensitive lobe. ''And here...'' A fingertip slid down her neck to the hollow at the base of her throat.

Did he know about the dress...and her sapphires? Was he aware of her subterfuge? But even as the idea occurred to her, she dismissed it as preposterous. Then all conscious thought fled as her body began to burn from within and a yearning filled her soul.

Why did life have to be so complicated? Just when she was about to embark on the adventure of a lifetime, and had committed herself to another man, why did she have to be swamped with desire for Gabe Cutter? Why did he have the ability to completely banish all thoughts of propriety with the merest glance?

Gazing up at him, she studied his stormy-gray eyes. Her hands lifted to rest on his hard chest. Her heart fluttered, then jolted into a gallop to keep time with his. Ignoring the voice of warning in her head that reminded her this man would never regard her as anything more than a passing amusement, she spread her fingers wide, testing the resilient musculature beneath the cotton of his shirt and the leather of her gloves.

"What have you done to me?" Phoebe flushed in embarrassment when she realized she had spoken the words aloud.

But he didn't chide her for her neediness. Instead, he bent to whisper near her ear, "I think I should be asking that question."

She shuddered as his breath stirred against her sensitive skin. "I shouldn't be doing this. I'm engaged to be married."

"Nor should I."

She started, trying to pull back. "You're married?" she asked, inexplicably hurt.

But when she would have fought free from his embrace, he stilled her with a low denial. "No. Not anymore."

Questions tumbled into her mouth, longing to be uttered, but she couldn't bring herself to ask them out loud. Not when the set of his jaw and the bleak shadows of his eyes made it clear that he didn't wish to talk.

Growing braver, she touched his jaw. When he didn't flinch, she continued, exploring his cheek and the faint abrasion of his beard. Then she delved her fingers into his hair, finding it whisper-soft and wavy.

She shivered, imagining the intimacy if *she* should offer to cut it for him.

"Why is this happening?" she breathed.

He shook his head, his hands sliding around her waist to draw her irresistibly closer.

"I shouldn't even be taking the time to talk to you. With the train being loaded, and cargo to store, I should be outside overseeing my men. I've put everything in jeopardy by staying this long." He dipped his head, training his eyes on her mouth. "But I don't seem to care…"

"Nor do I," she breathed.

Only a hairsbreadth remained, and yet he paused, seeming to search her features.

What did he see there? And what did he hope to see?

Panic flooded her being as she remembered that he'd admitted to being married at one time. Did she remind him of his former wife?

No. Please, God, no. If he was to be attracted to her, let it be for the person she was. Phoebe had grown so weary of trying to please her father during their infrequent visits. She'd tried, whenever they were together, to adapt her personality in an effort to gain his approval. She'd done her best to appear meek and mild, but she'd constantly failed. She didn't want to endure such hurt again.

"You are so beautiful," Gabe whispered, and she felt her soul take wings. "So, so beautiful."

"Gabe!"

The front door to the office slammed open, and the two of them sprang apart, Gabe swearing. Stepping away from her, he retrieved his hat from its position on the desk.

''What is it?'' Gabe's voice was tight and gruff.

A stocky man dressed in tailored traveling gear, with a pair of silver revolvers strapped around his waist, regarded Phoebe and Gabe with narrowed eyes. Although they'd managed to part before he'd rounded the door, he was clearly suspicious.

''We need your help with one of the boxcars.''

''Fine, Victor. I'll be right there.''

The man's gaze darted from Phoebe to Gabe.

''Problems?''

''No,'' Gabe said shortly. ''I was merely warning Miss Gray about her choice in chaperons.''

Victor's brows rose. ''So the women *will* be coming with us then.''

Ignoring the way her limbs still shook and her body burned from within, Phoebe declared tartly, ''Yes, we will. And the sooner Mr. Cutter and his men grow accustomed to that fact, the happier we all will be.'' Tilting her chin to a haughty angle, she said stiffly, ''Good day, gentleman.''

Victor grinned, touching a finger to his hat as she brushed past him.

''Good day to you, too, miss. I hope to see much more of you and your lovely companions throughout our journey.''

Phoebe slammed the door hard enough to make it rattle.

After several heavy moments, Gabe motioned for Victor to leave as well. ''Go tell the men I'll be right there.''

''Very well.''

Victor's tone was respectful, but his grin was a bit

too sly for Gabe's liking. Nevertheless, he turned on his heel and disappeared.

Following the man outdoors, Gabe paused on the top of the landing and watched as Victor swung into his saddle. Within seconds the man had expertly maneuvered his mount through the throng of people on the bustling roadway.

Phoebe, however, was having a much more difficult time in escaping. She obviously hadn't counted on the crowd that had gathered during the short time they'd been in the office. She'd been forced to stop on the boardwalk while a group of wagons jockeyed for position in the dusty street.

As she paused, rising on tiptoe in an effort to see another way across the street, Gabe tried—oh, how he tried—to eye her with overt suspicion. He repeated the litany that he had already told himself a dozen times that day: *Don't trust anyone. Don't trust her. She is masquerading as something she isn't, and heaven only knows why.*

But as she moved toward the sea of farmers and passengers waiting to board the train, a primal sensation curled in the pit of Gabe's belly—one that had nothing to do with worry or tension.

He recognized the urge for exactly what it was: need. A sensual hunger. Lust.

Not now, not now. Victor had interrupted them just in time.

But Gabe's body wasn't listening to his mind. He couldn't summon his vow to remain emotionally uninvolved from the fairer sex, nor cling to his need for solitude. He thought only of the anticipation that had thrummed through his veins that moment before Victor had stormed into the office. When Gabe and

Phoebe had been forced to part, he'd been filled with a rage at the man who had destroyed the sweet moment, and an overwhelming hunger for the woman he'd been about to kiss.

Before he quite knew what he intended to do, he took a step, then another and another until he was following Phoebe at a brisk walk.

The crowd surged around them both, no one really paying them any mind. In that element of chaos, there was a strange measure of privacy.

Without thought of the ramifications, Gabe reached out to snag her by the elbow, turning her to face him.

Her gaze collided with his, and instantly, he knew that he wasn't the only one to be so affected by their embrace. Pulling her tightly against him, he noted the way that her breath came in quick gasps and her body trembled.

"Why have you bewitched me so completely?" he whispered—so softly that he doubted she heard the words.

But the flare of heat in her eyes revealed to him that she had understood. Her own body swayed nearer, her hands lifting to rest upon his chest.

His instincts screamed at him to back away, to refuse to let the women board the train, to banish her from his life forever. She could only cloud his memories of Emily.

But his mind could not overpower his body. Slipping a hand around her waist, he drew her even more tightly against him, reveling in the feeling of a woman's body against his own.

Dear, sweet heaven above, how long had it been?

She offered no protest as he bent his head toward hers, his free hand tipping her face up to his. Slowly, gradually, he closed the distance between them until finally his lips touched her own.

At that tiny point of contact, a fiery heat inundated his body. Pulling her closer, he deepened the embrace. The world seemed to fade away, leaving only the two of them, the straining of their bodies, the joining of their mouths, the knocking of their hearts.

A train whistle blasted, causing both of them to jump apart. They stood for long moments, breathing heavily. Then, bit by bit, Gabe became aware of his surroundings. His responsibilities. His need to deny what had just happened and to put space between himself and the hunger she'd inspired.

"I've got to go," he rasped, his tone husky with emotions he didn't quite understand. "I've assigned a railway car to the brides and your chaperon. It will be the third to last car from the end of the train. I know you were originally allocated seats in the passenger cars, but after the last change of plans, those tickets were resold. It's the boxcar or nothing. You'll have to share some of the space with a few odd crates and trunks, but there should still be enough room for you to exist comfortably. Make sure you and the other women have all of your belongings loaded before the train leaves."

Unable to stop himself, he bent for another kiss, and another, delighting in the way Phoebe clung to him, her cheeks growing bright from the heat of their embrace.

Staring down at her, he wondered how the two of them had come to this point. Passion couldn't bloom this quickly. It wasn't right. If he had any honor at all, he should turn away and vow never to speak to her again. She was a woman who deserved a promise of a future, and that was something he could never give. But the emotions this woman inspired were much too powerful for such a solution. Instead, as he backed away, he knew by the acceptance in her eyes that they would meet like this again.

Whether or not it was wise.

"What did he say?" Betty asked as Phoebe hurried toward the knot of women waiting near the railway platform. "Is he insisting on meeting Mr. Potter?"

Phoebe shivered at the question, realizing that it wasn't what Gabe had said—or hadn't said—that occupied her mind. It was what he'd done. She'd been kissed—and thoroughly—for the first time in her life.

She wondered if her friends would be able to tell. Was she somehow outwardly marked by the experience?

Had anyone seen them?

Heaven knew that the embrace had branded her soul. So much so that she didn't know how she could ever be the same. Finally, she had been initiated into the wonders of passion, true passion, and the experience had shaken her to the core.

"Well?" Twila demanded when she didn't respond.

"He...didn't really say anything about Mr. Potter. At first he was worried that we might have hired a boy to accompany us. Once I had assured him we hadn't, he seemed...mollified."

Twila frowned. "He didn't hurt you, did he?"

"Hurt me?"

"You're flushed. Did you argue?"

"We exchanged...words, but he kept his bargain." Summoning what little bit of control she could muster, Phoebe forced herself to stop thinking of the way Gabe had held her, and to concentrate on the business at hand.

"We've been given a boxcar of our own," she said, hoping she didn't sound as breathless as she felt. "But we'll have to share the space with some miscellaneous baggage. We have less than an hour to get our baggage safely stowed and the boxcar made as comfortable as possible for the journey. Ladies, are we game for this adventure?" Phoebe asked, straightening her spine.

To her relief, all the brides, except for Doreen, quickly added their cheers of support. Mr. Potter snored from where he'd been hidden behind a stack of trunks.

"Then let's get to work."

The first order of business was to locate the proper car. Third from the end, it was battered and clearly had been in use for years, but to Phoebe's relief, it held no visible signs of having carried animals. Instead, the dusty confines were littered with spilled grain and bits of straw. Chinks of light striped the floor from areas where the boards were loosely fitted, and the air had a musty smell. But overall, the space was much larger than Phoebe had imagined it might be.

With some difficulty, the women half dragged, half lifted Mr. Potter inside, placing him on a blanket, which they then dragged to a far corner, away from prying eyes.

It took four trips to move everything from the spot where the omnibus had disgorged their belongings, but even Doreen proved she could work when she felt motivated enough to do so.

Using the crates that had already been loaded onto the boxcar, they formed a barrier, dividing the space in thirds. The rear portion was filled with baggage, with one small corner closed off with blankets suspended from a rope for a private dressing area. The middle part, near the door, became a "traveling parlor" of sorts, with trunks and wooden cargo boxes used as makeshift furniture. The last area, toward the front of the car, was also shielded with a blanket hung from a length of rope. Here, the women spread out a soft layer of straw covered with blankets for their beds.

By the time the hour had elapsed, the boxcar was cleaner than it had been in years and redolent with the smell of fresh straw.

"Well done!" Mable exclaimed just as another long shriek signaled that the time for departure was at hand.

For the first time since stepping from the ship, Phoebe felt a flurry of excitement. Soon, soon, she would be on her way…to another life, a husband….

The thought snagged in her consciousness like a burr, spoiling the joy of the moment.

A husband.

A stranger.

Moving to the doorway, she peered out at the last few passengers scurrying to board the train. From a spot near the locomotive, she saw a figure on horseback, and even from this distance her body instantly recognized him, her blood flowing with a molten warmth.

As if sensing her regard, Gabe pulled on the reins, turning his mount toward her, then moving down the length of the train in a slow trot. He rode effortlessly, betraying a lifetime of experience in the saddle. Watching him, she insisted to herself that there was no reason for her heart to knock in her breast in time with the thundering hooves, or her mouth to grow suddenly dry. But even as she called upon her innate level-headedness, she seemed to have lost the ability to do anything but watch Gabriel Cutter approach.

Once he neared the brides' boxcar, he slowed to a walk, then stopped his mount in front of them. She felt the sweep of his gaze and mourned the fact that she was dusty and had long ago removed the pretty bonnet and the decorative ribbon. For one instant, she almost wished that she had retained her family title so that she could face him wearing silk and sapphires.

But if she hadn't adopted another woman's name and another woman's identity, she never would have met him at all.

Gabe peered into the boxcar, noting the changes they'd made. His gaze moved from the arrangement of trunks to the supine shape snoring in the corner. "That's your escort?"

Phoebe doubted that even the shadowy interior of the boxcar could hide Mr. Potter's obvious inebriation.

"Yes, that's Mr. Potter."

She held her breath, knowing that the moment of truth was at hand. She had no guarantees that Gabe wouldn't decide to dump them all on the siding and signal for the train to leave without them. Just because he'd kissed her didn't mean that he would be willing to turn a blind eye to such an obviously unsuitable escort.

"Is he the best you could do?" Gabe asked, his eyes narrowing. The horse he rode pranced at the sound of the train whistle, but he quickly brought the animal under control.

Phoebe's gaze momentarily clung to the strong muscles of Gabe's thighs and the broad span of his hand as he calmed the roan gelding.

"On such short notice? Yes. That's the best escort we could find." Phoebe's words were defiant, daring him to renege on his word. But the quavering tone of her voice betrayed her fear.

Gabe caught her gaze, and for one tension-fraught moment it was as if they were alone. She could all but feel his eyes as they dropped to her lips...to the hollow at the base of her throat. Without a word, he reminded her of the embrace they had shared and offered her a promise of further delights to come.

Then, just when she feared her knees would buckle, he smiled and touched his hat with a glove-covered finger, saying, "Ladies."

Too late, Phoebe remembered the other women, who had gathered around her. Disappointment flooded her body as she realized there would be no private words.

No quick kisses.

Gabriel turned his mount and rode swiftly to the front of the train. Peering down the track, Phoebe watched as he expertly maneuvered the animal into a car near the front and disappeared. Within moments, she could hear the rusty rattle of doors being pulled shut.

"We'd best batten down our own hatches," Mable said.

Knowing that she couldn't continue to hang out of the doorway hoping for another glance of Gabriel Cutter, Phoebe helped to draw the heavy door closed.

It would be hours before the train would stop again. Taking a deep breath, she knew that she should use the time to steel herself against Gabe's effect on her.

Again and again, she found herself wondering what had caused him to grow so bitter. So angry at the world. What had hurt him in the past? Did it have something to do with the way his men watched him when he wasn't looking? As if they were suspicious of him for some reason?

Or was it a more personal tragedy? Had he loved and lost? Had someone scorned him?

She snorted at such a thought. Gabe would never be so affected by a woman's refusal. Phoebe couldn't imagine him suffering any lingering harm from a woman who would be foolish enough to let him slip away.

Or a woman foolish enough to let him go in order to marry another.

Chapter Seven

That evening the train stopped for a few hours' time at a humble railway station so that the passengers could avail themselves of the restaurant and washing facilities.

Weary from a long, bone-jarring ride, the women made their way first to the ladies' waiting room. There they pumped fresh water to wash their faces and hands, and paused before a speckled mirror to repair their coiffures.

"If only there were a way to dive in headfirst," Betty said forlornly as she bent over the basin, her hands plunged wrist-deep in the cool depths.

"At least we have a moment's peace and quiet away from—" Maude broke off, and the women exchanged glances, each looking as guilty as the last.

"Doreen does tend to tire the ear, doesn't she?" Edith finally whispered.

Twila moved to the only mirror, swept her bonnet from her head and tried to smooth back the strands of hair that had fallen from their usual tight knot. "Lordy, I've never heard anyone complain so much."

Phoebe sighed and moved to the window. Lifting

the blind, she watched the other passengers milling on the platform.

"If you're looking for the trail boss, he's already eating."

Phoebe stiffened as Doreen's strident tone announced her arrival in the washroom.

Assuming a bland look of innocence, Phoebe turned and said, "Why would I be searching for Mr. Cutter?"

Doreen's smile was filled with haughty amusement. "You can't seem to keep your eyes off the man." She sashayed into the room, looking far too fussy in a rose-colored dimity dress trimmed with yards of ruffles.

"*If* I have a habit of looking for the man, it's because I don't trust him not to throw us off the train midway through our journey. Mr. Potter didn't offer the best possible impression this morning."

Doreen sniffed. "Are you sure there isn't more to your fascination, Miss Gray?"

Phoebe felt each muscle in her body stiffen one by one. Had they been seen? Was Doreen a witness to the passion she and Cutter had shared? If so, would she decide to tell Phoebe's future husband that Phoebe had been unfaithful to him mere days before they were to be married?

"Frankly, I've come to the conclusion that Mr. Cutter is a bully and a rounder, with little regard for women or their plight in life."

Doreen's brows lifted. "Perhaps what you say is true. But if you should develop an...interest in the man, I'd be careful if I were you."

Phoebe knew she should ignore the woman's baiting, but something beneath her skin prickled as she realized that Doreen had information about Gabriel that she was dying to share with the other brides.

Nevertheless, it was Twila who took the bait. ''I don't know why you would say such a thing, Doreen. As unpleasant as the man can be, he has been a gentleman today.''

''Twila is right,'' Phoebe said. ''As much as we might dislike the way Mr. Cutter handled our travel arrangements, he has had our best interests at heart. You'd do well to remember that rather than peddling idle gossip.''

Doreen studied Phoebe as if she'd never seen her before. ''Just as I suspected. Despite your impending match, you have a hankering for the man.''

Phoebe crossed her arms impatiently. ''I fail to see how you came to such a preposterous conclusion.''

''I've seen the way you follow every move he makes with your eyes. We haven't made a single stop today without your going to the door to look for the man.''

''Nonsense. I'm merely curious, that's all. The man seems so...''

''Handsome?'' Betty breathed.

Phoebe started. She hadn't realized she wasn't the only one who had been taken by the man's flint-hard features.

''If I weren't engaged, I wouldn't be above a bit of flirting,'' Maude said from the settee.

''Maude!'' Mable gasped.

Maude peered at her sister from beneath the wet cloth she was using to wipe her face. ''Be honest, Mable. You wouldn't mind batting your eyelashes in his direction, either.''

Mable's cheeks flooded with pink, but she didn't deny it.

Edith whispered, ''The man is so...so—''

"Ornery," Phoebe supplied quickly—a touch too quickly if Twila's smile was any indication.

"They say he's a deserter."

Doreen's pronouncement fell like a rock into the stillness, the effects of the words spreading like ripples through the assembly. The other women froze in the midst of their tasks and stared at Doreen. Then, just as quickly, they turned toward Phoebe.

"It isn't true, is it?" Edith asked, clearly stunned.

Phoebe scrambled for an answer, but her brain was still stuck on the single word.

Deserter...deserter...deserter...

Of all the things she had suspected Doreen might accuse Gabe of being, this was not one she was prepared to deny.

Twila's eyes filled with tears, and Phoebe remembered her mentioning that her first husband had died during the war.

"Doreen doesn't know what she's saying. No doubt she's been gossiping."

"It isn't gossip, it's gospel. I heard his own men talking about it." Doreen flushed with excitement. "He was a cavalry scout during the war."

Edith and Betty gasped as if the news were somehow important.

Phoebe shrugged. "I don't understand."

Betty was the one who explained. "Sheridan's cavalry rode behind the lines to undermine the Confederates during the Conflict."

"Conflict?"

"The War between the States."

Phoebe supposed she should know more about America's most recent history, but news had been a precious commodity at Goodfellow's. Generally, those periodicals she managed to borrow from the other girls throughout the year centered on fashion and society. Vaguely, she remembered that America had been divided, North and South, each fighting one another in a devastating war.

''If that's the case, and the man was brave enough to ride behind enemy lines, I hardly think he would desert.''

''But he did,'' Doreen said with evident relish. ''Toward the end of the war, he abandoned his unit for more than six months.'' She now had the full attention of everyone in the room and reveled in it. ''According to his men, he rode off on patrol and didn't come back until the war was all but over.''

From what Phoebe had seen already, she couldn't imagine Gabe doing such a thing. He was a man who followed a strict code of rules—many of which were of his own making. How could someone like that run from battle and leave his compatriots to finish the work?

''I think that you've embellished on what was probably a one-day absence with good reason.''

''According to his men, he offered their commanding officer a tall tale as an explanation—that he'd taken time to ride by his home to see his wife and son, only to discover that they'd been killed by deserters earlier that day.''

The pronouncement had been made with a note of triumph, as if Doreen expected them to share in her disbelief. But the women were clearly stunned by the news.

''Poor man,'' Betty breathed.

Edith gasped.

Twila grabbed for her smelling salts and sank onto one of the spindly chairs.

Doreen held her hands wide. "You don't believe such an excuse, do you? I doubt the man was ever married at all. He probably made up the story so that he could plant his fields and stay for the—"

"Ladies..." The low drawl from the doorway sent ice water through Phoebe's veins.

Gabe.

She exchanged quick glances with the other women, praying that he hadn't overheard much. Turning, she sought his expression for some hint of emotion. But his features were as implacable as ever.

"It's time to get into the café. We'll be leaving in little more than an hour and there's a healthy crowd inside. If you want to eat you'd best go while you can."

Then, with a touch of his finger to his brow, he was gone.

"Did he hear us?" Betty whispered.

"What does it matter if he did?" Doreen said, planting her hands on her hips in open irritation. "The story he gave his officers isn't true, I tell you. He's a deserter, plain and simple—which means he isn't to be trusted."

"Be quiet, Doreen," Phoebe said impatiently.

Doreen gasped, her mouth opening and closing like a gaping fish. "You can't talk to me like that!"

"Oh, shush!" Edith snapped, surprising Doreen even more. To be chided by Phoebe was one thing, but to be chastised by the "mouse" of the group was even more startling.

The women waited until Doreen had flounced out the door and hurried in the direction of the café. Then, as if drawn by an unseen hand, they all crossed to the windows and stared at Gabe as he swung onto his horse and urged it in the direction of the train.

"It's true, isn't it?" Betty whispered. "That Mr. Cutter found his family murdered?"

The other women watched him with horrified curiosity.

"He isn't a man who would willingly desert," Mable said with utmost certainty.

"But *six months?* What would keep a man away for six months?" Twila whispered.

No one answered. The possible explanations were too horrible to be imagined.

"You ladies go ahead and find a table for us. I've got to check on something," Phoebe said to the other women as they left the waiting room and headed in the direction of the café.

Twila eyed Phoebe in concern. "You really shouldn't be alone, dear."

Phoebe waved aside the warning. "I'm just going to the telegraph office." She pointed to a doorway on the opposite side of the building. "I'll join you as soon as I'm finished."

"Holler if you get into trouble," Mable said with a grin.

"Better yet, wear this." Maude took a shiny whistle from her reticule.

"You carry a whistle?" Phoebe asked, eyeing the intricate piece.

"It's a nanny whistle. Mable and I did a stint with a family that had four sets of twins."

"Four sets?" Phoebe gasped in horror. Twins ran in her own family. Her father had been a twin, but his

younger brother by twelve minutes had drowned at sea fifty years ago.

Phoebe waited until the other women were out of sight before hurrying in the opposite direction. With all the delays the train had encountered so far, she was sure that Louisa's news would be dated. But at least Phoebe would be able to assure herself that the other woman was happy with her newfound life.

But after awaiting her turn in line, Phoebe discovered that no message had arrived.

Turning, she nearly ran head-on into a man's chest. In an instant, she knew who it was.

Gabriel Cutter.

Looking up, she glared at him with as much heat as she could muster. "You seem to have a nasty habit of taking me unaware."

"Perhaps it's because you have a talent for being in the wrong place at the wrong time...Phoebe."

The slight pause before her name caused her heart to grow sluggish in her breast.

What, if anything, had Gabriel overheard? Had she said anything to the telegraph operator that could give away her secret?

Phoebe mentally scrambled to remember what she had said in the last few minutes, but for the life of her, she couldn't think of anything other than this man's nearness, the warmth of his body seeping into her own.

"You'll never get anything to eat at this rate, Miss Gray."

She shrugged. "I can do without, if need be."

His eyes dropped down her body and she felt her cheeks grow warm. "It looks to me like you've gone without more than you should.'' He took her elbow. ''Come on. You can eat with me.''

As he led her through the waiting room to the café, she tried to remove her arm from his grip. ''This isn't necessary. I'll join the other women and—''

''The other women arrived too late to find a table together. They're scattered throughout the dining room. And since mine is the only table that is reserved, you'll have to eat with me.''

''No!'' Phoebe dug in her heels, forcing him to pull up short of the door. But if she'd thought the action would deter Gabe, she was sadly mistaken.

''Is something wrong?''

''Yes, there's something wrong,'' she whispered, looking around her to see if they'd captured anyone's attention. ''We've already been…indiscreet in public. I don't think it would be seemly to invite that kind of spectacle again.''

He laughed. Gabriel Cutter, the hardened, embittered trail boss for the Overland Settlers Company, laughed at her concerns—and the effect was astounding. For one brief moment, his features lightened and his eyes lost their somber cast. In that instant, Phoebe saw him as he must have been years ago, before the horrors of war and the deaths of his family members had made him hard.

''What do you think will happen, Phoebe? Do you think I'll ravish you in the middle of the dining hall?''

She huffed in indignation, finally wrenching free and folding her arms tightly beneath her breasts. The minute she did, she wished she'd remained still. Gabe's eyes dropped, then lingered on the tight tailoring of her bodice.

''I can assure you,'' he murmured in a voice so low

that even she had trouble hearing the words, ''that as much as I might wish to sweep the dishes from the table and take you there and then, I will restrain myself. You have my word.''

With that, he held out his arm as if he were a dandy about to take her to the theater. ''Shall we?''

Phoebe knew she should refuse again. She knew she should brush past him in a huff or turn on her toe and rush back to the train.

But like a fool, she also knew that she couldn't resist a few more minutes in this man's company. Even if she lived to rue her impetuousness.

The moment she took her place at the tiny table marked Reserved, Phoebe became suddenly conscious of her fellow travelers. Although the majority of those who dined in the same room were strangers, it was evident that they were curious about the man who was their trail boss and the woman he had chosen to be his companion during dinner.

Stiffening her spine, Phoebe pretended that she wasn't aware of their regard as she ordered blindly off the menu, then took a quick sip of the scalding coffee the waitress had poured without even being asked. From the corner of her eye, she saw Doreen smirking at her. Clearly, the woman thought that her suspicions about Phoebe and the trail boss had been correct.

In record time, the waitress returned with their food—bowls of steaming soup and platters laden with meat, vegetables and roasted potatoes.

Phoebe blinked at it all, wondering how she was going to swallow anything past the tightness gathering in her throat.

''This isn't right,'' she whispered under her breath.

"It doesn't taste good?"

"No, no, I mean—" She bit her lip, wondering if she was too sensitive to the quick glances being cast in their direction. "We are creating a stir."

Gabe, who had begun to eat the moment the waitress slipped his plate in front of him, momentarily stopped his chewing. His knife and fork hung poised over the thick steak on his plate. He glanced around the room. "I don't see anything 'stirring' at all."

He began eating again with the gusto of a starving man. "You're being overly sensitive."

She forced herself to act as normally as possible, cutting into the meat on her plate and arranging a tiny slice on her fork as the teachers at Goodfellow's had taught her. According to them, only a glutton would dare to put more than a bird's portion in his or her mouth at once.

Slipping the morsel into her mouth, Phoebe tried counting as she chewed, until it was impossible to prolong the effort any longer. But she didn't think she could have said what she'd eaten. Her senses were focused entirely on the man seated across from her, and on the awkwardness of her predicament.

She hadn't wanted anyone to know of her odd reaction to this man. She was destined to marry a farmer, and everyone knew it.

But she had only to spend a moment in Gabriel's company to become jittery and jumpy. Her body seemed to take on a life of its own, reacting to him in ways she never would have imagined possible. She grew cold, then hot. Her pulse skipped beats; her hands grew sweaty. More alarmingly, she couldn't seem to look away. Her eyes greedily roamed his features and a longing grew within her breast. She yearned for his attention, his approval…

His touch.

Could other people see that?

"Eat, Phoebe," Gabe said without looking up.

Her stomach rumbled noisily, reminding her that it had been some time since she'd eaten. Suddenly focusing on the food arranged on her plate, Phoebe craved the sustenance.

"Eat."

When she hesitated again, he added in a low voice, "I expect to see you clean your plate. If not, I may decide to force-feed you."

At his words, her temper flared. How dare he? How dare he treat her like…

Like her father would have done, using threats to bend her will toward her own. Her will stiffened and her self-consciousness evaporated.

Why was she so concerned about what others thought? Hadn't she learned anything? Hadn't she rejoiced in being free of the strictures society had imposed on her by her being born into an aristocratic family? If that was the case, why was she allowing idle gossip to ruin her day and her lunch?

Ignoring the other passengers, she began to eat—slowly at first. Then, as the flavors began to permeate her befuddled senses, she ate with the appetite of a thresher at the end of a hard day.

"Make sure you save room for pie."

"Pie?" Forgetting all her training, Phoebe spoke with food still in her mouth. She flushed, scrambling for her napkin.

"You appear as if you haven't eaten in a long while."

Too late, she saw that Gabe had finished. He was leaning back in his chair, watching her with those dark, hooded eyes.

"I—it's good," she said weakly, not knowing how to best excuse her behavior.

"I take it you're not accustomed to such hearty fare."

She held her breath. Had she made a mistake? Would the real Phoebe Gray have eaten food like this on a regular basis?

Deciding that he couldn't possibly find fault with her enjoyment, she said, "My meals were generally supplied to me by a less than imaginative cook."

He nodded to show that he understood.

As she began to eat at a more restrained pace, he continued to watch her. He was slouched in his chair in a posture that should have been relaxed and unassuming. But she had the sensation of his body being coiled and ready for action should the provocation arise.

"Is Phoebe your given name?"

Her knife clattered onto the plate. Her heart leaped into her throat, jamming there in such a way that she wished she had not eaten with such gusto.

"I beg your pardon?" she whispered.

Again, she had the impression of his eyes seeing right through to her heart.

"You don't look like a Phoebe to me. I wondered if it was your given name or a nickname of sorts."

Her fingers twisted the napkin under the cover of the table.

"Phoebe is my given name. Phoebe Abigail Gray."

"Hmm."

Her heart fluttered in her breast as a frown touched his brow.

"Whatever is the matter?" As soon as the words left her lips, she damned herself for speaking at all. She should leave the matter completely alone, change the subject and lead this man to more comfortable territory.

"As I said, you don't look like a Phoebe."

"Then what would you name me?" she asked with an airy unconcern she didn't feel.

"Something less...common."

"I don't know what you mean."

"Phoebe brings to mind farmers' wives, dairymen's daughters and backstairs maids, while you, on the other hand..." His voice grew low and deep, stroking across her nerve endings with sinuous grace. "You have an air of sophistication about you that is more in keeping with a lady of the manor overseeing a house of servants."

Did he know how close he was to the truth? Did he know how his words had instilled a fear in her that she could not quell?

"I've never been waited on by a house of servants." She did her best to make the retort carefree and filled with humor, but she feared that she merely sounded frantic.

"That's a pity." Again, his eyes became shadowed, and she shivered, knowing a portion of what horrors he had suffered in the past. "It would be easy to imagine you wearing silk and sapphires."

For one fleeting moment, she was back on the ship with the darkness closing in upon her. As if a phantom had touched her, she felt the caress of a man's hand on her hair and the soft whispered reassurances of a stranger.

"Cherry pie."

The image shattered as if it were a mirror tossed to the ground. The noise and clatter of the café filled Phoebe's ears as she stared blankly at the slice of pie the waitress had placed before her.

Phoebe would have pushed it away, but Gabe growled, "Eat it."

Knowing that he would not allow her to leave until she'd "cleaned her plate," she quickly scooped the sweet concoction into her mouth. But where she would have immensely enjoyed the tangy flavors only moments before, now she could think of only one thing.

Escape.

The moment she had finished, she wiped her mouth and pretended to glance at the watch pinned to her bodice.

"My goodness! Look at the time! I've got a few things I need to do before the train leaves." Jumping to her feet, she didn't allow herself to look in his direction. "If you'll excuse me."

Not waiting for his reply, she fled before she could embarrass herself any further and beg him to kiss her one more time.

Chapter Eight

When had this whole situation grown so complicated? Phoebe wondered as she found an isolated spot near some trees and collapsed onto the ground. It should have been such an easy matter to step into her friend's life. With no ties to bind her and no real needs other than to be away from the controlling hand of her father, she should have been able to board a train, travel West and marry Neil without so much as batting an eye.

Instead, she had been forced to fight for every inch of progress since stepping foot on dry land. She had fought to retain her rightful passage on the train. She had been embarrassed, bullied and seduced.

She squeezed her eyes shut, feeling sobs rising within her as she shied away from the worst fact of all.

She was attracted to Gabe Cutter.

But it was more than that. So much more. The pull she felt was deeper, hungrier, needier than any she could have ever imagined. It was as if a part of him had entered her blood. Until she had another taste of him, she could not rest.

Was she falling in love?

No. It wasn't possible. No one fell in love in such a short amount of time. Especially not with someone like Gabriel Cutter. Everything about him warned a woman not to get too close. He was a man who would spend his life alone—and judging by the tragedies he'd suffered, Phoebe couldn't blame him.

Yet...she still longed for more than he could give.

No.

No, no, no! She couldn't feel anything for him! Her future was set. She'd made promises that would have to be kept.

Phoebe felt rather than heard Gabe approach. Starting like a deer spotted by a hunter, she looked up...then could not look away.

The shadows in his eyes were tempered by a burning heat, one that was directed at her.

"What have you done to me, Phoebe Gray?" he rasped.

Then there was no time for words as he reached down to take her hand, pulling her into his arms. She clutched at his shoulders, needing his strength to hold her steady.

Desire flared white-hot between them as their mouths met. In an instant, the years of chaste charity-school learning vanished from her head and her heart. Gone were the warnings of the evils of men and the sins of the flesh. Gone was everything but this moment.

This man.

Her hands spread wide across the musculature of his back as he lifted her against him, taking her weight as if she were no more than a feather. Then he was setting her on the grass again, his body looming over hers, his kisses becoming deeper, hotter, more searching.

Phoebe lost all conscious thought of her surroundings or the consequences of her actions. She had only one overwhelming need—to get as close to Gabe as was humanly possible.

When he lifted his head, she gasped for air, her fingers fumbling with the buttons at the front of his shirt, until finally, the corded muscles were bare to her inspection. But even as she ran her fingers across his ribs, he was kissing her again, his body pressing into hers, his hips settling intimately against her.

She shuddered. In all her days, she had never dreamed that she could feel this way. Gabriel Cutter had stolen her reason. In his arms, she felt beautiful and powerful. Her body thrummed and her pulse pounded through her veins. She did not protest when he unfastened the buttons of her shirtwaist. Nor did she refuse him when his hand slipped inside to explore the tight drum of her corset, moving higher, irresistibly higher, until he encountered a breast covered by little more than the lace of her camisole.

She gasped, arching against him. Never had she felt so alive. So—

Without warning, Gabe tore free from her, leaving her alone and breathless in the matted grass as he rolled away, then sat up, raking his hands through his hair.

''Damn, damn, damn,'' he whispered, his eyes closing.

Long moments passed before Phoebe realized that Gabe wouldn't be returning to her side. Shivering, she clutched the gaping placket of her blouse. Hurt welled within her. Was she so horrible that a man would curse himself for touching her intimately?

Gabe turned at that moment. He must have caught the gist of her thoughts because his gaze grew gentle.

"No, Phoebe. Don't think that. Don't think that you're at fault in any way." He squeezed his eyes shut and took a deep, shuddering breath. "I'm the one who's to blame." He rubbed at the deep lines etched between his brows. "You deserve so much more and..."

Gabe suddenly stood and scooped his hat off the ground. "I'm not the man you think I am," he said harshly. "So let's just leave it at that."

Then, before she could ask what he meant, he strode away, moving swiftly toward the dark shape of the train in the distance.

Phoebe didn't try to stop him. She sensed an aching loneliness and a pain in the man that reached deeper than any one woman could fathom. Although a part of her yearned to make him smile, she knew she didn't have the right.

After all, she wasn't what she pretended to be, either. She had secrets of her own that could not be expressed. And although she might have the urge to try her hand at healing his wounded spirit, such thoughts were dangerous.

Her life was already far too complicated and she must remember first and foremost that when she had taken Phoebe's name, she had also accepted all of the responsibilities that came with it. She couldn't forget that Neil had paid for this trip West, and that once she arrived at her destination, she was obligated to marry the man.

But she wasn't married yet. She could change her mind.

No. She couldn't. If she refused to marry him, she would be honor-bound to reimburse the man for the expenses he had incurred in bringing her here. Even with the handsome price she'd received for her ring, she hadn't enough in her "emergency stash."

Moreover, she wouldn't disappoint Neil. She couldn't. He had made the arrangements in good faith—and judging by the letters she'd read, Mr. Ballard was already half in love with his bride-to-be.

Or rather, he was half in love with the woman he thought she would be.

Phoebe's heart grew heavy. Could he love her? And more to the point—could she learn to love him?

Or would she forever be haunted by the emotions inspired by a brooding stranger?

Gabe strode resolutely in the direction of the train, intent on checking on the gold. But he was only midway there when he saw Victor Elliot waiting to speak to him.

"Problems?" Victor asked as soon as Gabe was within earshot.

"No." Gabe knew his answer was much more curt than necessary, but he couldn't seem to tamp down the roiling emotions inside him—anger, frustration…

Regret.

"The women seem to be taking up a good deal of your time and energy, Cutter."

"Which is the reason I originally refused to let them come along. But they're here now and it can't be helped."

Victor grinned slyly. "We've been traveling for less

than a day. Are the women really such a trial? Or do you have other reasons for hovering over them?''

Gabe opened his mouth to refute the fact that he was spending too much time with the brides—or more specifically, one bride. But when he realized that the answer would be too telling, he made an impatient gesture and said, ''We've got less than five minutes before we head out again. Let's get to work.''

Phoebe soon discovered that the journey West held little resemblance to the trip she had expected. Barely two days had passed when she realized that she had vastly underestimated the rigors involved.

According to the pamphlet that she had studied about the Overland Company's proposed route, the settlers had been promised ''clean, comfortable and quick'' travel.

The reality proved to be far different. Where Phoebe had envisioned the excursion to be a straight shot from New York to Omaha to San Francisco, the train in fact stopped several times a day. Soon the excuses began to take on a similar tone—the railway crew had been forced to make repairs, supply the engine with water and coal, or make way for other traffic sharing the same lines.

Nor was the travel clean. Within minutes, the heat of the boxcar became unbearable, forcing the women to crack open the large door. As a result, smoke from the stacks soon covered everything with a gritty layer of soot, and the air became stagnant and unpleasant. The only relief came from the all-too-frequent breaks when the women were allowed to walk up and down the siding to stretch their legs or perhaps venture into booming railway towns to explore.

Sighing, Phoebe stretched and dropped from the boxcar into the chill morning air. Late the previous evening, the train had come to a halt due to flooding washing out a portion of the track bed. Employees of the railroad and volunteers from among the passengers had worked until dark on the repairs, and judging by the distant clang of hammers, the work had begun again.

As yet, Phoebe could see only a scattered handful of people milling about in the early morning gloom. Evidently, a night free of the usual noise and motion of the train had lulled many of the travelers into an uninterrupted sleep.

As for herself, Phoebe didn't know why she was so restless. Her rest had been fitful, and when she'd managed to sleep, she'd had dreams filled with disturbing images. Sensual images.

Phoebe shivered, but not because of the cool breeze that touched her hot cheeks.

It seemed that even her dreams weren't safe from Gabe's interference. Finally, in an effort to control her wayward emotions, she had abandoned all attempts to rest.

She mustn't forget there was a man waiting at the journey's end.

But even after chiding herself for being ten times the fool, Phoebe couldn't manage to focus on Neil Ballard. Knowing such thoughts were dangerous, she'd reread the letters he'd sent to his mail-order bride, and had studied his picture. He was kind, sensitive, funny and romantic. He spoke glowingly of Oregon, his land, and the home they would build together. He was everything any woman could want in a husband.

So why was her heart bent on playing with fire? Why did the presence of a man who was completely unsuitable prove ever so much more powerful?

Phoebe tried to convince herself that it was merely a matter of timing. Gabe Cutter was the first man to pique her sensual curiosity, that was all. If she'd met any other man so soon after leaving Goodfellow's, she was bound to have had the same reaction. Her emotions were a product of the moment, nothing more. The instant she met Neil, she would fall for him as well—and by reading his letters, she would know him ever so much better.

But even as she assured herself that her preoccupation with the trail boss was little more than a flight of fancy, her eyes fell on the man standing in a copse of willows.

He was stripped to the waist, his shirt tossed carelessly over a branch, the tops to his union suit hanging about his hips. A tiny shaving mirror was propped on another branch, as well as a shaving mug and a leather strop.

Phoebe stopped, her feet seemingly rooted to the ground as she watched the lather and whiskers being scraped away from the rugged contours of his jaw in slow, steady strokes.

Dear heavens, how could this man so overpower her senses? In an instant she grew warm and breathless. Her heart knocked impatiently against her ribs and her knees threatened to buckle. And the sensations merely intensified when she took in the careless waves of his hair and his broad, bare back.

She'd never known that the masculine form could be so beautiful. Hungrily, she traced the width of his shoulders, the defined crease of his spine and the narrow span of his hips.

As if of their own volition, her feet began to move.

Phoebe was sure that she made no sound. Nevertheless, Gabe must have heard something because he suddenly whirled, reaching beneath his union suit to draw a revolver from the waist of his pants and level it at a spot between her eyes.

Instinctively, Phoebe raised her hands in surrender, her heart jolting to a frightened gallop.

After what seemed like an eternity, he released the hammer and lowered the gun, setting it on one of the thick, gnarled willow branches.

"You're up early."

Phoebe didn't quite know how to respond. Her hands hovered in the air above her head as if they'd frozen there.

"You can relax. None of the women has been annoying enough for me to resort to violence...yet."

The remark instantly enraged her, enabling her to lower her arms and nearly—*nearly*—ignore the way he stood there, so close and so very bare.

"I see that you haven't yet summoned the necessary niceties to apologize for the way you've been so beastly to us from the very beginning."

One of his brows rose. "Beastly?"

"Yes, beastly. Instead of caring whether or not we were up to the challenges of traveling, you simply assumed we would prove a hindrance. Because of your narrow-mindedness, we are now making the trek in a cattle car rather than a passenger car."

If she thought she would get a reaction from the man, she was sorely mistaken. He merely folded his arms across his chest—that firm, golden chest—and studied her with brooding eyes.

"Life is full of disappointments, isn't it, Phoebe?" he murmured.

Phoebe ground her teeth together to keep from shouting in outrage. Obviously, the man didn't care that he'd inconvenienced any of them. But even though she might want to rail at him for the injustice of it all, she instinctively sensed that such an action would have little effect.

"Have you been following me again?" Gabe asked.

This time an indignant "oh" burst from her lips before she could stop it. "I'll have you know that there is nothing on this earth that could possibly convince me to follow you anywhere."

His eyes grew dark and she immediately regretted her hasty words. After all, why should he believe such a claim of disinterest when only yesterday she had lain in his arms and hungrily returned his kisses?

"Then what are you doing here?"

Phoebe was struck momentarily speechless. What answer could she give him that wouldn't be too telling? She couldn't possibly confess the truth—that she'd been drawn to him like a lemming to the ocean.

Frantically, she searched for a logical reply before saying, "Since you have denied my companions and I our rightful spot in one of the passenger cars, we must insist that you arrange for some type of water container to be placed in our boxcar."

"All right."

Phoebe had already opened her mouth to counter his objections with an argument when she realized that the man had agreed to the demand without a fuss.

Her breath left in a whoosh. "Well, then. Thank you."

"Is there anything else the lot of you would like? Breakfast in bed? Perhaps some feather pillows?"

She glared at him, then realized he was teasing. "That will be sufficient. For now."

He turned his back to her and peered into the mirror finishing the last few swipes of the razor before reaching for a towel to wipe the traces of lather from his face.

"You really should arrange for a haircut as well," Phoebe blurted. The moment the words escaped her lips, she could have kicked herself.

"Are you volunteering?" The question was a barely veiled challenge.

Knowing that she would never forgive herself if she allowed him to get the better of her, she said, "If you wish."

She hadn't thought that he would accept her offer. She'd been sure he'd merely meant to embarrass her. But to her astonishment, he draped the towel around his neck. Then he reached for the saddlebags looped over a branch and removed a leather toiletry kit. Unbuckling the case, he removed a pair of small, silver scissors and a comb.

"Here you are."

She took them because she had no other real choice. "You'll have to sit down."

He moved to a boulder a few yards away and she meekly followed, wondering how she had allowed herself to be maneuvered to this point.

She didn't know anything about cutting hair. She'd never done such a thing in her life.

Sweet heaven, don't let me make a mess of this or I'll never hear the end of it, she prayed silently.

Positioning herself behind the man, she briefly closed her eyes to gather her courage about her. Then she grasped a handful of hair and cut it off.

The sight of the skin on Gabe's neck—slightly lighter than the dark tan of his face—gave her a moment's qualm, but she didn't allow herself to stop. It was only hair, she reminded herself. If Gabe didn't like her efforts, he could grow it back soon enough.

The whisper-soft *snip, snip* of the sheers soon punctuated the early morning silence. After making a few obvious mistakes, Phoebe fell into a rhythm, alternating the clipping of the scissors with the smoothing action of the comb. Bit by bit, the waving strands fell away, accentuating even more the angular contours of his jaw.

With each moment that passed, Phoebe was made more and more aware of the warmth of his body, the spicy scent that lingered on his cheeks after his shave, the silkiness of the hair beneath her fingers. When she'd finished, she faced him, gazing at rugged features that had become so familiar, yet were completely transformed by the shorter hair.

"I'm done," she finally whispered, despite her efforts to prolong the job as long as possible.

He didn't speak, but merely gazed up at her with a look she couldn't define—one that held pleasure and pain, desire and something akin to fear.

No. Not fear. This man would never be afraid of anything.

His hands lifted to her waist, the fingers sliding to the hollow of her back. Then softly, irresistibly, he pulled her to him until his head rested beneath her breasts and his arms wrapped around her body. Just as quickly as he'd touched her, he released her again. Swinging a leg over the boulder, he retreated to the tree, gathered his belongings, then returned to his own boxcar without so much as a word.

As he disappeared into the shadows of the car, Phoebe's fingers slowly curled into her palms as if she could trap the lingering vestiges of his body heat.

She was shaken to the very depths of her being. After experiencing the tumultuous power of his kisses, Phoebe had thought that nothing more could surprise her.

She'd been wrong. So wrong. With that brief embrace, with the pressure of his head against her, she had discovered that this man could touch her emotions in a way that she had never imagined. There had been such a tenderness to his actions, such…

Vulnerability.

No, being vulnerable wasn't a description that could possibly be affixed to the indomitable Mr. Cutter.

Or was it?

Something had passed between them in those brief quiet moments. A nameless emotion rose within her, a bewildering mixture of joy and inestimable sadness, of longing and regret.

Think of Neil.

But even as she tried to summon the image of her husband-to-be in her imagination, it was completely swamped by the moment she had just shared with Gabe Cutter.

A moment she feared would haunt her for the rest of her life.

Chapter Nine

In the days to come, Gabe did everything in his power to avoid Phoebe, without success. Progress from New York had been slow. Time and time again the train was delayed, sometimes for genuine reasons, other times at his own discretion, allowing Gabe to check security and rotate his guards in a way he hoped would avoid suspicion.

Despite his own careful observations and the unending surveillance of his men, Gabe had been unable to pinpoint even the slightest curiosity among the passengers about the boxcars holding the gold shipments. There was nothing at all he could point a finger at as being suspicious.

Except a single passenger who had changed her name since the onset of her journey.

Again and again Gabe was brought back to that point. Why was the woman he'd originally known to be called Louisa now traveling under an assumed name? Could she be part of the Overland Gang? Or was the change an innocent coincidence?

As much as Gabe's instincts might tell him that she was harmless, he couldn't allow himself to drop his guard. And even as he convinced himself that as a man he would be better off staying away from her, he couldn't ignore the fact that as a Pinkerton, he would do far better to stay close and sound her out.

Which was why, after two days, when Gabe heard the sound of a pistol being fired from the direction of the women's car, he found himself riding along the siding in search of Phoebe Gray. Instinctively, he knew she was embroiled in the trouble and that his gun was responsible for the noise.

"Move aside, move aside!" he barked to the crowd that had already begun to gather.

Just as he'd suspected, the brides had formed a protective knot around Phoebe. When they reluctantly parted, Gabe noted that her cheeks were flushed scarlet.

Not for the first time, Gabe thought that her blushes should be a sign to him that she was innocent of any collusion with the Overland Gang. But as soon as the thought appeared, he pushed it away. He'd known women who could summon tears at the drop of a hat. How was he to know whether a blush couldn't be fabricated in much the same manner?

"Who would like to explain what happened here?"

The women exchanged guilty glances, then Phoebe was given a none-too-subtle shove forward by the bride Gabe recognized as being Doreen Llewellyn-Bowes.

"I—I..." Phoebe bit her lip, her cheeks taking on an even rosier tint. Her reticule hung heavily from her wrist, giving him no doubt as to where the revolver was still hidden.

"Yes?" Gabe prodded.

"I...could I speak to you alone about this matter?"

Gabe stared at her hard, knowing that he should refuse. He couldn't think of a logical explanation that would require privacy, but growing uncomfortable with the attention he was receiving from the other passengers, he nodded. Then, before she could object, he reached down, took her by the elbow and swung her onto the horse.

She was opening her mouth to squeal when he prevented the instinctive protest by urging his horse into a trot, then a gallop.

Squeezing her eyes shut, Phoebe wrapped her arms around his waist and held him in a viselike grip.

Gabe did his best to ignore the warmth of her body against his own—the sweet curve of her cheek, the softness of her breasts. She had washed recently, he knew, since her hair was damp and smelled of a flowery aroma.

Gabe rode until they had passed an outcropping of rock, then drew to a halt in a small grassy meadow. Knowing he would need a clear mind to deal with Phoebe Gray, he allowed her to slip to the ground. Moving in a much more leisurely fashion, he swung from the saddle, tethering the animal to a nearby branch.

"Explain," he offered shortly, folding his hands across his chest in a manner that he hoped would intimidate her.

Again her cheeks grew rosy, though Gabe resisted the urge to point out the fact to her.

"It was a mistake."

"Undoubtedly."

"I didn't mean to do it."

"I hope you're right."

She bit her lip and clasped her hands, apparently

choosing her words with care. ''I have a confession to make.''

Gabe felt his heart harden. So he'd been right. This woman had an ulterior motive to traveling on this particular train.

''Go on.''

She took a deep breath, keeping her head bowed. ''I can't shoot,'' she nearly whispered.

Of all the confessions that he had expected, this would have been the last. And yet he'd seen an example of her marksmanship. Was she attempting to lie to him again?

''I have a shirt that says differently,'' he stated.

''That's just it,'' she said in a rush. ''It was a mistake, a horrible mistake. I was aiming for the bedpost the other day and I nearly killed you!''

The hardness he'd felt melted away in an instant, and he had the sudden urge to laugh. ''Prove it.''

She blinked at him in surprise. ''I beg your pardon?''

''Prove it.'' He studied the area around them, then pointed to a tree barely twenty feet away. ''I want you to hit the center of that knothole. Try your best. I'll know if you're trying to pull the wool over my eyes.''

He watched the way she grappled with her reticule—exposing a neat black hole in the bottom in the process. Gripping the gun handle, she pulled the weapon out, then held it with apparent awkwardness.

Could such ineptness be feigned? Probably.

Holding her breath, Phoebe aimed the pistol with utmost care. Then at the last minute she turned her face away, shut her eyes and squeezed. The noise of the report caused her to jump, and the backfire nearly knocked her off balance.

Again he resisted the urge to laugh. "I think your claims of ignorance were an understatement."

She had righted herself and was trying to find the point of impact. Gabe pointed to a branch on a neighboring tree that had been cut in two by the bullet.

"Oh, my," she sighed. "I seem to be getting worse."

"I would tell you that I find it comforting to know you weren't trying to shoot me the other day, but I'm afraid your lack of skill is just as frightening." Walking toward her, he pointed to the tree. "Aim at the knothole again."

She cringed, anticipating the noise and recoil of the weapon before she had even cocked the hammer.

"Relax," Gabe murmured, placing his hands on her shoulders.

She started, seeming to grow even more tense.

Stepping closer, he caught the scent of flowers that clung to her hair. And even though his mind warned him against the dangers inherent in getting close to the woman—physically or emotionally—he slowly slid his palms down the length of her arms until he cupped her hands.

"Close one of your eyes and sight down the barrel."

He wasn't sure, but he thought she'd begun to tremble in his arms.

"Do you see the tiny piece of metal at the end?"

"Yes."

Her voice was barely a puff of air.

"Adjust the revolver so that ridge points directly at the knothole."

"Now what?"

"Pull back the hammer."

Again she struggled to cock the weapon with both thumbs.

''Are you still pointed at the center of the knot-hole?''

''Yes.''

''Don't think about the noise or the recoil. I'll steady you. Just squeeze the trigger very slowly.''

Bam!

This time he absorbed the shock to her body with his own. Except for flinching at the gun's retort, she kept her arms steady within his grasp.

''Where did it hit?'' she breathed—as if speaking too loudly would alter the results of their experiment.

''Dead center.''

''Are you sure?''

''Go see for yourself.''

He released her, still holding the pistol while she rushed the thirty feet to the tree, rising on tiptoe to explore the hole with her finger. Then she squealed in delight, running toward him and throwing her arms around his neck. ''I did it, I did it!''

It was at that moment that she must have realized what she was doing. But before she could back away, Gabe wrapped his arms around her waist, holding her still. Heaven help him, he knew he was being ten times the fool, but he couldn't resist her. Nor could he ignore the sensual need that rushed through his veins like a tidal wave.

When he tipped her face up, she didn't resist, either. Her eyelids dropped, her eyes becoming heavy with an unspoken promise.

''We shouldn't be doing this,'' he whispered.

''I know.''

''We're all but strangers,'' he insisted, more to himself than to her.

''Yes.''

''But I can't stop,'' he admitted softly.

''I don't want you to stop.''

Since her admission was as hesitant as his own, he moved slowly, stroking her cheeks with his thumbs as he bent toward her.

The first meeting of their lips was ever so sweet, filling him with a warmth that he couldn't explain. Automatically, he took a step toward her, deepening the embrace, demanding entrance to her mouth with a stroke of his tongue.

She seemed to melt into his embrace, opening her lips and straining toward him, her response filled with an eager desire.

Slipping his arms around her waist, he drew her tightly against his hips, even as he damned the fullness of her skirts and the barrier they provided. Seeking to assuage the hunger within, he caressed her waist, her back, her shoulders, memorizing the indentation of her spine beneath the taut boning of her corset. Impatiently he increased the intensity of their kiss, his heart pounding at the innocent sincerity of her response. He was ready to drown in the passion she inspired. In her arms, he knew that he would forget the pain he still harbored in his heart, if only for a short time.

As the meaning behind his last thought filtered through the storm of sensation, a chill filtered through his body.

Had he really sunk that low? Had he really reached a point where he would use a woman to selfishly block out the past?

Gabe extricated himself from her clinging arms. Although it was one of the hardest things he had ever had to do, he assumed a cool, noncommittal mask. If he could offer this woman nothing else, he would allow her to keep her pride. Let her think he was a bastard through and through. He'd been considered worse. But he would never let her guess the depths of his inexplicable need for her.

"We'd better go."

He watched the way she sought her balance, blinked, then slowly came to her full senses. His words must have hit her like a slap to the face, because she stiffened, her chin lifting to a defiant angle, her eyes growing dark with hurt.

"I want the pistol back," she said coldly—but the tremor of her voice gave her away.

Wordlessly, he extended it.

Snatching it out of his hand, she marched back to the spot where her reticule had fallen. Jamming the gun into the bag, she tightened the strings, then walked stiffly to Gabe's mount.

"Come along, Gabe," she said with the cool civility of a princess. "I really have a great many things to do while the train is stopped."

At dusk that evening the train finally pulled into Chicago, where they would spend the night and part of the following morning before resuming their journey just before noon. Despite the fact that the train had traveled little more than two hours that day, the bustling city was a welcome sight to Phoebe—especially after her latest run-in with Gabe. She needed to get away from things for a time. Although she was beginning to grow fond of the other women, their constant chatter offered her little time to mull over her future…

As was becoming her habit, the first place Phoebe visited was the telegraph office. Taking her place in line before the caged booth, she waited impatiently, praying that this time she would have some form of communication from Louisa.

As she stood there, a prickling sensation touched the back of her nape. Glancing over her shoulder, Phoebe searched the crowd that milled through the station house. For several days she'd felt as if she were being watched.

Seeing no one who seemed particularly interested in her or her errand, she stared straight ahead at the brass bars separating the telegraph operator from his customers. Stuff and nonsense. No one was following her. Why would anyone *want* to follow her?

Unless…

No, her father couldn't have discovered her deception so quickly. He'd been on his way to Italy in the hopes the climate would improve his health. It would be weeks before he could receive communication from Charles Winslow or anyone else in Boston.

Nevertheless, even as she convinced herself that she was worrying for naught, she desperately hoped to receive a message from Louisa.

"May I help you, miss?"

"Yes, I'm looking for a telegraph sent to Phoebe Gray."

The man peered at her from behind a pair of glasses balanced on the end of his nose. Then he opened a drawer and thumbed through the stack of envelopes waiting to be delivered to travelers like herself.

"Here you are," he said, sliding two telegrams toward her—*two!*

"Thank you!" Phoebe blurted with such delight that the man blushed. Then, pushing them deep into her reticule, she hurried outside, seeking somewhere relatively private where she could read them.

Phoebe was soon to discover that "privacy" was a rare commodity at the Chicago station. Nevertheless, after walking the length of the platform, she was able to find a relatively quiet spot amid a huge pile of baggage.

Sitting on a large trunk equipped with thick straps and shiny buckles, Phoebe opened her reticule. Reaching past the pistol, her gloves and a tiny coin purse, she drew out the first telegraph and tore it open.

> My Dearest Phoebe. Looking forward to your arrival. I have long awaited the day when we finally meet face-to-face. Our life together will be a happy one.
>
> N. Ballard.

The paper dropped from her fingers as if she'd been burned. Neil Ballard.

Why was it so hard to remember that there was a man waiting for her at the end of her journey? Intellectually, Phoebe knew she was destined to marry the man. Why couldn't she convince her emotions?

Tired of analyzing her behavior, she scooped the paper off the ground and wadded it into a ball. She was about to toss it into a barrel of trash when she felt the hairs lift on her arms and her neck.

She *was* being watched. Phoebe was sure of it.

Glancing around her again, she failed to find the

source of her disquiet, but this time she refused to ignore it.

Smoothing the paper, she tucked it into her reticule, deciding that now wasn't the time to read the second missive. Instead, she stood and brushed off her skirts.

Perhaps it *would* be better to join the other women for an afternoon of shopping. She was beginning to believe she shouldn't spend too much time alone.

Gabe had just finished riding the length of the train when he noted one of his men walking toward him with studied casualness. As soon as the Pinkerton noted that he had Gabe's attention, he stopped and moved into a space between cars, allowing Gabe to ride up next to him.

"You've been relieved by Kenton?" he asked. Since discovering that Phoebe was traveling under an assumed name, he had instructed a pair of men to follow her whenever she left the boxcar, whether alone or with the other women.

"Yep. He caught up with me just after Miss Gray made a trip to the telegraph office."

"Again?"

"Yes, sir. She's done the same thing at each of the stops along the way. This time was different."

"She finally received a telegram?"

"Two."

Gabe's mount shifted restlessly, but with a touch of Gabe's knees, the animal calmed.

"Any idea who they were from?"

"No, sir. She was about to throw one of them away when she changed her mind and stuck it in her bag. She never looked at the other one."

Gabe nodded, then offered, ''Get some rest,'' as he nudged his horse into a walk.

He was doing his best to keep away from Phoebe Gray, but damned if she didn't keep rousing his suspicions.

Chapter Ten

Nights were the worst time for traveling, in Phoebe's opinion. By evening, the boxcar was a black, impenetrable oven, with only weak light from the lantern hung from the ceiling, and a thin bar of starlight at the door, to provide some relief from the oppressive environment.

Already the other women had grown used to retiring as soon as the sun set. Within the hour, they had said their goodnights and fallen fast asleep.

All but Phoebe.

There was too much noise for her to sleep this night—or perhaps the problem lay in her own brain.

Stepping soundlessly over the recumbent figures of the other women, Phoebe took her accustomed spot opposite the doorway, which was left open a crack to let in fresh air. Wrapping a shawl around her shoulders, she sighed and reached into the pocket of her wrapper. She was itching to open Louisa's telegram, but since she'd known its presence would cause too many questions, she'd waited until she had a few minutes of peace and privacy.

Phoebe should have heard something from her

friend ages ago. For days she had tormented herself with all sorts of horrible possibilities. Slitting the seal with her fingernail, Phoebe hastily opened the message and held it up to the dim light emanating from the swaying lantern.

> Dearest Phoebe, Charles Winslow is a rat and a bounder. Except for letters of credit left at the hotel, I have been waiting for days with no sign of him. This does not bode well for a happy marriage! I have used Winslow's letters of credit to great advantage. Have greatly augmented my wardrobe with dozens of shoes and matching parasols. I bought a lapdog and have advertised for personal maid and companion, setting up interviews. Haven't I come a long way since my own days of service? As far as I am concerned, C. Winslow can remain in hiding. Hope you are doing well.
>
> Louisa Marie Haversham Winslow

Phoebe resisted the urge to laugh. Even in a telegram, Louisa's effervescent personality had touched every word. Phoebe could nearly hear Louisa saying the words aloud, her voice tinged with a hint of laughter. Nor did the tacit details of the missive escape her. On their long voyage to New York, Louisa had sworn that she wouldn't be shy about using Charles Winslow's money. She'd vowed to have a dozen pairs of shoes in every color imaginable—each with a matching parasol. She'd dreamed about outfitting herself with all of the accoutrements of a wealthy woman, from a tiny yapping lapdog to an entourage of personal servants. Evidently she was well on her way to realizing her dreams.

A momentary frown chased across Phoebe's features when she wondered why Charles hadn't yet made an appearance. As Louisa had stated, such rudeness would not help the relationship to start off on its best foot. But no matter. Louisa seemed content to spend the Winslow fortune for the time being, and Phoebe had no doubts that she could take care of herself in the meantime.

Greatly relieved by the news, Phoebe slid the telegram back into her pocket, then peered out at the darkened countryside. Even with a half moon and a sky full of stars, she could see little more than differing shades of black. Their next major stop would be Omaha, Nebraska, but she had no doubt that there would be smaller stops along the way.

Originally, Phoebe had been impatient at the delays. But after reading Louisa's letter, she found herself wishing that she could arrive in Oregon to find her husband-to-be had mysteriously disappeared. But the other telegram she'd received had dispelled any such hopes before they could be formed. Neil Ballard was eager for her arrival.

Sighing, she rested her head against the boxcar wall. In her mind's eye, she could picture the letters that Ballard had sent to her friend. His penmanship had been powerful and scrawling, giving the impression that he was a large, impatient man—a fact totally at odds with the short, mild-mannered, balding gentleman who stared from the depths of the photograph he'd sent.

Not for the first time, Phoebe assured herself that her life would be a good one. In his letters, Ballard had painted a picture of the home he had built with his own hands, the beauty of Oregon and the life they would lead together. He'd wanted a woman who would make his house a home, a helpmate to work beside him to tame the land.

Grimacing, Phoebe realized that she had changed since first reading those letters. Originally, she'd been excited by the prospect of helping a man chase the wilderness away. She'd found his letters thrilling and inviting, and she'd been sure that her life could be a happy one, even after marrying a stranger.

Now she wasn't so sure. Her heart had been touched in a way she didn't dare acknowledge as yet—by another man. She tried to tell herself that she was merely infatuated with Gabe—that she was bound to have been attracted to the first male who crossed her path after leaving the charity school.

But her protestations were weak. Instinctively, she knew that what she was experiencing was something out of the ordinary. She would never feel for another man like this.

The boxcar was silent except for the clatter of the wheels. In the darkness, she could just see the outline of Mr. Potter near the door. To date, he hadn't done much to fulfill his role of escort—proving in Phoebe's mind the needlessness of the women having a chaperon. And despite their efforts to keep him sober and respectable, he often managed to find liquor to drink. He'd vacillated between being roaring drunk, tipsy or unconscious ever since they'd left New York.

Phoebe's lips twitched in a smile. Despite his many vices, she was developing a soft spot for the old man. When he was coherent, Mr. Potter was warm-hearted to a fault. He visited with the women and told them his own sorry tale about losing his wife and children to an outbreak of influenza. Phoebe couldn't really blame him for growing melancholy and drowning his sorrows in drink. It was obvious from the way he spoke that he'd truly loved his family and continued to mourn their passing.

She grimaced, wrapping her arms around her legs.

She longed to "belong" to someone. Despite her vows to avoid being controlled by anyone again, she longed to become a part of a family. A real family.

Resting her cheek on her knees, she allowed her thoughts to wander. Soon she would have a husband, and one day, children.

Children?

In all her thoughts and dreams about her new life, she had never considered such a thing. Her imaginings had always ceased upon meeting Neil Ballard and becoming his wife.

A small shiver of fear coursed down her spine. Was she ready for such a drastic change to her life? Only weeks earlier, she'd been imprisoned in Goodfellow's charity school, and now she was contemplating becoming a mother.

So why did the thought fill her with such overwhelming dread? She wanted children—she'd always wanted them. Unlike her own father, she would be a loving parent who nurtured their hopes and dreams.

Again she shivered, realizing that it wasn't the dream of children that caused her to pause, but the man who would become their father. She had read Neil Ballard's letters over and over. His words were eloquent and filled with a sensitivity Phoebe had never known a man to possess.

Surely she could learn to love him.

Desire him.

Sighing, she pushed away another face that swam into her consciousness. Not that of a gentle farmer, but of a hardened trail boss.

Would she ever be able to forget him? Or would his features be permanently branded into her brain?

Phoebe pressed the palms of her hands to her eyes as if she could forcibly remove the image, but the action did little good. Even now, her body tingled with awareness for a man she barely knew. He had a power over her that she found bewildering and enervating.

Why couldn't she will her body and her heart to ignore the man? He would only bring her pain.

A sting of moisture came to her eyes, but she blinked it back. No. She wouldn't waste any more tears on the masculine sex. Hadn't she learned her lesson with her father? No one could be forced to love another person. And despite the passion that flared between herself and Gabe, she mustn't delude herself into thinking that he could ever love her. He was a man accustomed to movement, action and an element of risk. He would never be content with the simple life offered by a home, wife and family.

And she would not settle for less. She would have an unshakable commitment from any man she let share her life.

So why did the thought of the pain he must have suffered at the death of his family resonate within her own breast? And why did she sense that the passion she experienced was something she might never know again if she let him go?

Bit by bit the train began to slow. Peering out of the narrow slit in the door, Phoebe was able to see that dawn was beginning to touch the sky with a pinkish light. She could see no signs of a town as yet, so she supposed the train was stopping for water again.

Bracing her hands beside her, she waited until the train lurched to a stop on a secluded stretch of siding.

"Ten minutes! Ten minutes for water!" the distant engineer shouted.

Knowing that the ten-minute stop would invariably stretch into twenty or thirty, Phoebe crept toward the door. She needed to get out of the hot, airless boxcar, even if only for a few minutes. Once outside, she would be better able to push away her worrisome thoughts.

Moving carefully, Phoebe stepped over the supine figure of Mr. Potter and pulled the door open wide enough to slip through. She still hadn't found a graceful manner to move from the boxcar to the ground, so she glanced quickly in both directions. Seeing that no one else had braved the early morning hour, she gathered her skirts in one hand, then half slid, half jumped to the siding.

"Going somewhere?"

She spun on the loose gravel, peering through the shadows.

Gabe. Naturally, he would catch her sneaking out alone. Hours earlier, he'd lectured the women on how they were to stay in the boxcar unless the train stopped at an actual station. Even then, they weren't allowed to venture away from the train without Mr. Potter or another female companion.

"Yes, I—I..." She stopped, snapping her jaw shut. Why was she explaining her actions to him? There was nothing at all wrong with getting a breath of fresh air to clear her head, and a moment or two of privacy.

Lifting her chin to what she hoped was an imperious

angle, she stated sharply, ''I need to tend to...personal needs.''

If he was embarrassed by her frank admission, he didn't look it. Clearly weighing the validity of her statement, he finally nodded his head. ''Just see to it that you're back before the train leaves. If not, we'll go without you.''

It was clear from his tone that he had forgotten those stolen moments of passion in the orchard hours before. Her cheeks burned when she realized that she had not been able to put the memories behind her. With each monotonous clack of the train's wheels, her mind had returned again and again to the passion they'd shared.

Harrumphing softly, she whirled away from him and stalked off into the gloom. Yet even as she silently berated the man for being every kind of cad, she couldn't deny that deep down she was hurt.

How could he remain so unaffected? How was it possible for him to forget an event that, for her, had been earth-shattering?

She moved several yards away from the train, then finally sat on a boulder behind a copse of trees. From here she could hear the activity at the front of the train, but was isolated from view. A cool breeze toyed with the strands of her hair, and sighing, she closed her eyes and leaned her head back, wishing that she could loosen the tight plait and...

What was stopping her? Just because the teachers at Goodfellow's had insisted on students wearing their hair in a severe knot, that didn't mean their views should hold sway now. She wasn't Louisa Haversham anymore. She was Phoebe Gray—a woman who had never set foot in a charity school.

Needing something to ease the pounding of her head and the weary ache of her body, Phoebe surrendered to the impulse. Moving swiftly, lest she lose her resolve, she plucked the pins from her hair and used her fingers to comb the braid into rippling waves. Then, flinging the pins into the brush in an added show of defiance, she wound the strands into a loose braid, tying the end with a bit of ribbon that she pulled from the hem of her drawers.

Instantly, she felt freer. The air tickled the back of her neck and sifted through the locks of her hair to cool her hot, prickly scalp. If only she wouldn't be forced to return to the train and the stifling heat of the boxcar.

"Over here!"

Phoebe froze when a harsh whisper interrupted her reverie, followed by the scrabble of footfalls on loose rock.

Although the voice had been muffled, Phoebe instantly recognized that it belonged to a woman. Someone imperious and demanding. Doreen?

Blast it all. Was there no getting away from her? Wasn't it bad enough that Phoebe was forced to endure the woman's endless complaining while they traveled? Did she have to spend her few moments alone within earshot of her as well?

"...don't like meeting like this."

Phoebe froze when a deeper voice betrayed the fact that the woman was not alone.

But Doreen had never given any indication of knowing any of the other passengers. Instead, she'd seemed reluctant to have any interaction with the "riff-raff" as she called them.

"I have to see you," the woman said, and Phoebe

frowned, wondering if it was truly Doreen. The bossiness of her tone of voice was familiar, but not the inflections. ''It's been unbearable being away from you like this.''

Phoebe flushed when it became obvious that the couple was embracing—and quite passionately, too.

Heavens! Doreen was supposed to be marrying an Oregon merchant when they arrived. And yet here she was, kissing another man.

To Phoebe's relief, the couple seemed to separate.

''I need you so desperately,'' the woman gasped.

''Don't start!'' the male growled.

If it was Doreen who spoke, Phoebe was sure that she'd begun to pout, for her voice took on a wheedling tone. ''Then when? When can we...alone together?'' An intermittent breeze ruffled the leaves of a nearby cottonwood tree, obliterating part of the conversation.

''Not until I've done...here to do. We have only a few days before...arranged...gold heist. Granted, our progress...slow, but we still have...finite time.'' The man's voice lowered to a whisper.

''But that shouldn't...seeing one another.''

Phoebe heard the scuffle of shoes.

''Damn it...isn't a game! This is serious...''

Phoebe heard the woman sniff.

''...aware that the gold—

''...only a small part...plan!'' the man whispered fiercely. ''Don't you...stand? I mean to des... Gabriel...'' His whisper grew harsher, cooler, slicing through the twilight like the blade of a knife, but with the figures moving away from her, Phoebe was unable to catch even less of what he was saying. ''Then...mean to ki...him.''

What had the man said? Could he possible have muttered ''kill''?

Phoebe felt the impact of the words hitting her with the force of a slap. But before she could fully absorb their meaning or decide whether or not she had even heard them correctly, the shriek of the train's whistle signaled that any missing passengers should quickly resume their places.

The couple standing mere feet away from her exchanged more words, but the sharp toots of the whistle drowned out all but their tones and inflections.

For long moments, Phoebe stood rooted to the spot, wondering if the others had left or if they were still clinging together in a fierce lover's embrace. Bit by bit, the huffing of the steam engine grew from a faint panting to a pronounced chug.

She had to get on the train!

Moving as quietly as she could, Phoebe peered around the boulders.

Whoever had once stood there was gone now.

Lifting her skirts, she ran toward the boxcar. Glancing up the line, she saw Gabe clinging to the side ladder of his own car.

For a moment she stopped. She had to warn Gabe. He had to know that someone meant to kill him!

But as soon as the thought occurred to her, the train lurched.

There was no time now. Besides, she wasn't even sure that she'd heard correctly. She hurried on toward the boxcar.

Phoebe was only a few yards away from her goal when she felt a blinding pain in her head. Then she was falling to the ground, where the sharp gravel bit into her hands, her cheek.

Dazed, she tried to move, but her body wouldn't comply with her commands. Distantly, she heard the train engine building steam, the wheels creaking as they began to roll.

"Please," she croaked, reaching out. But even to her own ears, her voice was little more than a whisper.

Tears welled in her eyes. They were going to leave her! Gabe had promised as much if she wasn't back in time, and no one else would discover her absence until later.

Sobs welled within her and she tried to push herself upright.

"Wait," she panted.

Footsteps strode across the gravel, harsh and purposeful. A distant part of her brain acknowledged that she'd been hit on the back of the head, and helplessly she wondered if the culprit had come to finish the job.

"Keep away from me," she growled, trying to push herself to her feet. Her head throbbed and she felt the sticky warmth of blood seeping down the back of her neck.

"Damn it, Phoebe! I warned you about missing the train!"

Relief shuddered through her, and summoning the last of her strength, she threw herself into Gabe's arms.

Then the world around her dissolved to black.

Bit by bit, Phoebe became aware of a hazy glow of light somewhere in the distance. It shot from one end of her field of vision to the other, then back again, lulling her into a sensation of well-being.

Moisture touched her brow, offering a blessed coolness to the heat of her skin.

"Louisa...Louisa..."

Frowning, she considered the name being called. It sounded strange to her ears somehow.

Then, without warning, a pain shot through her head from the back of her skull and she cried out.

The warmth beneath her moved, and she became conscious of a pair of arms holding her.

"Phoebe, what happened?"

The low voice caused her eyes to flicker and her heart to pound with sudden awareness.

It was her stranger! He'd found her!

But as she blinked and her eyes focused on her surroundings, Phoebe realized that it wasn't the mysterious stranger from the ship, but Gabriel Cutter.

Her head continued to throb, the ache centering low in her skull. But when she would have touched the area, Gabe stopped her.

"You've got a gash beneath your hairline. I've stopped the bleeding, but you'll need to keep the cloth on it a little longer before we clean you up."

Feeling weak as a kitten, she allowed Gabe to have his way. Her hand dropped against her chest and she closed her eyes again, trying to remember what had happened.

"Would you like to tell me about it?"

She grimaced, trying to remember something, anything, before this moment, but her mind proved uncooperative. "I stepped out for a breath of fresh air and then..."

But the pounding in her head made remembering impossible. "I...can't..."

A lump lodged in her throat. And then, as if a dam had broken, she began to sob—huge, wrenching cries that attested to the tension she'd experienced the past few days, the worry she still harbored for her friend, and the pain of her injuries.

To her relief, Gabe didn't press her for details. With a tenderness that would have astounded her earlier in their acquaintance, he stroked her hair, brushing it back from her cheek.

"Lie still for now," he murmured, shushing her as if she were a child.

Then he was holding her close, his arms a bastion of strength in a world she didn't completely understand. And for a moment, she felt safe.

Cherished.

Perhaps even loved.

Chapter Eleven

Gabe stared down at the woman in his arms, watching as the swaying of the railway car and the lantern overhead lulled Phoebe to sleep.

Bowing his head, he tucked his face against her own, absorbing the warmth of her body and the gentle rise and fall of her chest.

She would never know the terror that had spread through him when he'd lit the lantern and discovered her neck and clothes covered with blood. Ripping one of his spare shirts into pieces, he'd carefully wiped at the gash at the back of her head until he'd been able to ascertain that the injury was superficial and far from mortal.

In that instant, a relief such as he'd never known had rushed through him. If he wasn't already sitting on a bed of straw, cradling her, he was sure that his knees would have given away.

Without warning, he'd been reminded of another woman he'd held in his arms. Dear, sweet Emily had already been gone when he'd found her, but he'd still held her close, willing the warmth to return to her body. All for naught.

And yet…

As he held Phoebe in his arms, Gabe discovered that the memory wasn't as overwhelming as it had once been. Not too long ago, thoughts of his wife and son had been enough to swamp him with despair. In an effort to wipe away the sights and sounds, Gabe would volunteer for another difficult assignment or spend the night at the Golden Arms Hotel nursing a bottle of whiskey.

But tonight, though Emily's memory brought an ache to his heart, Gabe's overriding concern centered upon Phoebe. He found himself wanting little more than to hold her, and he prayed this moment would last forever.

He was surprised by his own reaction. He was generally a man who found it hard to sit still and wait. Yet here he remained, marveling in the velvety texture of her cheek and the fiery color of her hair in the lamplight.

She shifted in her sleep and the waves of red-gold fell away from her neck, revealing the bluish tinge of a bruise beginning to form. A slow anger rose within him.

Although he had tried to convince himself that Phoebe's misadventure was nothing more than an accident, he didn't believe it. The location of the gash and the length of the wound made it unlikely that she'd simply fallen. If so, there would have been other scrapes and bruises. The conclusion was inescapable. Someone had hit her. Moreover, Gabe feared that she'd been hurt because of him.

Tonight, the Overland Gang had tipped its hand. By threatening Phoebe, they had made things personal. Either Phoebe was innocent of being involved in the robberies, or she had hit upon the perfect way to allay suspicion.

Gabe shook that thought away. No one would purposely allow herself to be hurt so severely. Somehow, although Gabe and Phoebe had tried to keep their attraction to one another discreet, someone must have noted his uncharacteristic attachment to the woman. No doubt they were attempting to weaken his will or distract him by threatening the first woman he had been attracted to in years.

When would he learn that his lifestyle was a danger to any woman who entertained his company? Hadn't he learned his lesson with his own wife?

Unconsciously, he tightened his fingers on her arm, as if wanting to protect her through sheer will alone. It wasn't until she winced in her sleep that he realized what he was doing and loosened his grip.

Dear sweet heaven, she was so beautiful. So beautiful and…

Innocent?

He still had no explanation why a woman wearing silk and sapphires would answer to the name Louisa on board the same ship that had transported the gold, and then, within the space of a day, change her name and appear on his train.

Yet despite all common sense, he was beginning to trust her. She was…

Intriguing.

Alluring.

Frightening?

Gabe balked at the last observation, but he could not ignore it. Yes, this woman frightened him. She terrified him. He who had seen battle and death and anguish was now cowed by a slip of a girl. Not so much because of who she was, but because of the way she made him feel.

This redheaded woman was melting the ice around him, forcing the walls around his heart to crumble. And try as he might, he couldn't seem to push her out of his life. She obsessed him like a secret hunger. Only by sating himself with her laughter could he begin to feel a little less like a starving man.

Sighing, Gabe rested his forehead against hers.

"So what do I do?" he whispered into the darkness.

But as the moments wore on, Gabe realized he had no answers, only more questions. As morning broke, he began to fear for his own heart and his own sanity.

When the train shuddered to a stop once more in order to take on more water, Gabe knew it was time to get her back to the other women, where she belonged. She wasn't safe with him.

But he couldn't let her go.

Not just yet.

Light seeped into Phoebe's consciousness, urging her to awaken, but she resisted the sensation, knowing instinctively that consciousness would bring pain.

"Phoebe?"

She frowned to herself, struggling to make her way through the darkness. She knew that voice from… where?

Her stranger?

"It's Gabe Cutter."

In an instant, the dregs of sleep vanished and she blinked. Bit by bit, her surroundings came into focus, bringing with it them the smells of hay, soot and dust.

Her hand moved to the ache at the back of her skull,

and she hissed when her fingers encountered a soft bandage.

"Leave it alone," a deep voice uttered brusquely. Strong fingers wrapped around her wrist, pulling her arm to her side.

Blinking again, she saw that Gabe was sitting on the floor beside her. With a rush of shame, she remembered clinging to him with overt neediness.

She grimaced and reached for the blanket draped around her waist. A gasp lodged in her throat.

Where were her clothes?

Phoebe quickly snatched the blanket up to her chin.

"W-what happened to my traveling costume?"

His expression remained inscrutable, concerning her even more. Had she done something in her dazed condition to make him think that she…that they…

"You opened your wound again and the blood was getting on your things, so I removed them."

He had removed them. *He* had touched her bare flesh and disrobed her, leaving her in little more than her chemise, petticoats and corset.

She regarded him with undisguised horror. "How could you have done such a thing?"

His brows lifted ever so slightly and she was sure she saw a glint of humor in his steel-gray eyes.

"As I said, you were bleeding all over your clothes."

She grew hot, then cold, then hot again. "B-But it isn't proper for a man to—"

"I've been married, Phoebe. I can assure you that I didn't find anything new."

She gasped at the effrontery. But even as she opened her mouth to chide him, she closed it again.

She couldn't possibly win an argument about this subject, so why bother?

"What time is it?" she asked quickly.

"A little past noon."

"Noon!" Her mouth gaped, but she had to force sound to move past the sudden dryness of her throat. "W-why didn't you take me back to the brides' boxcar?"

"I didn't want to move you until I'd had a chance to ensure that you didn't have a serious injury."

"Then take me back at once now."

This time his lips twitched. "As you've no doubt noticed, the train is moving."

Phoebe bit her lip, feeling a wave of embarrassment rise in her cheeks.

"It seems you have a penchant for blushing, Phoebe."

She dragged the blanket even more tightly against her chin.

"A gentleman would immediately turn his back so that I could dress again."

"As you have probably deduced, I'm no gentleman."

The breath locked in her chest.

His expression grew stern, but his gaze held a sensual heat that she couldn't ignore. As his eyes raked her form from head to toe, she felt their fiery heat. When he spoke again, his voice was like velvet over gravel.

"I'm a bastard through and through. I'm the wrong kind of man for you or any other woman. You should have taken one look at me and arranged for another train."

''But I didn't,'' she whispered after a beat of silence.

''No. You didn't. And that makes you a very foolish woman.''

''Why?'' The word was a bare puff of sound.

''Because I've never been good at minding my manners or doing the proper thing. And right now—'' his voice dropped to an intimate murmur ''—I'm remembering the way you felt in my arms all through the night.''

A new kind of heat swept through her body, settling low in her belly. Not for the first time, Phoebe was at a loss for something to say. She didn't have any experience with men and the emotions they inspired. Or rather, the emotions this one man inspired.

Her gaze locked with his for an infinitesimal moment. Then she became fascinated with the rough-hewn angles of his face, the shadow of whiskers darkening his jaw.

And those lips… Was it so wrong to want to feel them against her own once more?

Her heart started a galloping beat at the mere thought. Her breath came quick and shallow. As if he were sensing her thoughts, Gabe's regard become even more intense, until time seemed to have stopped and the cacophony of the rattling train faded.

There was only this moment and the heat of his eyes.

Without her being aware of who moved first, the distance between them melted. His arms wrapped around her shoulders, drawing her to him. His head dipped and his lips lowered to brush against her own—once, twice, then with a hunger that neither of them could ignore.

Phoebe's hands slid around his waist and over the firm musculature of his back. Eagerly, she met each of his advances with one of her own, kissing him with a passion that she never would have thought she was capable of feeling.

What was she doing? The man had all but told her she wasn't safe in his company.

But she couldn't seem to find the will to care. A fire was building within her, one that would soon be impossible to stifle.

Gabe suddenly drew free, gasping for breath. Phoebe grabbed at his shirt to steady herself, feeling emboldened by the pounding of his heart.

"Make no mistake, Phoebe," Gabe muttered, his voice curiously gruff and trembling. "I'm not a marrying man. Nor am I the sort to come courting for years on end. I can't promise you anything but this moment."

An inexplicable shaft of hurt pierced her heart, but she pushed it aside, pride rising to the surface. "I don't remember asking you for any promises, Gabe." She slid her fingers through the silkiness of the hair that tumbled over his collar. "I am capable of taking care of myself."

"Thank God," he whispered as he drew her to him again, his mouth taking hers in a crushing embrace.

Phoebe willingly melted into his arms. She ignored the little voice that warned her she was making a mistake. She would be married to a staid farmer soon enough. Was it so wrong to enjoy her freedom until then?

When Gabe leaned back, taking her with him, she didn't resist. Nor did she demur when he pushed aside the blanket and began to tease the bare skin of her shoulders and arms. Lightning flashes of delight traced from those points of contact to her very core, until she was trembling and nearly frantic with desire.

Heedless of the consequences, she began to tear the buttons of his shirt from their holes until his broad chest was laid bare. Trembling with passion, she traced her fingers down the hard length of his abdomen, then back up again, finding the dark patch of hair and—

A ring.

Phoebe became still, so still. Breaking away from Gabe, she looked down at the ring, seeing its delicate filigree work and catching a peek of the inscription.

...love, Gabe.

Love.

Immediately, she was doused by an icy wave.

Love. This man had once loved a woman so intensely that even years after her death he wore her ring—just as he continued to wear his grief. Instinctively, she knew that Gabe had sworn never to love another woman.

Not even someone like me.

A noise that sounded uncomfortably like a whimper burst from her throat. Rearing back, Phoebe automatically reached for the blanket, shielding herself from his gaze.

"Your wife's ring?" she breathed.

Gabe reached for it as if he'd forgotten it was there. But as his fingers curled around it and his knuckles grew white, she knew that he was thinking of his former wife and regretting the passion he and Phoebe had shared.

"Yes, it's Emily's."

Emily.

For some reason, knowing his wife's name made Phoebe feel even more guilty, ashamed...and somehow not good enough.

Ducking her head, she began to retie the ribbon of her chemise. Sweet heaven, she had nearly lost control! If not for the hard shape of that ring, she probably would have...

What? What would she have done?

The shame intensified as Phoebe realized she would have given this man everything—her passion, her virtue...perhaps a small piece of her heart.

Swallowing hard, she whispered, "I think I'd better get dressed."

She reached for her clothes, but was stopped when Gabe's hand clenched around her wrist.

"My wife is dead, Phoebe. Nothing has changed between us. We haven't done anything wrong."

She sniffed against the tears that were beginning to form. "Haven't we?" Wrenching free, she snatched up her bodice and shrugged into the sleeves. Then she swiped at her eyes as her vision blurred. "Somehow I doubt you've ever put her completely to rest. You mourn her as much now as you did the day she died. Your heart is so crowded with grief and regret that you have little room for anything else, let alone an ounce of fondness for me."

Phoebe lifted her chin to dare him to refute her statement. She nearly withered beneath his icy stare, knowing immediately that she had gone too far this time.

And who was she to judge him? Wasn't she hypocritical in criticizing his devotion, when she herself longed for a love that could endure beyond death?

To her intense sorrow, Gabe didn't say a word. Instead, he rolled to his feet and strode to the far side of the boxcar.

"Gabe, wait!"

If he heard her, he gave no indication. Instead, he yanked open the door, causing a flurry of soot, dust and straw to sting her eyes.

By the time she cleared her vision, he was gone, the heavy thud of his footfalls overhead marking his passage to the car behind them.

Instantly, the strength fled from her body and Phoebe slumped onto the floor, allowing the tears to fall. Her heart felt as if it had been wrenched from her body and her breath came in choked gasps. But as she cried, she didn't know what she mourned most…

Gabe's ever-present grief for his late wife?

Or the fact that he would never care for Phoebe herself with the same intensity?

Chapter Twelve

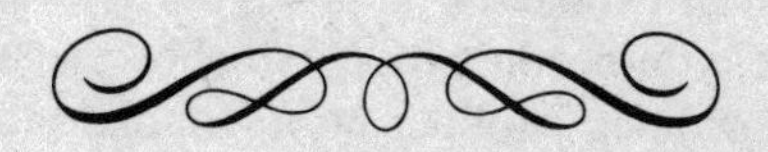

Phoebe woke the next morning to discover that the train was underway and she'd been left in the care of the other brides. Frowning, she rued the fact that her storm of weeping had exhausted her so much that she hadn't awakened on Gabe's return or his posthaste delivery of her to the brides' boxcar.

"She's waking up," Betty called in a whisper that could have risen the dead.

"Oh, my dear," Twila sighed, quickly replacing the cloth on Phoebe's forehead for a fresh, cool one. "You had quite a tumble at the water stop."

"Tumble?" Phoebe echoed, her mind fuzzy and refusing to grasp even the simplest concept.

"Yes, Mr. Cutter explained to us how you'd taken a walk the other night and fell as you were trying to hurry back to the train in time. He barely managed to lift you into his own car before the engine picked up speed. Otherwise, the two of you would still be marooned on the siding somewhere."

Phoebe's brow creased. Gabe had told them that she'd fallen? But he had to know that she'd been hit! Hadn't she told him that she'd been hit?

She winced as a shaft of pain threatened to split her skull in two. Her hissing inhalation immediately sent the other women into motion. Edith brought her a tin cup of fresh water, Mable and Maude fussed over the pallet where she lay, Twila freshened the cloth on her brow yet again. Even Doreen deigned to offer a few kind words, while Potter stood a few feet away, wringing his hat in his hands.

"Please, you needn't fuss," Phoebe insisted.

But the women paid her no mind, and after a time, Phoebe stopped protesting. In truth, she was tired and achy and confused, and their ministrations helped her feel better.

Nevertheless, she couldn't help worrying over Gabe.

Yesterday, she'd allowed her body to betray her. She'd been so consumed by sensation that she had forgotten what had happened to her on the siding.

She hadn't fallen; she'd been pushed! Moreover, she had heard someone making threats against Gabe's life.

She furrowed her brow. As much as she didn't want to talk to the man again, she had to speak to him about what had occurred. He had to know that her injuries weren't an accident. Even more importantly, he needed to be forewarned.

As soon as the train stopped, she would have to find him.

"I'd like to have a word with you if I could."

Gabe barely glanced up as Victor approached him. He didn't really have the time or the patience to deal with the man's petty concerns. Gabe was quite certain that the man wouldn't have been satisfied if the Ninth

Pennsylvania Regiment had been guarding the gold. He had complained nonstop since joining Gabe and his men. The man was a complete nuisance. And if Gabe had his way, Victor would be left on the siding somewhere along the way.

"What do you need, Elliot?"

"I just wanted you to know that I've wired Josiah about a grave lapse in security that I've noted during the journey."

Gabe flicked a glance in Victor's direction, and then returned his attention to the pistol he was cleaning.

His lack of response obviously irritated the man because he sat stiffly on a bale of hay and reached out to grab Gabe's wrist.

Gabe grew infinitely still, his whole body tensing. "You obviously don't know me well, Mr. Elliot," he said quietly, his voice harsh with anger. He gazed pointedly at Victor's hand. "If you did, you'd know that I've shot men for less than that."

Victor released him so quickly Gabe's skin might have been made of molten metal. But rather than backing away, he continued. "I don't like how you're handling the situation, Cutter," he whispered harshly. "You've got agents lollygagging around here when they should be guarding the shipment."

"The gold is well hidden and under the constant surveillance of six men."

"But that's only half of the agents you have available!"

"Tired men make mistakes, Mr. Elliot." Gabe's eyes narrowed as he met the man's furious gaze. "We can't afford mistakes."

"Then shouldn't they be sleeping?" Elliot asked with a wave of his hand at the men who played cards.

"What my men do on their time off is their business. I only ask that they be rested, fresh and ready to respond at the least hint of trouble. If they wish to ease the tension with a game of cards, I can hardly fault them for having a little fun."

"They are *gambling,* Mr. Cutter."

"Then perhaps I'd better join in the game," Gabe said wryly.

Elliot's eyes flashed. "Still, I suppose it's better to be caught gambling than womanizing."

The silence grew heavy with barely controlled tension.

"I've seen you and that woman," Elliot hissed. "You've hardly been discreet about it—even going so far as to keep her in your boxcar for more than a day. Do you honestly think that Overland Express is paying for you to spend more time with that…that *tart* than guarding the gold?"

Gabe moved so quickly that the other man didn't have time to escape. Reacting purely on instincts he'd developed in battle, Gabe twisted Victor into a chokehold, then whipped a knife from the scabbard strapped to the outside of his boot, and leveled it at the base of the man's throat.

"The woman you have maligned is a *lady* through and through, Elliot, and I'll have you remember that."

Silence descended over the car as the men in the far corner became aware of the way their boss held Victor Elliot at knifepoint.

"A *lady* wouldn't be seen with the likes of you," Elliot hissed.

At that moment, Gabe would have willingly plunged the blade into the other man's throat. But as the truth of Elliot's words echoed in his brain, he slowly released his grip.

No, a lady *wouldn't* be seen with the likes of Gabriel Cutter. So why had Phoebe allowed him to hold her, kiss her? She was beautiful, unspotted by scandal and good through and through. While he...

He was a bastard and a deserter.

"I think you'd better join the men," Gabe said through clenched teeth.

For once, Elliot seemed to understand that he'd crossed beyond his authority. Standing, he touched the drop of blood that welled from a tiny nick in his throat. His hands balled into fists and his body trembled with barely concealed rage, but he finally backed away...leaving Gabe to the blackness of his own thoughts about Phoebe and the increasing tension he felt concerning the gold.

Gabe didn't know how or why, but he sensed that the relatively easy time they'd had guarding the shipment was about to end. Come morning, they would cross into Utah Territory. By late afternoon, they would be in Ogden, one of the major railway hubs this far West. And then...

Wide-open desert, alkali flats...a whole lot of nothing. The perfect spot for the Overland Gang to make its move. Once telegraph lines were cut, the train was virtually helpless, and Gabe would have to rely on the men around him.

Overall, he'd been pleased with the agents assigned to his team. Even Luke Peterson, the boy Gabe had bargained on being a weak link in their operation, had shown himself reliable. His apparent nervousness around Gabe had disappeared, to the point where he'd begun volunteering to help when the need arose.

Nevertheless, Gabe couldn't trust any of them. Except for the men he had handpicked to guard the real shipment of gold, he was surrounded by strangers and adversaries—not the least of which was Victor Elliot.

Gabe stared at the man, noting the way Victor pretended to concentrate on his hand. But the way he visibly seethed gave him away. Gabe had no doubts that he'd made an enemy tonight. A powerful enemy. Gabe wouldn't escape retribution of some kind.

But at this point, he really didn't care.

This run was his last. As soon as the gold was delivered safely and the Overland Gang had been uncovered and apprehended, Gabe intended to resign from the Pinkertons. He was tired of trying to prove himself. For years, he'd been trying to live down his desertion. He'd run from one job to another in an effort to show the world he was brave.

While in reality, he'd only been running from himself.

Slipping the knife back into his scabbard, he began snapping the pieces of his revolver together. No more running. It was time he settled down. He was a man who loved working with animals. He'd taken most of the money he'd amassed over the years, and bought a little spread out West. Maybe the time had come to settle down and raise horses.

The idea spread through his being like warm butter. His land was in a valley twenty miles south of San Francisco, where the grass was green and the water sweet. He'd have a house and a fine barn, and one day he'd pass it on to his son—

He grew still, his heart clenching in pain.

No. There would be no wife. No son.

His jaw clenched and his breath hitched in his

throat. Damn, he mustn't think about that now. The job. Only the job. He had vowed never to give his heart away, and he'd best remember that. He would never allow himself to experience the pain of losing yet again.

When the train stopped again, word spread like wildfire—the passengers would have an hour before resuming their journey.

Phoebe was the first to jump down from the boxcar. She needed to check the telegraph office for a message from Louisa. Then she intended to find Gabe.

But as she strode into the station house, she discovered that her spurt of energy was short-lived. By the time she'd made her way through the airless confines to the telegraph operator, her head was pounding with such ferocity she could barely think. To make matters worse, she felt as if she were being watched again.

Scowling, she turned in a circle, trying without success to pinpoint the source of her discomfort.

Who was following her? And why? A cool fist closed around her heart.

"May I help you?"

Phoebe started. She'd been so deep in her thoughts she hadn't noted that she'd reached her turn at the wicket.

Attempting to appear unconcerned, she checked for any messages that had been left for her.

The clerk searched through the stack of envelopes and handed her two envelopes. "Next!"

Grimacing, Phoebe supposed that Neil Ballard was probably responsible for the second telegram. Without bothering to look at it, she shoved it deep into her pocket. Then, curious about whether Louisa had met

Charles Winslow, Phoebe quickly moved to a grimy window and slit open the letter.

"You should be in bed," a deep voice interrupted from a point over her shoulder.

Again she jumped, quickly tucking the telegram out of sight as she whirled to face Gabe.

"Have you been following me?"

He frowned. "I have no idea what you mean."

She sniffed indignantly. "Someone has been following me each time the train makes a stop."

"Who?"

"I thought perhaps you were responsible."

He offered her a derisive smile. "I've got better things to do than follow the movements of a contrary woman who hasn't sense enough to lie down when she should. I merely came to wire the home offices about our latest delays." Gabe scowled at her, his hands on his hips. "Let's get you back to the train."

Before she could utter a word, he had grasped her by the elbow and was pulling her irresistibly outside.

Phoebe tried to wrench free. "I'm fully able to take care of myself," she insisted.

"It doesn't look that way to me."

She flushed under his regard. Because of the gash at the back of her head, she'd braided her hair into two plaits like a child.

As soon as they'd stepped outside, she dug in her heels, refusing to go any farther. "I don't know why you're suddenly so concerned about my welfare. You wasted no time getting rid of me this morning."

He scowled. "I had work to do. The job always comes first."

She stiffened, the words hurting her more than they

should have done. The pounding in her head increased. "Why did you tell the other women that I fell?"

"You did fall."

"No, I was hit from behind."

Gabe shook his head. "There was no one out there but you, Phoebe."

"There was! I heard them talking! I heard them threatening to kill you!" His gaze grew keen, but otherwise he offered no reaction.

"If that's the case, then your companions are stuck somewhere in Nebraska, because you and I were the only ones to board the train."

"But—"

Gabe's voice softened ever so slightly. "You were hurt, Phoebe, and now your mind's playing tricks on you. No one else was out there."

She blinked, feeling an inexplicable sting of tears. He didn't believe her—which meant that he wouldn't even listen if she tried to tell him a tale of gold and revenge.

"I'd best be going," she said, forcing her trembling muscles to draw herself erect.

She'd taken only a step before Gabe said, "Get off the train, Phoebe. We'll be stopping in Ogden for two days to unload a third of the passengers, reorganize the train and ready everything for the second leg of the journey. You and the other women need to get off the train and make other arrangements, do you hear me?"

Phoebe stared at him in horror. Gone was the man who had cared for her the other day, and the lover who had lain with her in the grass of the orchard. In his place was the hardened, embittered trail boss she'd encountered the first time she'd met him.

"Take care to follow my advice, Phoebe."

She felt a shiver trace down her spine.

"Or what?"

"Or you may regret not taking the chance when you had it."

The cattle car was cramped and airless—a less than satisfactory meeting place, but one that would have to do for the time being.

Looking up from the bin of oats that he used as a makeshift table, the leader of the Overland Gang gestured to the map he'd spread out.

"We'll hit here, two hours out of Winnemucca." One by one, he pointed to each of the four men. "You'll rig the charges to the tunnels, here and here. You'll unhitch the rear cars here, as soon as we've nearly reached the summit. Don't wait too long. We want to roll free of the blast in plenty of time." Pointing to the last two men, he said, "You two will be with me. We'll be on top of the last three cars, waiting."

"You're sure the gold is in one of those cars?"

"Damn sure. Despite his show of force around the crates he's loaded onto the first boxcar, it's near these last three where Gabe has been spending most of his time and attention."

"But what about—"

"It's a dummy shipment, I tell you. I've already checked. Besides, Gabriel Cutter is much too smart to transport this payroll shipment with an open guard of Pinkertons." He tapped a diagram of the train. "No, it's here somewhere. And if I were a betting man, I'd wager it's in the same car as the mail-order brides." He looked up, pinning the only woman in the gang with his stare. "Which is where you come in. You've got to search that car."

"I've tried, and I—"

"Just do it. Every bag, every trunk. Then I want you to find out how that Gray woman is involved with the whole affair."

"She doesn't know anything."

He offered a sharp laugh. "That woman is in on this, I can feel it. There's no other reason why Gabriel Cutter, a self-proclaimed woman hater, would be so involved with her. Go through her things with special care."

She nodded, biting her lip.

"Now get going. By the time we reach Ogden, I want all of the information you can give me."

It was nearly dusk when Gabe leaned out of the boxcar, grabbing the ladder bolted to the side. Ignoring the wind and the soot, he climbed to the roof, then began jogging toward the rear of the train. As he moved, he ignored the wind that whistled in his ears and the sick twisting of his stomach as he jumped from roof to roof.

Landing on the boxcar that held the brides, he padded as quietly as he could across the top, then settled on the car holding Miles and Green. After using the butt of his rifle to knock against the roof in a signal to the men inside, he descended the ladder and climbed through the small opening they'd made for him.

"Any problems?" he asked, his gaze skipping from Miles's beard-covered jaw to Green's ruddy features. Except for rare occasions, the men hadn't left the crates since the train had departed from New York.

"Nothin' so far, Cap'n," Miles said. His lips twisted in a wry smile. "But we've been getting some interest."

"What sort of interest?"

Green shrugged. "Neither one of us can pinpoint anything specific. We've just got the creepy-crawlies."

Gabe knew exactly what he meant. His own instincts had been whispering to him that the Overland Gang was getting ready to make its move. Such premonitions were further heightened by their arrival in Utah Territory. The past three raids had occurred in the miles of desert to be found between the main hub in Ogden and the California border.

"I don't think we've got much time," Gabe said.

The other men nodded, their grip tightening on the rifles they held.

"We're ready for a fight," Green said with a grin.

Gabe took one last look at the crates, then headed for the door. "Once in Ogden, I'll meet up with the men I've arranged to have join you. By the time this boxcar leaves the station, it will be fully loaded with agents that only you and I know are on board."

"Y'got a password so's we know who's to be let on?"

Gabe thought for a moment, then said, "Louisa."

The two men exchanged glances.

"Louisa?" Miles repeated.

"Yeah. A password like that can be worked into conversation without sounding odd."

But even as he swung outside to make his way back to his own boxcar, Gabe knew that he'd chosen the name as a talisman of sorts.

Phoebe was better off marrying her farmer from

Oregon. She would disappear from Gabe's life as quickly as she had come, leaving him with a few happy memories to dwell upon. He was a lucky man for having been given that much.

He could only pray that the good fortune she'd brought his way would continue through the next forty-eight hours.

Chapter Thirteen

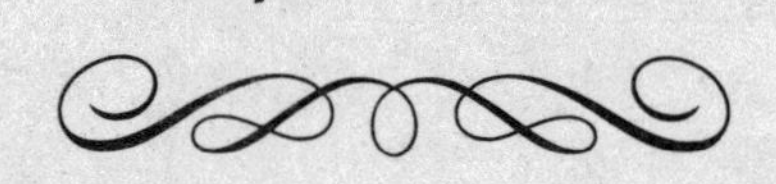

Phoebe was not surprised when she didn't see Gabe for the rest of the day. She had no doubts that he was avoiding her—and in a way, she was glad. The fact that he thought her wound had been caused by a fall upset her. And his studied indifference cut her to the quick. The man had all but told her that he didn't care that she'd been hurt, only that she'd inconvenienced him in the process.

Sniffing in outrage, she dropped to the floor and pulled the telegrams from her pocket. Finally, the women had begun to busy themselves with other things.

Opening the sealed envelope to the first telegram, Phoebe read quickly, almost guiltily.

> Just apprised of your delays. Don't fret, my love. The days will speed past and we will be together for a lifetime.
> N.B.

Phoebe grimaced, pushing away the guilt that flooded her. Neil was obviously a sensitive man, a loving man.

So why couldn't she set her sights on the upcoming marriage without hesitation? Why did she feel as if the lessening miles were stealing her one true chance at happiness?

Phoebe crumpled the telegram into a ball and threw it out the open doorway. But as soon as the wind caught the paper, she felt small and mean.

Refusing to think any more about Oregon or Neil Ballard, she grasped the second telegram and ripped it open. Once again, a long rambling message from Louisa assured her that her friend was not wanting for money.

> Still no sign of Charles Winslow. Growing impatient. Have bought all of the bits and bolts necessary for a wealthy woman, leaving nothing to do. Now have a ladies' maid named Chloe and continue interviewing for companion. So far, I find them all hopelessly dull. Hope your journey is proving delightful.
>
> Louisa Marie Haversham Winslow

Smiling to herself, Phoebe tucked the note in her pocket so that she could hide it in her trunk at the first opportunity. Although she supposed it was foolhardy to keep such letters, she hadn't been able to destroy the previous telegram. The link to her friend was too dear.

"Troubles, lass?"

Phoebe started, then smiled at Mr. Potter.

"No. Everything's fine," she said blithely—even as

she wondered what had happened to Charles Winslow to prevent him from retrieving his bride.

The old man stared at her for several long minutes, enough to make her feel uncomfortable. Then he looked away.

"That's good, then. I wouldn't want anythin' to happen t'ye."

By the time the train reached Denver the journey had definitely begun to take its toll. Tempers were frayed, even among the women.

Ignoring the bickering that had begun to increase along with the heat, Phoebe jumped from the boxcar. Although the train would stop only long enough to replenish water and coal, she needed space and fresh air.

As she strode toward the end of the car, Phoebe knew that she couldn't blame the other women for the heavy mood that had descended on them all. For the most part, they were friendly, helpful and supportive. But as they crossed the halfway point of their journey, their nervousness about meeting their husbands-to-be had increased, making them all feel as if they were sitting on pins and needles.

"Phoebe!"

She stiffened, hearing a horse trot toward her.

Drat. She'd hoped to work out the kinks in her muscles before Gabriel Cutter took it into his head to send her back.

Not wishing to betray her irritation, she turned, forcing a pleasant smile onto her lips.

"Gabriel. How nice of you to stop and say hello."

It was obvious by his scowl that he hadn't been

fooled by her attempt. ''I thought I made it clear to everyone that this stop would be a brief one.''

''Indeed you did. I wasn't planning on going far, merely up and down the length of the train.''

''I'm surprised that you aren't indulging in a bit of target practice.''

She shifted uncomfortably at his none-too-subtle reminder of the afternoon she'd accidentally shot his pistol.

''I can assure you that your revolver is safely tucked away in my purse, which is, in turn, put away in my trunk.''

He continued to glower at her. ''I don't suppose you stored it with the hammer cocked.''

She tightened her lips. Trust him to believe she was too idiotic to know how to properly store things.

''No, the hammer is not cocked.''

He stared at her for long moments. ''Just make sure you return the revolver to me with the last bullet still in the chamber.''

For a moment, she didn't know what he meant. ''*Last* bullet?''

''Yes, ma'am,'' he drawled. ''I was especially careful during our shooting lessons to leave you with a single bullet. That's enough to fire a warning shot if someone should climb into your boxcar by mistake, but not enough to prove much of a threat.''

Her hands balled into fists.

One bullet. How could she have been so stupid? She'd thought that Gabe had truly cared about her safety when he'd taught her to shoot and had allowed her to keep the gun. Now she realized that the entire episode had been nothing more than a clever ploy to disarm her.

This time Gabe grinned openly. ''Good day to you, Phoebe.''

Touching his finger to his hat, he urged his mount into a trot, leaving her in a cloud of dust.

''I swear, one of these days...'' she muttered to herself. But she was unable to complete the threat. She might grumble and toss indignant comments his way, but deep down, she knew she was powerless to do anything to discourage Gabe.

As she glanced over her shoulder, she was forced to admit that he was the one with the power. Even now she trembled slightly from their exchange. A warmth suffused her body. Her fingers seemed to tingle.

All because he'd taken a moment to talk to her.

Damn you, Gabe Cutter. Damn you for being so appealing.

As the train pulled to a stop in Ogden, Utah, the brides laughed in delight and quickly gathered their things. They had eighteen hours—a day and a half!—to rest from their journey before continuing on toward Winnemucca.

With so much time available to them, the brides were eager to avail themselves of the amenities to be found in a local hotel where baths and laundry services were provided for weary travelers.

Their destination was also important for another reason. Ogden signaled the fact that the cross-country trek was more than two-thirds of the way completed. Even taking their slow progress into account, the railway journey should end within a few days. From there, it was only a day's coach ride to Oregon.

Where they would all be married.

A heavy dread filled her. The farther West Phoebe traveled, the more she seemed to feel its oppressive weight. But try as she might, she couldn't seem to reconcile herself to the fact that this train trip *would* end—and when it did, she would be honor bound to marry a stranger.

Listening half-heartedly to the other women's chatter, Phoebe knew she should be preparing herself for the moment she met her new husband. The others were busily sewing and embroidering, using the long hours aboard the train to augment their trousseaus, while Phoebe...

Phoebe spent most of her time thinking of Gabe.

He was shutting her out of his life, and that thought hurt more than it should have done. Once again she could feel him erecting emotional barriers between them—and even though she knew, intellectually, that he was doing the right thing, her heart wasn't nearly so compliant.

She was beginning to care for him far too deeply, and that fact frightened her. Before meeting Gabe, she had never known what it felt like to truly love another. Now she feared that she would never experience such a depth of emotion again.

Pushing that thought resolutely aside, Phoebe tried to reassure herself that she would grow to care for Neil with the same intensity, but her mind refused to concentrate.

"Are you coming, Phoebe?"

She shook her head. "I need to send a telegram."

Doreen's lips tipped up slyly. "You seem to spend a good deal of time at telegraph offices along the way. If we didn't know any better, we might think you were up to something nefarious."

Phoebe stared at her, wondering again if Doreen had been the woman she'd seen on the siding that night she'd been hit.

"I promised a friend that I would keep her apprised of my progress."

"It must be a very dear friend," Doreen drawled in a voice that dripped with innuendo.

"As a matter of fact, she is. We're much like…sisters rather than mere friends. We shared a cabin on the voyage to New York."

"Then we'd best not keep you from your errand," Maude said smoothly, effortlessly shooing the other women ahead of her. "We'll see you at the hotel when you've finished."

"Yes, yes. I'll catch up with you before water can be boiled for a soak."

As the other women stepped onto the platform, Phoebe quickly gathered a change of clothes, her soap and a bath sheet. After slipping a few coins into her pocket to pay for the telegram, she hurried outside.

Thankfully, the Ogden station had a series of raised platforms that removed the necessity of jumping from the boxcar to the ground. But since Phoebe needed to get to the opposite end of the train yard, she had to skirt around the train, descend to the tracks, then cross several more sets of rails before climbing a second set of stairs to yet another raised platform.

By the time she had traversed half of the boardwalk, her friends had been swallowed up by the chaos of a whole new group of passengers waiting for their train. In the distance, Phoebe heard the shriek of another locomotive's whistle and the squeal of metal against metal as it tried to slow its headlong rush toward the station.

Obviously eager for their journey, the crowd surged forward, trapping Phoebe. Rising on tiptoe, she tried to spot what door she should take into the station, but she couldn't see much of anything but people.

Sighing, she glanced down at her things to ensure she hadn't dropped anything. She really was looking forward to a bath. She planned to spend half the day immersed in—

A sudden push at her shoulder caused Phoebe to lose her balance. Screaming, she dropped her belongings and threw her hands out to stop her fall. But it was too late. Her body had already twisted awkwardly and she fell hard, her hip striking the metal rail, her head banging against the gravel. In a sickening montage, she saw the train growing nearer, ever nearer. Yet even as her brain scrambled to send an order for her body to move, she was rooted to the spot, knowing that there wasn't time.

Horrified, she heard the squeal of the train's brakes, the shriek of the whistle. And then, just when she was sure that she had taken her last breath, a body fell roughly over hers. A pair of arms wrapped around her waist and she was rolling, rolling, out of the path of the oncoming train and onto the sharp rocks of the shoulder.

For a moment everything seemed to stand still, and she was aware of little more than the arms that surrounded her. Then time jolted into gear and the world began rushing madly around her. She became aware of the air rushing against her cheek as the train sped past them and shuddered to a stop. There were shouts and screams, then blessed, blessed quiet.

Phoebe's body shuddered with a quick breath that was half sob, half laugh of relief.

She was alive. Alive!

Her eyes squeezed shut as she reveled in the warmth of the sun on her cheek and the ache of her own body. Instinctively, she knew who had saved her from certain death, and at that moment there was no place she would rather be than in the circle of his embrace.

"Damn it, what in hell were you doing?"

The harsh whisper jolted her back to the moment, as did the hands that drew her upright until she was standing within the circle of Gabe's arms. Blinking, she stared up into his angry features. His eyes blazed from a face that seemed harder, colder than ever.

"Were you trying to kill yourself? Is that it? Do you have a death wish? This is the second time I've had to pick you up off the siding in as many days!"

He took her arms, shaking her, and her head throbbed from her day-old injury as well as from the new bruises and scrapes that were beginning to make themselves felt. Then he hauled her close, hugging her to him as if he wished to squeeze the breath from her body.

"Damn it, Phoebe, why would you jump?"

"Jump?" she echoed weakly. "I didn't jump."

At his look of disbelief, she added more forcefully. "I *didn't!* I was pushed!"

It was clear that he didn't believe her—just as he hadn't been willing to listen to her claims that she'd been struck on the head.

Tears welled in her eyes and she pushed against him with all her might. "Leave me alone from now on, do you hear? You aren't responsible for me. I don't even know you—especially after the way you've been so beastly to me the last couple of days. Obviously, you don't give a hoot about me other than how my injuries might reflect on your job, so just stay away. Stay away, I say!''

All at once, Phoebe became aware of the fact that she was screaming at the man, barely making sense. When she saw that her outburst was witnessed by the passengers who had streamed around the back of the train to assure themselves of her safety, she swiped at her tears, picked up her skirts and ran.

She was through with Gabriel Cutter, once and for all. It was time to turn her head and her heart toward the man waiting for her at the end of her journey.

Gabe brushed the dust from his trousers and headed in the opposite direction.

If he hadn't dismissed his man in order to follow Phoebe himself, Gabe hated to think what might have happened. The bolt of fear he'd experienced at Phoebe's first scream stunned him—and that pang had been nothing compared to the horror he'd felt when he'd realized the train was heading straight toward her.

Sighing, he supposed he should have handled the entire episode more carefully. When he'd realized that he'd reached her in time and that she was safe and unharmed, his body had been flooded with relief. But his relief was swiftly followed by a wave of powerlessness and remembered terror. Not thinking, he'd lashed out at her for her carelessness. But he had also touched her face, her shoulders, then hauled her tightly against him, needing to reassure himself of her well-being.

He was suddenly struck by just how much he had begun to care for this woman. Instantly, his heart had filled with fear.

He couldn't love again.

He couldn't lose again.

But even as the thoughts raced through his head, he turned to find Phoebe in the crowd. Immediately, he located her delicate shape. The other brides had gathered around her and were ushering her in the direction of a nearby hotel.

Damn it, what was he going to do? Twice in two days someone had tried to harm her. He'd tried to play down the seriousness of the events when talking to Phoebe, but deep down, he'd known someone was targeting her.

Because of you.

No. The Overland Gang didn't work that way. They struck quickly and violently, then ran with the gold. They didn't play a game of cat and mouse.

At least they hadn't operated that way before.

Automatically, Gabe's eyes searched the rail yard, looking for anything that might be out of place. Tension had been building within him with each passing moment. The Overland Gang was here; he could feel them. Judging by their desperate attempt to harm Phoebe right in front of Gabe's eyes, they would be making their move soon.

It was up to Gabe to make sure that he and his men were prepared. As much as he'd grown to care for Phoebe, he couldn't become distracted by this latest attempt at violence. He had to pretend an aloofness he didn't feel.

Otherwise, the Overland Gang might take it into their heads to use Phoebe as a pawn.

Unless she's somehow involved in it all.

Just because Gabe had developed a fondness for this woman did not mean that she was automatically innocent. At the very least, she was guilty of deceit.

So what should he do about it? Should he stand by and wait for her to tip her hand?

No.

Turning on his heel, Gabe moved in the direction Phoebe had gone. The time had come to apply a little more pressure on this mysterious woman. Somehow, some way, he must find the means to make her confess her secrets.

Chapter Fourteen

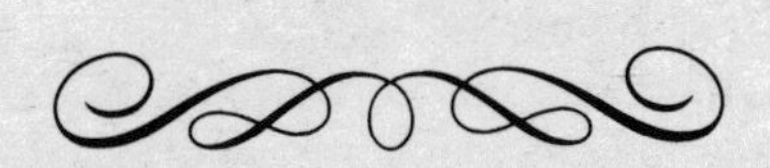

It was only after Phoebe had managed to undress that she saw the full extent of her injuries. A massive bruise was already beginning to form on her thigh and hip. Her elbows were scraped and the palms of her hands pocked with tiny cuts.

Tamping down the sobs that threatened to tumble from her throat, she turned to the large tub near the windows.

Heaven, sheer heaven.

When the hotel owner heard about Phoebe's near miss with a train, she had insisted that Phoebe use the bridal suite rather than the more public bathing facilities.

"You'll need a bit of silence and perhaps a nap," she'd insisted when Phoebe had tried to demur. "I'll send Heber up with the hot water right away, as well as a bite to eat. Then I insist you linger in the tub at least an hour and take a little nap on the bed."

"But—"

The woman held up a hand. "I won't take no for an answer. Consider this the first of many wedding gifts you're sure to receive."

True to the woman's word, hot water and a tray filled with fruit, crustless sandwiches and muffins arrived within minutes. Despite the warm weather, a fire was laid in the hearth and the curtains drawn until Phoebe was enclosed in her own private world. Then, after all the errands had been performed, Phoebe had turned the key in the lock and padded toward the cheval mirror to undress.

At that moment, she could think of nothing she wanted more than to follow the woman's instructions. She planned to soak in the freestanding tin tub until her skin wrinkled and the water turned to ice.

Dipping a finger into the bath, Phoebe added a touch of cold water to make it bearable, then, seeing that a separate privacy curtain could be drawn to encircle the tub, she pulled on the panels until she was completely enclosed.

Slipping into the tub, she cried out as the hot water touched her raw flesh. But gradually, she sank down until only her head emerged.

Heaven, sheer heaven, she repeated.

Then and only then did the tears begin to flow.

Phoebe awoke with a start, and her eyes darted around the small alcove holding the tub. Lifting a hand, she smoothed the damp hair away from her forehead and shivered. She wasn't quite sure when she had drifted off to sleep, but she'd been there long enough for the water to have grown cold.

Standing, she reached for one of the voluminous bath sheets stacked on a nearby table.

Despite her nap, she still felt weary to the bone. But her exhaustion had less to do with the bone-numbing traveling she'd endured than the aftereffects of shock and emotion. She had come to the realization that her life at Goodfellow's had ill prepared her for the real world. She'd been instructed on the importance of goodness, service and mercy. But such pedantic studies had left her with very little knowledge of the realities of life.

Biting her lip to keep the tears away, Phoebe wound the bath sheet around her body, then draped the end over one shoulder. Perhaps if she sat by the fire and dried her hair, she would be able to push away the nameless panic that gripped her. Despite her long soak, she still felt anxious and emotional.

Reaching up, she pushed aside the curtains.

"It's about time you finished," an all-too-familiar voice drawled. "I was beginning to believe that you'd drowned."

Gasping, Phoebe clutched the bath sheet higher against her neck.

"What are you doing in here?" Her gaze bounced from the indolent figure lounging in a nearby chair to the door that she was certain she'd locked.

"Let me give you a piece of advice," Gabe said. "Never leave the key in the lock. It's far too easy to retrieve it and open the door from the outside."

"What are you doing here?" she demanded.

"I wanted to make sure that you weren't suffering any ill effects from your experience this afternoon."

Her jaw dropped and she stared at him in disbelief. "For that, you broke into my room?"

"I was very concerned."

"You could have knocked!"

"I was sure you wouldn't let me in."

She huffed in displeasure. "And in that respect, you would have been right!"

"Just as I thought. So we're both better off now that I've taken matters into my own hands."

Phoebe felt her knees begin to quake—as much from the man's overpowering presence and the memory of his embraces as from the shock of finding him here.

"I think you'd better leave."

Gabe watched her for several long moments, but he didn't move.

"You've already assured yourself of my safety."

"Perhaps." He stood then, moving toward her with a catlike grace, reminding her of the caged lions she'd seen in the zoo. "However, I would be neglecting my duties if I didn't take a closer look, don't you think?"

Phoebe pointed an imperious finger. "No, I don't think so at all."

"Since I'm in charge, it really doesn't matter what you think."

Phoebe huffed in indignation, backing away from him. In doing so, she tripped over the folds of her bath sheet, nearly stumbling.

"Get away!" she said, pointing to the spot where he should have remained.

But Gabe ignored her.

Her avenues of escape were disappearing rapidly, since she had literally backed herself into a corner.

"You have no right—"

"I have every right to assure myself of your well-being. As leader of this excursion, I have to consider the needs of one person against those of the many. If you are in need of medical attention, I may have to forbid you from continuing the next leg of the journey."

"You wouldn't dare!"

He continued as if he hadn't heard her. "And since the rest of the bridal party would then be incomplete, I would be forced to leave all of you behind."

Phoebe balled her hands into fists, then hissed when the action brought a quick gasp of pain.

Gabe's eyes narrowed. "So you *are* injured."

She gave him her haughtiest stare. "I can assure you that my injuries are minor, merely bruises and a few scrapes."

"I don't want your assurances. I want to see for myself."

She stared at him in horror, lifting the sheet even higher. "Never!"

"Then I'll arrange for your things to be removed from the train."

"No!" Her blood ran cold, then hot. Would she be forced to bare herself in front of this man in order to continue her journey?

She took another step back, intent on dodging around the tufted settee. But her foot caught the hem of her sheet, pitching her backward.

Before she even realized what was happening, Gabe had snagged her wrist and pulled her tightly against him.

"I seem to be continually bailing you out of mishaps," he murmured into her ear.

A storm of sensations swept through her body as she found herself absorbing the warmth and strength of his body without the multitude of layers she normally wore.

Gabe seemed as stunned as she by the contact. The hand at her back spread wide, nudging her even closer, dipping low on her hips.

"Let me go," Phoebe whispered. She'd meant to

sound commanding, but the words resonated with a sudden awareness.

Naturally, Gabe ignored her. His gaze dropped to the swath of bare flesh above her towel, and a smoldering gleam touched his gray eyes.

A streak of molten sensation trailed in the wake of his stare as he examined her from the hollow of her neck to the soft curve of her shoulder, her elbow and finally the palm of her hand.

Briefly, he met her eyes. Then he bent his attention to the raw surfaces of her palm. ''You're hurt.''

Her heart was pounding so hard in her breast that she was barely able to respond. ''It isn't life threatening.''

''You never know.''

Before she knew what he meant to do, he'd lifted her palm to his lips.

Instinctively, she curled her fingers. ''What are you doing?''

''When I was a boy, my mother would make such injuries better with a kiss.'' He slipped his thumb beneath her fingers, forcing them to open.

''But you aren't my mother,'' she insisted weakly.

Again his steel-gray eyes grew dark. ''No. I'm not.'' Then he bent to press his lips to her palm.

The caress was so gentle against her sensitive skin that she shuddered. A lightning bolt of desire spread through her system, settling low in her belly.

''Please…''

He looked at her through dark lashes. ''Please what?''

''Please don't.''

''Why not?''

She bit her lip. "Because it makes me feel so..." He watched her so intently that she couldn't continue.

"Are you in pain?"

Yes. Yes, I'm in pain. But the ache had nothing to do with her scrapes and bruises.

His grasp tightened, drawing her so tightly against him that she could feel the buckle of the holster he wore.

"What do you want from me, Phoebe?"

She scrambled desperately to remember the many demands she'd intended to make of him. But try as she might, she couldn't consciously direct her thoughts. She was being stormed with a thousand emotions and sensations, all of which centered on this one man.

"What would you have me do, Phoebe?"

"I..." Unconsciously, she swayed toward him.

He bent toward her slowly, filling her with an aching anticipation.

"Tell me," he murmured.

Her own hands had been pressing against his chest in an effort to put space between them, but in that moment she lost her will to resist.

Lifting on tiptoe, she slid her arms around his neck, pulling his lips down to her own.

The moment they touched, their embrace became fierce and hungry. Phoebe surrendered to the wild tide of passion, her lips parting, her hips arching against him.

How had she come to this point? How was it possible for her to lose her resolve and her control at a mere touch? A glance? She had been raised in an atmosphere of piety and strict morality. And yet none of that seemed to matter the moment she stepped into his arms.

She made no demur as his fingers burrowed beneath the sheet at her back. Nor did she resist when he deepened the kiss. Where he led, she followed, her body seeming on fire.

In all her life, she never would have imagined that she could have felt this way. Her body throbbed with a molten desire. Each nerve seemed acutely attuned to him. There was nothing but this moment.

This man.

Her fingers grabbed at his shirt, bunching it at his back as she pulled the fabric free of his waistband. But when she sought to caress his bare flesh, she was disappointed to find the thin woolen layer of his union suit instead.

Whimpering, she wriggled her hands between their bodies, struggling with the buttons of his shirt, then the buttons of his union suit until she reached bare flesh.

Gabe drew back, his breath hissing in her ear. "Don't," he groaned.

This time it was her turn to smile in triumph. "Don't what?" she asked, her fingers pausing in their exploration.

"Don't...stop...."

His lips grazed her chin, her ear, causing a flurry of gooseflesh to travel down her arms. But he didn't halt there. Bit by bit, he slipped lower, discovering a sensitive spot on her neck, then the curve of her shoulder.

Gasping, she abandoned her own foray, clutching at his shoulders as her limbs seemed to lose their strength. Knowing that she would be lost if she continued, she whispered, "No...we shouldn't."

Gabe's lips continued their descent to the swells of her breasts.

"No. We shouldn't," he echoed.

"I don't even know you."

"That's true."

"And I'm about to be married."

For the first time he paused, a frown appearing between his brows. He didn't say a word, but she felt him withdraw emotionally, then physically.

As he dropped his arms and backed away, she felt immediately chilled. Instinctively, she tightened the sheet as it threatened to fall.

"I'm sorry," she whispered.

"For what?" He stared at her, his eyes hard.

Phoebe bit her lip. Although she knew she'd done the right thing in bringing their passions to a halt, she couldn't seem to help feeling bereft. Empty.

Unable to respond, she watched in secret torment as Gabe became distant and detached.

"I—"

A knock at the door interrupted her words before she could string them together in logical form.

"Phoebe, are you there?" a voice called through the wooden panel.

"We wanted to check on you before we went back to the train."

Instantly, Phoebe recognized Maude's and Mable's voices, and she stared at Gabe in horror, knowing that if she hadn't pushed him away, the women might have arrived just as she gave herself to Gabe without a second thought.

"Phoebe?" Maude called again.

"Phoebe, are you all right?"

She gazed at Gabe in desperation. "What do I do? I've got to answer them."

He nodded in the direction of the door.

As she moved to talk the other women, Phoebe automatically ran her fingers through her tousled hair.

"I'm here," she called out. "I fell asleep in the tub, that's all."

There was a moment's silence, then Twila asked, "You're sure that you're feeling well?"

"Yes. Yes, I'm fine. Just tired."

"You hit your head when you fell," Betty called.

"You didn't black out, did you?" Edith asked.

"No, no," Phoebe hastened to reassure them.

Faintly, she heard a murmur in German and she closed her eyes in distress. All of the brides must be waiting outside her door.

"Open the door, will you?" Maude asked. "None of us would feel right if we left without seeing for ourselves that you've suffered no ill effects."

Phoebe's heart leaped to her throat and she frantically searched the room for a place where Gabe could hide. But before she could find a possible solution, she suddenly realized that he was gone.

Gone?

Again she scanned the room, wondering how he could have hidden so quickly.

It was then that her gaze fell on the open window opposite the bed. The sash had been lifted and a gentle breeze toyed with the curtains.

Had he jumped?

"Phoebe?"

Knowing there was no time to investigate, Phoebe opened the door. Thankfully, despite his unorthodox entry into her room, Gabe had replaced the key in the lock.

As soon as the wooden panel swung wide, Phoebe found herself the subject of the other brides' scrutiny. Inwardly, she prayed that her face wouldn't reveal her lack of control, her overwhelming passion for a man who had just jumped out a window in order to protect her honor.

"You look tired, dear," Twila said after several long moments.

Phoebe tucked a lock of hair behind her ear. "Yes. I—I thought I'd rest a little on the bed before going back to the train."

"We were going to invite you to go shopping with us, but I think you're right about taking a nap," Maude insisted. "Come along, ladies," she called. To Phoebe, she added, "We'll check back with you later this evening to see if you'd like to join us for dinner."

"That would be wonderful."

Phoebe waited until they had turned the corner of the hall before shutting the door and running to the window. There, she discovered that it wouldn't have been necessary for Gabe to jump. Her hotel room looked out upon a grassy garden, and a small balcony had been built on this floor to take advantage of the cool breezes. From there, Gabe must have climbed down the support posts to the ground below.

As if to give credence to her theory, her gaze suddenly fell on his tall, familiar form in the distance. He was watching her from beneath the portico of a building across the street. Sensing her gaze, he tipped his hat ever so slightly.

Suddenly frightened by the burst of emotion that

innocent gesture inspired, Phoebe dropped the sash and slid the latch into place.

She needed to be alone, completely alone. She would take her own advice and sleep the afternoon away. Perhaps then she would be better able to ward off any unwanted advances.

But as she hurried to the door, locked it and deliberately set the key on the bedside table, she couldn't completely ignore the mocking inner voice that chided her for insisting Gabe's caresses had ever been unwanted.

The chance to wash and relax in a bona fide room had been a precious one—perhaps the best few hours since she'd boarded the train to head West. Although Phoebe was well aware of the fact that the grime would reappear as soon as their journey resumed, at least she'd had an opportunity to feel more human—if only for a short length of time.

Climbing into the boxcar, she carried the cloth holding her toiletries to the far corner where her own trunks were stacked. Thankfully, most of the items she'd taken with her had scattered on the platform when she'd been pushed, so the other women had been able to gather them up. They'd been dusty, but no real damage had been done.

Running her fingers through her still-damp locks, Phoebe headed to the spot where her trunk stood against the wall. It felt so good to have the soot and dried blood washed away. Now all her hair needed was a good brushing.

But mere feet away, she stopped short.

Where was her trunk?

Her reticule?

Gabe's revolver?

Turning in a circle, she wondered if her things had been moved. But try as she might, she couldn't find them.

Her heart began to pound and she vainly tried to calm herself. But even as she tried to convince herself that the items had merely been misplaced, a panic began to swell within her.

The missing trunk held the blue silk gown and the other finer pieces of clothing Louisa had convinced her to take—along with her mother's jewels and the hidden stash of coins sewn in the lining of the skirt.

"No," Phoebe whispered aloud. "No!"

She heard the sound of hooves on the siding and turned in time to see Gabe riding past the open door.

Was he responsible for this? He had insisted that the women should get off the train here in Ogden. He'd even threatened to leave them here if Phoebe couldn't prove she was healthy enough to make the journey. Had Gabe or one of his men decided to press the issue by tampering with her bags?

Her fury erupted. Damn them. Damn them all. Why couldn't Gabe and his cohorts let her and the others continue their journey in peace? Why had they decided now, at the tail end of their journey, that the women should leave the train?

An icy chill ran down her spine at an even more horrible thought. Were Gabe and his men responsible for that attack on the siding? For her being pushed from the platform?

Her hands balled into fists. Ignoring the fact that her hair still hung around her shoulders and she wore little more than a skirt and shirtwaist, she jumped from the boxcar and ran in the direction of Gabe's distant figure. The closer she got, the more she was sure that he was responsible for the theft. After all, it was his revolver that was missing. Who else had even known she had it?

"You did this, didn't you?" she called out to him when she was only a few feet away.

He expertly turned his mount, eyeing her from narrowed eyes. The sudden heat that filled his gaze made her instantly conscious of her casual state of dress and the embraces they'd shared short hours earlier.

Refusing to allow herself to be dissuaded, she marched toward him, stopping close enough so that she could grasp the reins to his mount. The horse shied away from her, but she held it steady.

"I want my things back this instant!"

"Let go of the reins, Phoebe."

"Not until you tell me what you've done with my things!"

He leaned forward, his voice becoming steely. "Let go of the reins, or I will have no qualms at all about forcibly removing your hand."

His tone was so chilling, his address so formal, that she automatically let go.

He cast a quick glance about to see if they had drawn any unwanted attention, and she realized at once that he wouldn't have used her first name if his men were near. In a way, his manner stung. Evidently, he would go to great lengths to ensure that no one could suspect him of impropriety.

Gabe swung down from the saddle. Taking her wrist in a grip that was firm but not punishing, he led her away from the train to an alleyway between two supply buildings.

"Perhaps you could take a deep breath, calm yourself and—"

"I will *not* calm myself. You've stolen my things and I want them back!"

"I don't know what you're talking about."

"My trunk is missing. And my reticule!" She poked her finger into the hard span of his chest. "And *your* revolver! Don't even dream of telling me it's a coincidence!"

"You *lost* my revolver?"

His scowl was so thunderous that she grew still, panic swamping her again. "You didn't take my things?" she asked weakly.

"Hell, no."

"And you didn't arrange for one of your men—"

He gave a curt bark of laughter. "This may come as a surprise to you, but my men have better things to do than terrorize a passel of brides-to-be."

"But you said you would force me to leave the train."

His eyes narrowed. "Only if you proved to be too injured to travel." His gaze dropped as if he were seeing her wrapped in little more than a sheet. "As we both discovered, you are more than able to travel."

She flushed in awareness and embarrassment. But before she could indulge in memories of their moments of passion, a mewling sound of distress slipped from her throat.

Gone. Everything was gone.

What was she going to do? She had depended on a few sentimental scraps of her old life—and the money! What was she going to do without any money? She was bound to need something during the rest of her journey. With sudden horror, she realized she didn't even have enough to attempt telegraphing Louisa. Phoebe was well and truly isolated from everything she had ever known and every shred of comfort she had once enjoyed.

Sobs welled within her, choking her at first, then gaining strength until she nearly foundered from the weight of her grief.

She turned to run away, but Gabe stopped her. Before she quite knew what had happened, she was enfolded in a strong pair of arms, and the warmth of his body was seeping into her own.

Although she had sworn to stay away from him, she was unable to control her neediness. She clung to him, craving to feel protected and secure. When she had dreamed of freedom, she hadn't realized at what cost it would come. She had always thought herself resourceful enough to survive on her own, but with each day that passed, she'd been made more and more aware of her vulnerability. She had nothing, absolutely nothing. She had the fare to California, but no money to buy food for the trip. She had a packet of letters written by an unknown farmer, but no guarantees that he would learn to care for her once she arrived.

She sobbed again, huge piteous sobs that wracked her body and robbed her of the ability to breathe.

What was she going to do?

She must have said the words aloud, because Gabe dipped his head so that his breath touched her hair. "I can help. I'll give you enough money to tide you through until we can discover what happened to your things."

She shook her head. "No, no. I won't be a burden to you or anyone else."

His fingers spread over her back. ''You aren't a burden.''

''Nor will I take charity!''

He sighed. ''Then consider it a loan.''

She balked at the very idea. ''No. I can't do that. It wouldn't be right.''

He tucked a finger under her chin. ''You will take the loan and that's the end of it.''

''But—''

''How are you going to manage otherwise?''

Since he put it so bluntly, she knew she had no other choice than to take the offered money. She was only a few days away from the end of her journey, yet she'd failed to provide for herself.

She sniffed, embarrassed by her outburst. Wiping the tears away, she said, ''I insist that you put our arrangement in writing. And as soon as my things are found, I'll pay you back—with interest.''

He shook his head, drawing back to gaze at her. ''I don't think I've ever met anyone so stubborn.''

''It's not stubbornness that makes me insist on the terms.''

''Then what it is? Pride?''

She averted her gaze. ''No. I've had little opportunity to indulge in self-importance.'' She hesitated before saying, ''I simply won't be beholden to anyone. Especially a man,'' she added in a low voice. Fearing she had said too much, she broke free and hurried back to the boxcar.

There must be a clue somewhere to lead her toward the thief. And once she'd found him…

She just might be tempted to shoot Gabe's revolver again. But this time, she intended to improve her aim.

Chapter Fifteen

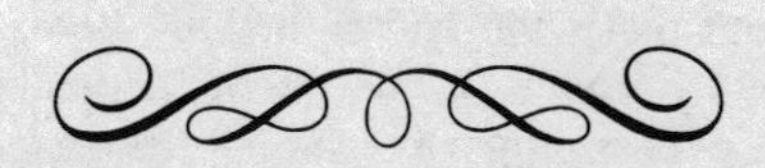

By nightfall Phoebe had discovered nothing new about the theft of her things. The women had clucked in concern and helped her to search the boxcar again, to no avail. Even Mr. Potter had patted her back and offered a few words of concern. But Phoebe's heart continued to beat heavily and her stomach to knot with worry.

Who could have done this to her? Who? She must been targeted for the crime, since none of the other women's belongings had been taken.

Wrapping her arms around her waist, Phoebe leaned in the open doorway of the boxcar. The night was still and a cool breeze brushed her cheeks. Up and down the length of the train, tiny fires had been made on the siding as the occupants took advantage of their stay in Ogden. Children cavorted around the boxcars, while men and women sat on trunks and crates, enjoying the stars overhead.

Distantly, Phoebe heard music and laughter. She could sense a measure of excitement in the air. For some, the journey was over. For others, there remained only a few days before they reached their goal.

And what about her? She'd spent very little time during her journey thinking of the man who would meet her at the end of the line. Whenever she tried to focus on her upcoming nuptials, her heart fluttered with panic and her hands grew cold.

Could she do it? Could she actually marry a stranger?

When she and her friend had decided to switch lives, it had seemed an easy enough matter. Phoebe would be exchanging one stranger-husband for another.

So what had changed in the intervening days?

Gabe. Try as she might, Phoebe couldn't stop thinking about him. The mere sight of him in the distance caused her heart to flutter. When he touched her…

She was lost.

"Good evening, ladies."

Phoebe's eyes flew open as the subject of her thoughts strode into the glow of their fire.

"Good evening, Mr. Cutter," the women said in unison. All of them cut their eyes toward Phoebe, then back to Gabe.

An awkward silence fell, then he said, "Will you excuse Phoebe for a moment? She and I have some business to discuss."

Phoebe's cheeks blazed with heat as the other women eyed her indulgently. Even Doreen seemed mildly amused.

Before Phoebe knew what he intended, Gabe slid his hands around her waist and lifted her from the boxcar to the ground. Then, maintaining a firm grip on her hand, he led her away from the train and into the darkness.

Phoebe supposed that she should chide him for embarrassing her in front of the other brides, but she couldn't. A comforting warmth was spreading from his hand up her arm, to her heart.

They had gone only a short distance before Phoebe saw Gabe's horse tethered a few yards away.

"Where are we going?" she breathed.

"Someplace where we can be alone."

Phoebe offered no protest as he placed her in the saddle, then swung up behind her. Instead, she reveled in the warmth of his body as his arms surrounded her and he clucked softly to his mount.

"I thought you'd shout at me for my high-handedness," Gabe said after several long moments.

Phoebe shook her head. "I'm tired of arguing."

"But you came with me. I thought you'd slap my face at the mere suggestion."

"No."

He gestured to his saddlebag. "I've got the money I promised."

She still burned with embarrassment at the thought of having to borrow money from anyone, let alone Gabe, but she merely said, "Thank you. I'll repay you as soon as I can."

"There's no rush, Phoebe."

"I'm hoping my things will be found."

He didn't answer, conveying with his silence that the likelihood of such an outcome was slim.

Phoebe took a breath, then said, "I'm sorry about what I said to you concerning your wife. I had no right to say such hurtful things."

He paused, then she felt his chest rumble against her as he said, "But they were true. I still mourn the passing of my wife and my son."

Her heart twisted in her breast. Would anyone ever love her that completely?

Long minutes later, Gabe drew the animal to a halt at the edge of a river. Arching trees spread over the bank and moonlight sparkled on the placid ripples.

After dismounting, Gabe reached to help her to the ground. But his hands lingered, his head dipping as she came to rest against his chest.

"I don't know what you're doing to me, Phoebe," he whispered into her hair. "I swore that I would never allow another person to affect me this way."

She bit her lip, clutching at his waist.

"What I'm doing is wrong," he continued. "You are about to be married, while I..." He shuddered. "I don't know where I'll be after this job."

Phoebe gazed up at him in concern. "You won't be a trail boss anymore?"

He hesitated. "No. I won't be a trail boss anymore."

"I see."

Phoebe tried to picture Gabe in any other line of work—shopkeeper, farmer, cowhand. But somehow the pictures would not form.

With a sinking heart, she realized that his pronouncement was yet another reason to avoid involvement with this man. He had his own worries and she could only add to them.

Drawing away from him, she stepped to the water's edge. The thick grass cushioned the soles of her shoes and the whisper of the trees soothed her battered spirit.

"Tell me about Emily."

If he seemed surprised by her request, he gave no indication. Sinking onto the grass beside her, he rested an arm on an updrawn knee.

"She was my childhood sweetheart. We were barely sixteen when we married."

Phoebe knew that it was not at all unusual for couples to marry so young. But in reviewing her own life, she couldn't imagine becoming a wife at such a tender age.

"Emily was quiet and shy, very sensitive."

Everything that Phoebe was not.

"She loved to cook and garden. As the years passed, she longed to become a mother, and feared she would never see the day. But in time, Nathaniel was born."

Phoebe saw the way his hand closed into a tight fist, and she worried that he would stop his narration. But after taking a deep breath, he continued. "Nathaniel was all boy—brash and vibrant and full of life. He loved snakes and frogs and bugs. Poor Emily had to harden her reaction to the beasties he brought into the house. But we loved him all the more for his adventurousness."

"So he was like you?" Phoebe murmured.

Gabe looked up at her, his face softer than she had ever seen it before.

"I suppose. But he had Emily's sweetness as well."

He rubbed at the creases between his eyes. "I never should have left them unprotected. I begged Emily to go farther north until after the war. But she wouldn't leave her home to vagrants and marauders, she said. I taught her how to shoot…but it wasn't enough."

Phoebe sank onto the ground beside him. Cupping his cheek, she forced him to look at her. "You can't continue to blame yourself for their deaths."

"It was my duty to protect them."

"But it was Emily's decision to stay. Even after you'd gone, she could have moved north at any time."

It was clear that such facts held little sway with him.

"Did she love you?"

She felt him shudder.

"More than I thought possible in another human being."

"Did she want you to be happy?"

He offered a choked laugh. "Her whole world seemed to revolve around me, but I didn't acknowledge that fact until it was too late."

Phoebe bit her lip, then said, "Would she want you to be so unhappy now?"

He didn't answer—not that she'd expected him to do so. Instead, she watched the change of emotions that he didn't try to hide.

"No," he finally admitted. "I don't suppose she would." He reached out, caressing Phoebe's cheek. "But knowing it and reconciling myself to live any other way are two different things."

Phoebe felt tears sting her eyes. Never had she encountered anyone in such pain. She could only wonder at what horrors Gabe had found when he'd returned home so long ago. Without asking, she knew that Emily's passing had not been an easy one, that she had probably been brutalized by the deserters to inflict such scars on Gabe's heart.

Phoebe also didn't know how to help him.

Leaning forward, she placed a kiss on his lips, gently, barely touching him. But it was enough to cause him to pull her tightly toward him. Shifting, he laid her on the grass and looked down at her, caressing her cheek.

"When did you grow so wise?"

She shook her head. "I'm not wise at all. If I were, I wouldn't be here now...with you."

And then there were no more words. Slowly at first, they reached for one another, caressing, exploring. Phoebe read Gabe's features with her fingers as if she were blind, tracing each dip and hollow, knowing that she would look back on this evening and remember each detail. Much like her stranger on the boat, she would relive the moments whenever life seemed lacking.

"I shouldn't be doing this," Gabe whispered against her cheek, her throat.

"Neither of us should."

"But I don't think I can stop."

"I don't want you to stop."

Then there was no need for words. The velvety evening enfolded them in its cloak and the burbling river provided its gentle melody.

There was no haste to their lovemaking. Instead, they deliberately prolonged each moment. Phoebe soon became infinitely familiar with the sharp planes of his face, the breadth and strength of his shoulders, the narrow expanse of his waist. Likewise, she gasped beneath the stroking of his hands, the caress of his lips.

In the stillness of their private world, there was no need for shame or shyness. As Gabe knelt, drawing her to him, Phoebe pushed the shirt from his shoulders, then shrugged off her own jacket. Peppering tiny kisses on his shoulders, she allowed him to help her with her skirt, shoes and corset, until she wore little but the gaping chemise and pantalets.

"You are so beautiful," Gabe whispered.

With those words, she felt beautiful. Beautiful and

bold. Resting her hands against his waist, she spread her fingers wide, absorbing the taut muscles and the leashed strength. Slowly, tantalizingly, she traced the faint line of hair up, up to the broader patch at his chest.

When his arms slipped around her, pulling her close, she sighed beneath the heady rush of passion that flooded her veins. Tipping her head up to his, she waited for his kiss and was not disappointed. His mouth settled over hers, teaching her the intricacies of love. White-hot desire burned in her, increasing her urgency until she clung to him, pulling him to the ground beside her, greedily seeking the satisfaction that only he could give her.

There were no thoughts of the future or the obstacles that faced them. They had already passed the point of no return. There was only this night, their lovemaking.

When Gabe rested his weight upon her, gently preparing her for his entry, she had no regrets. In that instant, she knew that she was holding the only man she would ever love. She would carry Gabe in her heart from this moment on, no matter what the future might bring.

And then, without warning, they ceased to be two straining bodies and became one—one soul, one heart, one mind. Gabe paused, whispering in her ear, ''I'm sorry.'' But before she could wonder if he was sorry for the twinge of pain she'd experienced or the future heartache that would come of this night, she wasn't sure. Soon there was no time at all to think as Gabe rocked against her, bringing her closer and closer to a precipice of pleasure, until finally she was tumbling, tumbling into an abyss of heat and sensation.

When, soon after, Gabe reached his own pleasure, she held him tightly against her, wondering how she would ever let him go. She didn't fool herself that this night had changed anything. Gabe had warned her that he wasn't the marrying kind. Nor would he make her any promises.

So why did she continue to wish that things could turn out differently for them both?

Nearly all of the brides had retired for the evening by the time Phoebe returned from her rendezvous with Gabe. Mable and Maude were the only souls awake in the boxcar, but upon seeing Phoebe, they yawned and padded to their own pallets.

"We just wanted to make sure you returned safe and sound," Mable said wearily.

"We also made bets on the amount of whisker burn you would have."

At Phoebe's gasp, the women giggled and slid beneath their blankets.

"You've no idea how your eyes light up when you see Mr. Cutter. Isn't that true, Maude?"

"I've never seen such a reaction in a woman before."

"But then we've never met a man such as Mr. Cutter," Mable remarked, yawning again.

"True, true. He really appears to be such a hard man, but I bet he's warm as molasses once…a body gets beneath…that shell…"

The words trailed away into silence. Within minutes, their steady, even breathing signaled that they were asleep.

Sighing, Phoebe undressed, washed and slid into a cool nightgown. But as she settled into her own bedroll, she found herself unable to sleep. Her body thrummed with remembered passion and her mind kept replaying the events of the day—the accident on the platform, her despair, Gabe's lovemaking.

A frown briefly crossed her brow. She could no longer claim to be a virgin. For a woman who had promised to marry another, she supposed she should worry about her compromised state.

No. She wouldn't think about it. Not now. She didn't know what the next few hours would bring, let alone the coming days. She refused to waste energy stewing over something that couldn't be changed.

What was she going to do? she asked herself over and over.

But what could she do? Events had been taken firmly out of her control. She had no more hope of a happy ending than she'd had of stopping the train that had barreled toward her.

When she closed her eyes, Phoebe could see the locomotive, hear the shriek of its whistle. Only at the last moment had Gabe's strong arms pulled her swiftly away from certain disaster.

A whisper of movement caused Phoebe's thoughts to scatter. Pretending to be fast asleep, she kept still and quiet. If someone was coming to check on her, she didn't want to explain her late evening or the way her cheeks were red from the rasp of Gabe's jaw.

The rustling came again, and peeking from beneath her lashes, Phoebe saw a shape disappear behind the curtained partition. A hint of Doreen's perfume as the woman retraced her steps to the door left Phoebe in no doubt as to her identity.

Although it was not unusual for the brides to leave the car in order to "heed the call of nature," there had been something furtive about the woman's actions. But the car's interior was so dark that Phoebe hadn't been able to see who it was.

It was then that she heard the deep murmur of a male voice. In an instant, she remembered the evening she had become an unwitting witness to a lovers' tryst, with Doreen and…

And who?

Phoebe's skin grew cold as she remembered the threats she'd heard—those that she'd thought were directed toward Gabe, but that she had since convinced herself she had misinterpreted. What if she hadn't been mistaken? What if this meeting was an effort to further such plots?

If she were to hear them talking again, would something they said help her to decide once and for all whether she should confront Gabe with the knowledge?

Climbing to her feet, Phoebe quickly slipped into her skirt and basque. Then, moving as quietly as she could, she stepped over Mr. Potter's supine shape and lowered herself to the ground.

Listening intently, she searched the shadows. Where had they gone?

Her heart pounded in her throat. The night was so still, so quiet…so dark.

A muffled giggle floated through the air and Phoebe immediately moved toward the outbuildings at the edge of the track. Was it Doreen's distinctive laugh she'd heard, or someone else's?

Ahead of her, she saw a pair of shadows moving into an alley next to one of the hotels. Tiptoeing closer, Phoebe strained to hear what they were saying.

"…sure the gold…hidden…"

"I swear, I've been through...everything..." The woman's response was interrupted by soft sounds of kissing.

So there *was* a hidden stash of gold somewhere on the train-and whoever Doreen was kissing suspected it had been hidden in the bride's boxcar.

"...not there...swear."

"...Ga...Cutter..."

A burst of music from the distant dance hall caused Phoebe to silently curse. She needed to hear what they were saying!

"...doesn't suspect...darling..." the woman was whispering. "You'll have...revenge soon...when—"

A sudden shadow streaked through the darkness from the alleyway, causing Phoebe to rear backward, a gasp ripping from her throat. Just as quickly, the yowl of a cat revealed that the animal had been none too pleased to find Phoebe lurking in the darkness.

"Damnit!" the male whispered.

Phoebe's heart thudded against her ribs as she heard the unmistakable sound of a revolver's hammer being cocked.

Dear sweet heaven, she was going to be killed. She would be found lurking in the alley—and there was no possible way to justify her presence there.

But feminine laughter slid through the darkness. "...jumpy...as the cat."

"...can't...too sure..."

"It was a cat." The woman's voice grew lower, huskier. "...have...way...relax you..."

Phoebe's face grew hot when it became obvious that the couple in the alley had found a sensual means of diversion. Hoping that their ardor would remain unabated, she backed as quietly as she could away, then hurried in the direction of the train.

She had to find Gabe. Perhaps he knew something of the gold being mentioned. Even if he didn't, he needed to know that someone intended to do him harm.

Phoebe was unable to locate Gabe that night—or all the next morning. With each hour that passed, she grew increasingly frantic, wondering if something had happened to him. But finally, just before the train was scheduled to leave again, she saw him tending to his horse at one of the corrals at the edge of the railway yard.

Offering an excuse to the other brides about questioning Gabriel about her missing trunk, she hurried through the dust toward the enclosure. Once there, she paused without speaking, needing to fill her senses with the sight of him.

Dear heaven, he was a beautiful man. The hot sun had caused a sheen of moisture to gather on his skin, highlighting the angularity of his features. His broad shoulders strained against the fabric of his shirt, and the musculature of his thighs was evident as he bent to check the leg of his gelding.

As if sensing her regard, he slowly lifted his head. Not for the first time, she was struck by the patent desire that entered his gaze when he looked at her. He might deny that he felt anything for her, and he might do his best to resist the emotions that flared between them when they were together. But in that single glance, he told her that his attachment to her was far more than physical and he wasn't as unaffected as he might pretend to be.

"I need to speak to you," she said when he stood and brushed the dust from his trousers.

He glanced around, making her aware of the men who stood only feet away from them.

"I haven't found your trunk, if that's what you've come about."

Although it was the same excuse she had offered her companions, the absence of her things had been pushed aside by her concern for this man.

How was it possible that in just a few days she had come to care for him so deeply?

"I think that someone is trying to kill you," she blurted, then gripped the railing of the corral in embarrassment. She had carefully rehearsed what she meant to say, but all of her preparations had flown out the window the moment she assured herself that he was unharmed.

Gabe raised his eyebrows. Clearly, he thought she was offering him an excuse to talk in a more private setting. "Oh, really? And just who would that be?"

"I—I don't know. Last night, I was near the alleyway by the hotel—"

"You were wandering around last night?" Gabe interrupted. "Alone?" His voice was filled with alarm.

"Well, yes. Doreen was sneaking out of the boxcar to meet someone." She frowned. "At least, I think it was Doreen. I smelled her perfume. It's very distinctive—almost too floral and sweet, if you know what I mean."

Phoebe bit her lip, realizing that she was beginning to babble.

"So you took it into your head to follow her—alone—only hours after you claimed that someone had pushed you in front of a moving train?"

Phoebe stamped her foot. ''I didn't 'claim' anything. Someone *did* push me!''

''So you reacted to that event by trotting around town, in the middle of the night, all by yourself.''

''Stop it! It doesn't matter what I did or why I did it. What matters is that there's someone plotting to steal a cache of gold, then get their revenge on you.''

Gabe became infinitely still.

''Who?''

''I—I don't know. I followed Doreen, but I didn't get a good look at her companion. I only know it was a man.''

Gabe scowled. ''The area is crawling with men.''

''Yes, but this gentleman has to be a member of our party. I overheard him speaking with Doreen once before—the same night I was struck from behind. At the time, I thought he meant to do you harm, but I convinced myself that I'd misinterpreted things. But after the snatches of conversation I heard last night, there can be no mistake about the matter.''

''What about the gold?''

She blinked, wondering why Gabe seemed so unaffected by the thought that someone intended to kill him.

''I—I don't know anything about the gold. But the man with Doreen seemed sure that it was hidden somewhere on our boxcar.'' She frowned. ''Is there gold hidden on our boxcar? Is that why my trunk was stolen? Was someone looking for gold when they decided to take my things instead?''

''Get back to the train.''

Her jaw dropped. ''I beg your pardon?''

Gabe didn't move, but the air between them seemed to suddenly blister with tension. ''Get back on the train and join the other brides. You've heard nothing, know nothing, do you understand? All of you are to stay in your boxcar unless I send an escort to accompany you."

Hurt, Phoebe took a step back. She wasn't sure what she'd expected, but at the very least, she'd thought she would encounter a little gratitude on his part.

Or a sense that he hadn't completely forgotten the lovemaking they'd shared the previous evening.

Phoebe opened her mouth to object, but one look from Gabe prevented her from speaking. Suddenly, she realized that he wasn't arguing with her. He wasn't insisting that she was imagining things or that she'd misinterpreted an innocent conversation.

That meant that there really was a stash of gold hidden on the train.

And Gabe wasn't the only one who was in danger.

Suddenly unable to bear the hard flintiness she saw in his eyes, Phoebe laid her hand on his arm. "You've been avoiding me. Is it because of the gold?"

Chapter Sixteen

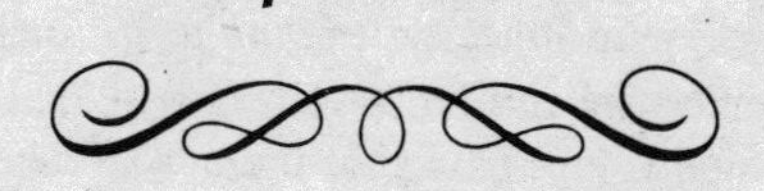

"You shouldn't be seen with me," Gabe muttered gruffly, barely glancing her way.

"I know."

Her admission took him by surprise.

"I've been telling myself the same thing for most of the journey. After all, I'll be married as soon as we arrive in Oregon. I have a good man waiting for me. One who spent a great deal of money to bring me here from England. And yet..."

He saw the way she stared at the horizon, as if the answers she sought would suddenly be written on the brilliant sky.

"I can't seem to help myself. You've overtaken me like a fever, driving all reason away."

When she would have moved a step closer, he shook his head, warily surveying the milling crowd. "No. Not yet."

At her hurt look, he added, "Give the brides an excuse, then slip into the car holding my horse. Do you remember the one you were in that night you were hurt?"

She nodded.

"I'll arrange to spend the next leg of the journey there, where we can be alone."

Gabe spent the next few minutes cursing himself for his hasty promise to Phoebe.

He didn't have time to meet with her. Once the train left Ogden, he needed to be on his guard more than ever. If the Overland Gang was true to form, they would make their attack before the train reached Reno.

But even as he reminded himself of that fact over and over again, he knew that there was nothing more he could do. Unbeknownst to the rest of the passengers, the second to last boxcar had become a rolling fortress. A dozen agents had slipped inside to augment Miles's and Green's security, bringing with them enough ammunition to level a city block.

There was nothing more Gabe could do.

And he needed to see her, hold her.

Gabe turned to find Luke Peterson behind him, his rifle held loosely in his arms.

"Was there something you needed, Peterson?"

"N-no, sir, I..." The boy kicked at a rock with his toe, then said in a rush, "I just w-wanted to th-thank you, sir."

"For what?"

"For giving me this chance." He hurried on when Gabe would have spoken. "I know that you were surprised when you first met me and that you felt I was too young for the job. But you let me stay on and prove myself, and I appreciate that, sir."

Gabe wasn't sure what sort of response he was supposed to give to a pronouncement like that, but it was obvious that Luke was waiting for him to say something.

"Keep up the good work."

The boy beamed at him. ''Yes, sir! And if you ever need anything—anything at all!—don't hesitate to ask.''

After offering one more awkward bob of his head, he spun on his heel and jogged to his post on the third boxcar.

As Gabe watched the boy go, he felt a twinge of worry. Despite his willingness to volunteer, Luke Peterson was little more than a baby. When the Overland Gang made their move, would Luke be prepared?

Moreover, had Gabe done everything in his power to ensure that the gold and the passengers would arrive safely in California?

Closing his eyes, he offered a brief prayer. So much rested on his preparations up to this point. Heaven help them all if he hadn't done his job thoroughly.

Phoebe didn't know what she had expected to happen once she sneaked into the boxcar full of horses. Heaven knew, Gabe wouldn't be treating her to tea, biscuits and a spot of gossip, as the other brides would. Nor was he likely to pull her into his arms and make love to her when it was obvious he was preoccupied with other matters.

What she hadn't expected was an empty car. Except for eight horses tethered at the far end of the boxcar and penned in by a makeshift rope barrier, she was alone.

Beneath her feet, the train shuddered, then began to move. Eyeing the open doorway, Phoebe prayed that Gabe would soon appear.

But no one came.

Bit by bit the locomotive built up steam, hissing and

chuffing until finally the world rushed past the door in a blur of color.

Sitting on a layer of straw spread over the floorboards, Phoebe wound her arms around her waist, cursing herself for being every kind of fool. She tried to tell herself that Gabe wasn't interested in anything but the passion they shared. That he didn't look upon her as anything more than a meddlesome female who had found her way beneath his skin.

But even after having repeated such assertions time and time again, she wasn't prepared for the hurt she felt upon being left alone.

Why had he lied to her?

And why, oh, why hadn't she stayed away from him?

Because he makes you feel alive.

A sob rose to her throat when the thought tumbled through her head. Moisture pricked at the backs of her eyes.

Yes, that was it. This man had the ability to make her feel more joyful, more vibrant than she ever had before. In his company, she truly felt like a woman. He had only to touch her to make all of her past hurts slip away. In his arms she felt beautiful and needed—and that knowledge filled her with a power like none she had ever experienced before.

Was it so wrong to revel in such emotions?

The train was at top speed now, the ground outside the door beginning to blur—a fact further emphasized by the tears that filled her eyes.

And then, without warning, she saw his shape, watched as he descended the ladder at the side of the car and swung into the doorway.

Without thinking, she rushed toward him, throwing herself into his arms.

He took her weight effortlessly, carrying her farther into the boxcar, his mouth already dipping for a kiss. Then passion ignited between them, and there was no thought of anything but their embrace.

"I love you," Phoebe whispered when they parted for breath.

For a moment she felt Gabe stiffen, and she feared he would draw away completely. But then his head dipped again. He kissed her slowly, deeply, bringing tears to her eyes with his tenderness.

And although he didn't say the words, she knew he loved her too.

Long moments later, Gabe lifted her in his arms and laid her in the straw, his own body settling beside hers. But when she thought that he would continue the sensual exploration he had begun, she was sadly disappointed. Instead, he held her against him, her head resting on his chest.

"Gabe, I—"

"Shh." He stroked her hair and took one quick, deep breath. "We're going too fast, too far."

Phoebe bit her lip, knowing he was right. Her cheeks flamed when she realized that she would have thrown caution to the wind if the choice had been left to her. She would have made love to him despite their unsettled futures and surroundings.

But just as quickly as her embarrassment overtook her, it dissipated. Beneath her ear, she could hear the furious beat of Gabe's heart.

He, too, was on the brink of surrendering to utter desire.

An emotion such as she'd never experienced rushed

through her veins and she tipped her head up toward the streak of sunshine spilling through the doorway. As far as she was concerned, the next leg of the journey could take an eternity. She needed only this moment and Gabe's strong arms wrapped around her.

"What would your husband-to-be say if he could see you now?" Gabe said after several long moments.

She smiled against his shirt, surprised at the hint of teasing she heard in his voice. Gabe was generally so hard and serious that this flash of humor excited her in ways she never would have thought possible.

"He would probably shiver in his puritanical shoes."

Gabe chuckled. "He's a religious man?"

Phoebe shrugged. "I've no idea."

"So you decided to marry him on a whim?"

"No..." But she *had* decided to marry Neil Ballard on a whim; otherwise she would be in Boston right now, living another life.

"I suppose you could say my decision was slightly blind, but careful nonetheless." She sighed. "I'll learn about him soon enough."

Gabe's hold tightened a fraction. "I thought you were anxious to join your beloved?"

She considered that remark for a moment before answering noncommittally. "I believe in fate."

"And what does fate have to do with anything?"

She peered at him under her lashes, wondering what he would think of her if he knew the entire story. Would he believe that she came from a family with none-too-distant ties with royalty? And would he believe that she had given away her birthright for a taste of the very life she was leading today?

"In the past weeks I have become a firm believer

that if a person waits long enough and wishes for something hard enough, some dreams will come true.''

''A very romantic outlook on life.''

''Perhaps. But a body can take only so much bleakness.''

''And what do you know of bleakness?''

She opened her mouth to tell him everything, then hesitated. To do so would break the promise she had made in adopting Phoebe's life. As far as anyone would ever know, she had spent her life as a servant, nothing more.

''I know enough.''

It was clear that Gabe found her answer less than satisfying, but she refused to add anything more. After all, she knew very little about him. She didn't know the foods he liked or the dreams he had.

She pushed herself into a sitting position, turning slightly so that she could study him more completely. The time had come for her to learn more about Gabriel Cutter.

''Why do many of the men on the train fear you?'' she asked softly.

Gabe's eyes narrowed. ''You're imagining things.''

''No. I'm not. They fear you and...dislike you. Quite intensely.''

''Perhaps they don't approve of my methods of leadership.''

She shook her head. ''No. There's more to it than that.'' She regarded Gabe's flint-hard features and the lock of hair that fell over his forehead. For the first time, she was able to see a hint of vulnerability in the granitelike features. ''There are rumors about you.''

A muscle flicked in his cheek.

"They say that somehow you disgraced yourself during the war."

He remained silent, but the gray of his eyes darkened to the color of steel.

"Why would they say such things if they aren't true?"

This time when he met her gaze she found it difficult to fathom the intensity of the emotions she found there—self-disgust, anger and a haunting sadness that tugged at her heart.

"What happened?"

"I would have thought you'd heard enough gossip to fill in the details."

"Perhaps I don't want gossip. Perhaps I want the truth."

Silence spun between them and Phoebe felt a thread of tension draw tighter and tighter in her breast. She had meant to see how much he would willingly tell her of himself. But she suddenly realized that she longed for more, so much more. She had become intricately involved in this man's life. Over the past few days, she'd been drawn into the depths of his mysteries as surely as a fly ensnared in a spider's web. She could not disengage herself—and had no wish to do so. This man was so complicated. He was dangerous, cold, hard and embittered. But she sensed that much of his nature was merely a shell he offered to the outside world. And she longed with all her heart to see what he hid from those around him.

The silence continued for so long that Phoebe was sure she had her answer—which was that she should kindly tend to her own affairs and leave Gabe to tend to his own. But after several minutes, he sat up and reached for the bundle of belongings stacked neatly in the corner.

Unbuckling one of the compartments in his saddlebags, he removed what looked like a large leather envelope and handed it to her.

"Open it."

"What is it?"

"You'll see."

Even as curiosity bubbled within her, Phoebe hesitated. Instinctively, she knew that Gabriel Cutter was about to allow her a glimpse into his past.

Did she really want to know this man's innermost secrets?

And by knowing the truth about the shadows in his eyes, would she find it impossible to leave him when the time came?

Realizing that she had no real choice in the matter, Phoebe lifted the flap and reached inside. Feeling the hard edge of another leather-bound case, she withdrew the object, knowing immediately what it was.

The item was small, about the size of a deck of playing cards, and hinged in the middle. Inside, she knew, the case held a pair of photographs. It was the type of miniature album given to loved ones when they were about to take a journey…

Or go to war.

She glanced up at Gabe, but his eyes were on the case.

Biting her lip, Phoebe ran her thumb over the design imprinted on the cover—the image of an eagle carrying a pair of flags in its talons. The well-worn surfaces and the spotted stains that could have been blood led her to believe Gabe had carried the pictures with him in battle.

Unlatching the tiny gold hook, she opened the case, then held her breath.

Finally, she began to understand that the rumors she'd heard had been true.

From the depths of the photograph on the left, a woman stared back at Phoebe, her eyes dark and obviously filled with love.

"She's beautiful," Phoebe whispered.

"As I told you before, we were childhood sweethearts. Emily was born a few miles away from where I grew up—the only daughter of the local minister. I first set eyes on her when my mother insisted that I be sent to school."

Phoebe swallowed hard against the tightness that threatened to cut off her breathing. His voice had lost its hard edge. The softness bespoke a deep and abiding affection for his wife.

Phoebe's gaze slid to the second photograph. Immediately, her eyes filled with tears as she saw Gabe wearing a dark blue uniform, his eyes alight with laughter despite the serious expression demanded by the photographer. In his arms, he held a chubby baby boy.

"Oh, Gabe," Phoebe whispered, her voice choked with emotion.

Then she began to cry—not just for the man he had been, but for the woman and child he had loved so much.

Suddenly, she understood everything. She knew how a man could cast his good name to the wind and disappear for six months. She could finally see how threats of a court-martial and possible execution for desertion could fail to move a man in the depths of a terrible grief.

"You must have loved them so much," she whispered, the words barely intelligible.

Then she was back in Gabe's arms, clutching at him, willing him to feel the empathy and the echo of pain that swelled within her.

In that instant, she realized just how much Gabe had loved his wife and son.

And loved them still.

A shaft of pain shot through Phoebe's heart and she swallowed against the tears that rose in her throat. As much as she might want to consider a future with Gabe, she knew that such a thing was not likely to happen. He cared for her; she was sure that he did. But there could be no happily-ever-afters between them. Gabe carried far too much pain in his heart to allow himself to agree to marriage.

And Phoebe knew that she could never be content with anything less. She couldn't live her life feeling that she was second best to a dead woman.

Biting her lip to keep from crying out, Phoebe turned away from Gabe. Resolutely, she made her way to the boxcar.

Her decision was made.

In less than three days time, she would become Neil Ballard's wife.

Chapter Seventeen

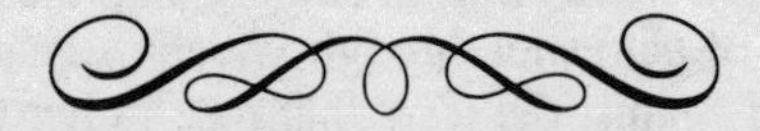

"All aboard!"

Gabe's heart began a slow, measured thudding as the conductor moved down the long line of cars, warning passengers that the train was about to depart.

Luke Peterson jogged toward Gabe. "Everything's ready, Mr. Cutter. All of the men are in place."

Gabe nodded and gestured for the lad to take his own place on the second car along with the rest of the security detail. "Take care of yourself, you hear?"

"Yes, sir!"

As the boy loped away, Gabe prayed that the next few hours wouldn't find the inexperienced Pinkerton dead.

Because the time had come to take the offensive. Gabe was sure that the Overland Gang intended to make their move sometime within the next twenty-four hours.

But they would never get their chance.

Gabe intended to be the first to attack.

"All ready?" a voice asked from behind.

Gabe didn't bother to turn, recognizing his old friend immediately. "It's about time you got here," he said without looking up. Instead, he twirled the chambers of his revolver to ensure it was fully loaded. "I've stalled this train about as much as I could. Any more water stops and I'd have a mutiny on my hands."

From beneath a battered hat, Josiah Burton grinned. "Then let's get back on the road."

Gabe and Josiah Burton climbed into the boxcar that Gabe had used throughout the entire journey.

Almost immediately, the train started to hiss and pant. Metal squealed against metal as the locomotive's wheels fought for purchase. Then there was a jarring shudder, a lurch, until finally they began to move, slowly at first, then faster and faster.

Without wasting time, Gabe dug into his saddlebags, removing a holster and revolver. Strapping them on, over the set he already wore, he began uncovering a rifle for Josiah, and several boxes of ammunition.

The two men checked their weapons in a silence fraught with expectation as the train built up speed, racing into the late afternoon shadows.

"What have you been able to piece together?" Josiah finally asked, when they were finally satisfied with their preparations.

Gabe pointed toward the front of the train. "The dummy shipment is still on the second boxcar. We've had a little interest over the past week, but not much. I think most of the curiosity has come from the passengers, who've wondered why that particular car has become home to so many men." He allowed himself a quick grin. "I doubt the Overland Gang has given it a second glance, just as we planned."

"So what do we do now?" Josiah asked.

"We hit them at their weakest link and hope the man will squeal on his partners in crime."

"And who did you have in mind?" Josiah asked.

Gabe moved to the door and grasped the ladder with one hand before meeting the gaze of his employer.

"Victor Elliot."

Josiah's eyes widened in disbelief. "Victor! Have you lost your mind?"

But Gabe wasn't listening to him. He was already climbing the ladder and beginning his journey down the length of the train.

The wind was hot against his face as Gabe took up position on the ladder outside the boxcar that had been used as the Pinkertons' bunkhouse throughout the journey. Glancing across the roof, he patiently waited until Josiah had gained a similar foothold on the opposite side of the car.

It was clear that Josiah still had his doubts that one of his handpicked executives could be involved in the heists, but Gabe had no second thoughts whatsoever. For three nights in a row, he had trailed Victor as he'd rendezvoused with several figures Gabe had been unable to identify in the darkness. There had been a distinct stealth to the man's movements, as well as a notable sense of anxiety whenever he'd been near Gabe.

But what had sealed Victor's fate was the telegram that Gabe had received only that afternoon. Ironically, it had been the attempt on Phoebe's life in Ogden that had caused Gabe's suspicions to harden. That day, he'd sent a message to a friend in New York asking him to nose into Victor's financial records for the past few years. Today, Gabe had received a response.

Victor's holdings were above and beyond anything

that he could have earned as an Overland Express employee. Moreover, the largest deposits in his bank account had been made within weeks of the last three heists.

Victor was involved up to his ears, and Gabe knew it. All that remained was to see how long it would take the man to crack and reveal the identities of his compatriots.

Gabe held up his revolver as a signal to Josiah, mouthing, ''On the count of three.''

Josiah nodded to show that he understood.

Silently Gabe counted. *One, two...three!*

Then, swinging through the door that had been left open to catch the fresh air, he charged toward Victor.

At the same moment, Josiah swung into the car from the opposite side, cocked his rifle and held it steady on the other men, who had jumped up from their card game and reached for their weapons.

''Nobody move!'' Josiah shouted.

''Listen to the man!'' Gabe ordered. Then he grasped Victor by his collar and jammed the tip of his revolver beneath his chin. ''Start talking, Victor.''

The executive mewled in distress, his hand groping behind him for the pistol he'd left on a nearby crate.

Adjusting his gun a fraction of an inch, Gabe pulled the trigger. The noise was deafening in the enclosed car. The smell of spent gunpowder mingled with the earthy odors of sweat and straw.

Victor yelped, his face growing pale as a streak of blood appeared at the side of his hand.

''Next time I won't be so forgiving,'' Gabe growled, pressing the revolver into Victor's cheek. ''Who else is a member of your gang?''

Victor's mouth opened and closed like a fish out of

water before he finally managed to choke out, ''I—I don't know what you're—''

''Don't!'' Gabe ground the revolver into his flesh hard enough to make the man wince. ''It's over, Victor. I've got copies of bank records showing that you've got more money stashed away than you're worth. Ironically, the timing of each of the major deposits coincides with stolen Overland Express payroll shipments. I also have a fellow in New York who spoke to your landlady and a couple of the girls from the Golden Arms Hotel. It seems you made it quite clear that you wouldn't be coming back.''

Victor whimpered, his gaze darting past Gabe's shoulder.

One of the Pinkertons dodged toward the doorway. Without hesitation, Josiah took aim and fired.

The agent crumpled to the ground, a pool of his blood seeping into the straw.

''Anyone else want to confess his involvement in the Overland Gang?'' Josiah shouted in obvious anger, his rifle swinging from man to man.

Gabe turned his attention back to Victor. ''As you can see, Mr. Burton doesn't take too kindly to traitors or thieves, Victor.''

The man clutched at Gabe's hand in supplication. ''I—I'm not...I didn't actually *steal* anything, I swear!''

''No, but you fed them the information, didn't you, you lying, sneaky, son of a bitch!'' Josiah shouted from the doorway.

Victor squeezed his eyes shut, knowing he had no real defense.

Gabe pressed the revolver even tighter into his cheek. ''I bet you never knew Josiah had a temper, did you? That's what made him such a fearsome opponent during the war.'' He dropped his voice to an icy whisper. ''Josiah spent more time behind enemy lines than I did. He had a reputation for making even the most ardent Confederate talk.'' Gabe tightened his grip on Victor's shirt, causing him to gasp for air. ''Of course, no one ever talked after Josiah was finished with him.''

''I—I—''

''Save yourself, Victor. Prison is a whole lot better than lying six feet under.''

''A-Andrew Styles!'' Victor blurted.

At the sound of his name, another Pinkerton tried to bolt. He hadn't taken two steps before Josiah shot him in the knee, sending him sprawling onto the straw, screaming in pain.

A sob of terror tore from Victor's throat. From outside, the train's whistle squealed as they approached the tunnel through Beckman's Pass in the Sierra Nevada Mountains.

Gabe started when he heard the thunder of footfalls passing overhead.

Damn it! He'd told his men to hold their positions, no matter what happened. But then Gabe realized that the footsteps were continuing on as the unknown men vaulted onto the next car—the one containing the women.

''It's too late,'' Victor shouted. ''It's too late!''

In that instant, an explosion ripped through the train.

Gabe felt himself being lifted bodily and thrown against the opposite wall. Automatically he lifted his arms to shield himself as debris and splintered wood scattered throughout the railway car.

Seconds seemed to drag like hours. In sickening

slow motion, Gabe saw a gaping hole appear at the rear floorboards of the car, heard Victor's screams as he tried to stand, then fell through to the rails underneath. A muffled thump was followed by a jarring screech as the boxcar suddenly left the tracks and began twisting and turning, throwing men every which way until the damaged coupling gave way. The car skidded through the dust before finally coming to rest yards away from the track.

Gabe fought against the blackness that threatened to overtake him. Taking deep gulps of dust-laden air, he pushed himself to his knees and from there to his feet. Shaking his head to clear it of the numbing effects of the blast, he gazed around him in disbelief. Three Pinkertons were dead. One began screaming that he was pinned, and two more stumbled to help him.

''Josiah!'' Gabe shouted.

Josiah appeared from the siding next to the tracks. A long gash bisected his cheek, but other than that, he appeared only dazed.

''Damn it, Cutter! Look what they've done to my train!'' he shouted.

From the opposite direction, they heard the screech of metal on metal as the locomotive applied the brakes in an effort to stop before any more of the damaged cars could be jounced from the track.

Gabe signaled to some men who had moved a friend free of the wreckage and carried him to a sheltered spot beneath a Joshua tree.

''Head back toward the train and gather our mounts!'' he shouted to those who could walk. ''What members of the Overland Gang remain will be with the last three cars they let loose!''

''Damn it, Cutter, look what they did to my train!''

Josiah shouted again, his face reddening with potent fury. He turned to regard the three boxcars that were rolling backward down the hill at a furious pace. "They'll have the gold before we can ever catch up to them!"

Gabe began sifting through the wreckage, frantically searching for his revolver. "Don't worry about your damned gold, Josiah."

"But if they've got wagons waiting, they'll have time enough—"

Gabe spied his revolver and grabbed for it, jamming it into his holster. Then he began running in the direction of the stalled train. "There is no gold to steal, Josiah!" he shouted over his shoulder.

"What?" Josiah began running as well. "What the hell do you mean, there's no gold?"

"The real shipment of gold was never loaded on this train. I gave Miles and Green special instructions to switch the crates they'd guarded from England with identical ones filled with lead the day they moved the shipment off the boat. The real payroll was sent West with the Union Pacific under heavy guard that same day. I received a telegram in Ogden stating that the cargo arrived without incident."

Josiah stopped in his tracks, breathing hard.

Gabe barely gave him a second glance as he saw the horses being unloaded. Pausing to catch his own breath, he met Josiah's stunned look with a grin. "You asked me to deliver the gold safely. I did that."

"But...you didn't tell *me* what you were up to? Damn it, Cutter, you—"

Gabe reached for the reins to his mount just as one of his men galloped up beside them, leading a pair of horses.

"I couldn't tell you, Josiah. You're trusting to a fault at times and I knew you had a leak somewhere within your own company."

"But..." Josiah swung into the saddle, then swore again. "You sent my payroll with the *Union Pacific!* They're my competitors, damn it!"

Gabe spurred his horse into a gallop. "We don't have time for that now. We've got to get to the women before all hell breaks loose. I've got an army of Pinkertons on the boxcar with Miles and Green. But I hadn't counted on the brides being caught in the crossfire."

Phoebe groaned, pushing herself onto her hands and knees. Feebly, her brain tried to grasp what had happened. There had been an explosion, knocking them off their feet, and then the boxcar had begun to roll backward down the hill.

Distantly, she remembered the screams of the other women, the rush of air coming through the doorway, the feeling of utter helplessness. Without warning, the boxcar had left the tracks, bouncing and tumbling. Trunks and boxes had been thrown free; straw and dust had made the air too thick to breathe.

And then silence. A horrible, deafening silence.

"Get up."

Pushing the hair from her forehead, Phoebe ignored the pounding ache of her own body and glanced behind her. Her eyes widened in disbelief as she saw the woman who pointed a pistol at her head.

"Edith?"

Dear, gentle Edith seemed to change before her very eyes. Gone was the shy youngster who was afraid of the marriage that awaited her in Oregon. In her place was an embittered woman who had lived through her own brand of pain.

"Get up. You're coming with us."

Phoebe frowned in confusion. "I—I don't understand."

"Cutter will be after us as soon as he realizes that his gold isn't nearly as safe as he thought it would be. We need you to come along with us to ensure that he doesn't try to be a hero."

Phoebe's eyes narrowed as she caught a sparkle of light. Her sapphires. Edith had stolen her mother's sapphires!

"*You* were the one who took my trunk," Phoebe gasped.

A cold smile crossed Edith's features. "You didn't suspect me, did you? I made sure of that—I even went so far as to leave it at one of our rest stops after I'd emptied out the contents and transferred them to my own bags. In fact, I'm certain that if you thought anyone other than Gabriel Cutter had stolen it, Doreen was the most likely candidate."

A strangled cry came from the opposite end of the boxcar, and Phoebe noted that Edith had already rounded up the other women. A burly man dressed in the rough clothes of a farmer held them in the sights of his revolver.

"I made quite sure that you would suspect her," Edith said, taking Phoebe's arms and twisting it so that Phoebe was forced to stand. "I even wore her perfume once when I suspected you were watching me."

Doreen's mouth opened and shut in outrage.

"But all of that's of little consequence now."

"Who were you meeting, Edith?"

"I really fail to see how that's any of your affair," she whispered close to Phoebe's ear. "Outside!"

Since the boxcar had come to a stop on its roof, Phoebe had to climb over crates and debris before finally stepping into the sunshine. When she did, it was to see a pair of men crouched in the dust, their weapons leveled on what had once been the last two cars of the train.

"Miles and Green! Come out with your hands over your head!" one of the men shouted from behind a rock.

"What are they doing?" Phoebe whispered, refusing to move even when Edith pressed the revolver to her back. Gabe's revolver.

"Phoebe! Phoebe, get down!"

The cry was so faint and far away that Phoebe wondered if she had imagined it.

"Phoebe! Down, down!"

Again she searched the horizon. Gabe was there somewhere, and he was telling her to get down.

"Move!" Edith said, pushing her forward.

Phoebe reacted purely on instinct. Lunging forward as if she had tripped, she fell to her stomach and quickly rolled away from Edith.

In the same instant, the door to the boxcar was wrenched open and the air became filled with gunfire. Screaming, Phoebe wrapped her arms over her head as the ground around her was peppered with bullets.

And then, just as quickly, silence fell.

Trembling, she lifted her head cautiously, just as a pair of boots skidded to a stop in front of her. Squeezing her eyes shut again, she began screaming. But her cries stopped short when a pair of strong arms lifted her upright and she was cradled against a masculine form that had become as familiar to her as her own.

"Gabe?"

"Are you hurt?" he gasped against her hair.

"No. No, I'm fine."

He crushed her even more tightly against him, only releasing her when his name was called.

She looked up to see a tall man striding toward Gabe. Phoebe's brow furrowed in recognition. She knew the gentleman. He'd been on the same boat as she and Louisa, sharing a first-class compartment with another man. Occasionally one of them had joined the group at the captain's table, but strangely enough, although the men shared a cabin, they had never dined together.

"Ma'am." The man touched the brim of his hat, then turned to Gabe. "I doubt any of them will be giving Overland Express any trouble in the future."

"How many?"

"There were only three of them." He gestured to the fallen forms near the boxcar. "Those two there, and the girl."

Phoebe glanced behind her to see Edith cradling her shoulder. She sobbed openly, blood seeping from between her fingers.

"Damn you," she shouted. "You've killed him!"

Staggering upright, she ran forward, falling upon one of the men. Weeping hysterically, she turned him over, dragging his head onto her lap.

Gabe stiffened. "Peterson," he whispered in disbelief.

"He hated you," Edith screamed. "He wanted to see you ruined."

Gabe eyed the woman in open disbelief. "Why?"

''Because you promised to take care of him during the war. He was nothing more than a child and you said you'd keep him safe.''

Phoebe felt Gabe shudder against her. ''The boy...'' he murmured in recognition. ''We'd adopted a drummer boy who was cut off from his regiment.''

''When you didn't come back, he had no one to watch over him. Eventually he was captured during one of the raids and was put in prison. They whipped him and beat him to try to make him talk, but he didn't say a word. He was so sure that you would find a way to set him free.'' Edith was hysterical now. ''But you never came back! He vowed that he would make you pay, that he would drag your name through the mire and harm anything you had ever grown to love.''

Gabe's arms dropped away from Phoebe.

''You couldn't have known, Gabe,'' she murmured.

But it was obvious from the cast of his features that he was remembering the boy Luke Peterson had been...and he was blaming himself for the man that boy had become.

Gabe finally turned to his men and ordered, ''Get them all loaded on the train. Let's get out of here before the sun goes down.''

Edith gaped at him. ''What about the gold?''

''There is no gold!'' This time it was Josiah who answered. ''The gold is already safely in the hands of my many employees.''

Edith stared at him in disbelief, then shouted, ''No! We couldn't have done all of this for nothing!''

Gabe's rein on his temper visibly snapped. ''Yes, you did all of this—'' he waved his hand ''—for nothing! You've killed innocent men who were only trying to do their job, and if you'd had your way, you would have killed Phoebe as well!''

Edith began to laugh, softly at first, then more and more wildly until Phoebe began to wonder if the woman were becoming unhinged.

''We didn't try to kill her! We didn't have anything to do with the attempts on her life!'' Her laughter became the cry of a wounded animal as she held Luke against her. ''It was Potter. Luke saw him.'' Her expression was that of a madwoman. ''The very man you hired to protect us was your attacker,'' she cried.

Chapter Eighteen

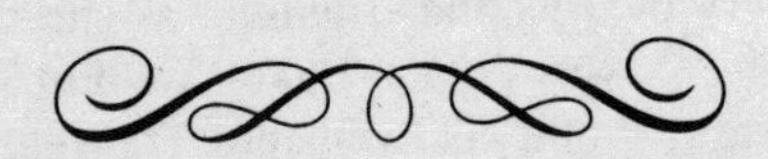

Phoebe gasped.

Mr. Potter? Mr. Potter had been trying to kill her?

Lifting her skirts, she ran toward the boxcar. Her heart hammered in her breast and she was nearly afraid to uncover the truth. She was horrified to think that she had unwittingly endangered her life as well as the lives of her friends.

But how could such a thing be true? Mr. Potter had been so kind during their trip! Several times he had asked about her well-being. Had she overlooked important clues? Had she been blind to anything but her burgeoning feelings for Gabe?

So much had happened since she'd left England. In the broad scheme of things, very little time had passed, but it seemed like an eternity. She had loved and she had lost. Uncovering the truth behind the accidents she had endured during her extraordinary journey was the only comfort she would be afforded.

Eager for answers, Phoebe stepped into the boxcar. But as she moved into the shadows and her eyes adjusted to the change, she discovered Bertram Potter lying in the rubble, gasping for breath. A crimson stain spread across his chest.

"What happened?" she breathed.

"He was crushed by one of the trunks," Maude murmured. Sadly, she stroked Potter's brow, trying to ease the old man's pain.

Phoebe caught the man's eyes and he quickly looked away. "Why, Mr. Potter?" she whispered as she stood above him. "Why did you want to kill me?"

Bertram's eyes closed again and he trembled beneath a wave of pain, but it was clear he'd heard her. "Take...pity on me, lass...." he said softly, his breath rattling in his throat.

"*You* were the one who hit me? The one who pushed me in front of the train?"

He nodded.

"Why would you do such a thing?"

"Because I—" He gasped, holding his breath. When finally his features released their tight grip, his eyes held a hint of panic.

"Yer uncle paid me to kill you...an' another fellow t'kill yer sister."

Phoebe shook her head impatiently. "I have no uncle, and I have no sister."

"Ahh, but you do." Potter's expression grew sad. "Yer from Haversham stock, you and the other girl y' traveled with. Yer twins, according to yer uncle."

"I don't have—" Phoebe stopped.

Her twin?

Her uncle?

She grew suddenly still when she remembered that Oscar Haversham had once been a twin himself. But according to her father, his brother had died at sea nearly twenty years ago.

''Ahh,'' Bertram sighed, his eyes growing heavy. ''Now y' see what I'm tryin' t'say. Yer uncle Horace an' yer father had a...fallin' out. Yer uncle was s'pposed to inherit, not yer father. When he refused to share the family wealth, yer father refused t'speak t'him again.''

''But my father is the marquis. He *did* inherit.''

Potter nodded. ''After yer uncle disappeared.''

''Disappeared?''

Potter hissed as a spasm wracked his body. Then he said, ''Yer uncle liked the sea.'' He grimaced. ''I served under him a couple o' times. But one year he went t'sea an' never came back. Everyone was told the ship went down in a storm.''

''Then how...''

'''Twasn't true. The ship was fired upon an' sank by an unknown vessel. Yer uncle was believed dead, but he actually survived.'' He squeezed his eyes shut and breathed hard. ''He's been waitin' for his chance t'take control again, bidin' his time until he could make a move to claim the family title. But by the time he'd reclaimed his health, yer father had married and been blessed with twin girls, so he waited.''

Potter coughed and blood sprayed from his mouth to dot his cheeks.

''For twenty years?''

Potter nodded. ''See, yer uncle had no choice in the matter. When the marriage broke up...yer mother took one twin, yer father t'other. Yer uncle couldn't make a move until he found all of the possible heirs t'yer father's estate.'' Potter's lashes flickered. ''It wasn't until this past year that Horace was able to find t'other girl.... Couldn't make a move against yer father until then.''

His body shuddered. ''When you an yer sister made the journey t'America together, yer uncle Horace considered the arrangement a godsend. At last he would have a chance t'wreak his revenge.'' His eyes grew sad. ''I was paid...t'see y'didn't finish yer journey alive.'' His brow creased and tears filled his eyes. ''I'm...sorry. So sorry...'' The strength faded from his voice. ''I'd about changed...m' mind on the boat. Spent my fare...on whiskey and women... Didn't think I'd get...caught...fer stowin' away....''

He coughed again and the flecks of blood became more distinct. ''When I was sent...t'jail...thought that was the end of it.'' His lips twisted in a grimace that could have been a smile. ''But then...y' arranged...t'set me free.'' He took a gulp of air and moaned. ''What's a man t'do...when he's been offered...a fortune for a job well done?''

''What about...my sister?'' Phoebe asked, the words sounding foreign to her. Sister. She had a sister. A twin.

Potter's skin was growing deathly pale. ''I can't help y' there. Someone else was t'follow her. I don't know who.'' He grimaced. ''Yer father made it easy...havin' y' travel together.... Horace wanted y' dead. I didn't want... I shouldn't...''

Phoebe watched in horror as the man grew lax. His breath escaped in a deathly rattle and his eyes lost their sheen, staring blankly in front of him.

From what seemed like far away, Phoebe heard one of the women sniff. Maude bit her lip and rested Mr. Potter's head on the floor, gently closing his eyes.

''He was such a nice man,'' Phoebe whispered. ''But he tried to kill me. How could a person so gentle and sweet want to kill anyone?'' she asked hoarsely.

"Even a saint can have his heart hardened with enough money, and Mr. Potter was far from being a saint," Gabe murmured.

Phoebe shivered, staring at the man she had unwittingly trusted. How could she have been so stupid?

A chill seeped into her soul as she realized how close she had come to death. And for what? An old vendetta with an uncle she hadn't known was alive?

Gabe wrapped an arm around her. "Come along, Phoebe."

She would have remained rooted to the spot, unable to move, but Gabe's arm circled her waist, taking most of her weight as he drew her away from the wreckage and into the sunshine.

For several long moments she stood motionless, soaking in the heat of the sun, trying to take in the confession she'd heard. She had an uncle, she thought again in disbelief. An uncle who was trying to kill her.... And a sister!

A twin.

Suddenly, it was all too much to bear. Turning into Gabe's arms, she began to sob—huge wrenching sobs that tore through her body and revealed the depths of pain harbored in her tattered soul.

Once again she had been betrayed. First by a father who didn't love her, then by an uncle who wanted her inheritance, and then by friends who would have seen her dead.

"It isn't fair!" she suddenly blurted in anger. "I haven't done anything to deserve this!"

Gabe pulled her tightly against him, his lips brushing her hair. "Shh, Phoebe, shh."

Refusing to surrender to the warmth of his embrace, Phoebe lifted her head. She stared at Gabe through a haze of tears, knowing instinctively that he would abandon her, too.

Gabe had endured his own brand of tragedy—a deep, haunting pain that she could never fully comprehend. But rather than work through his grief, he seemed determined to wear his sadness like a badge of honor. In his eyes, there would never be another woman like Emily. He had closed off his heart to all but the most necessary emotions. And as much as Phoebe might wish for Gabe to love her, body and soul, as she did him, she knew such a thing would never happen. Gabe would never allow himself to feel that deeply again.

A pain lodged in her chest. Instinctively, Phoebe knew that she could force the issue. She could eventually weaken Gabe's resolve. She might even convince him to marry her one day.

But he would never love her wholeheartedly. And Phoebe didn't think she could bear the pain of knowing that he would eventually draw away from her. He might even learn to hate her in the process. In time, he would begin to regard her as the woman who had come between him and his grieving.

"No, I can't—" Unable to say anything more, Phoebe tore away from him. Ignoring the rending of her heart, she ran toward the train that would take them West. And although Gabe cried out to her, she pretended she didn't hear.

If he couldn't love her completely and irrevocably, then she was better off marrying a stranger.

Phoebe was careful to avoid Gabe as the women were escorted back to the train. Since their own boxcar had been virtually destroyed, they were given seats in one of the passenger cars by a group of missionaries who insisted on moving to one of the other boxcars.

Peering through the windows, Phoebe watched Gabe and his men from a distance as they salvaged what trunks and crates they could and loaded them onto the undamaged cars. Then, to her astonishment, she saw one of his men climb a telegraph pole.

"What are they doing?" Twila muttered, echoing Phoebe's thoughts.

"They must be sending a message."

A message. What would it say? "I've done my job. I'll be leaving at the next stop."

Despite the fact that she had refused Gabe's offers of affection, Phoebe shivered. Hour by hour, mile by mile, her time with him was drawing to a close.

She could only hope that she would have the strength to leave him when this journey finally came to an end.

By the following afternoon, Phoebe discovered the gist of the message that had been sent from the top of that telegraph pole. Besides relaying a report on the well-being of the gold, Gabe had also provided for the mail-order brides. When the train pulled to a halt in San Francisco, the women learned that their husbands-to-be had been brought to meet them at the company's expense.

The brides were thrown into a flurry of preparations. In no time at all, blankets had been strung over the windows to provide them some privacy. Soon the railcar smelled of perfume and singed hair from the curling irons placed in the chimneys of lanterns.

The excitement grew to a fever pitch—so much so

that Twila's smelling salts made the rounds with all the brides.

All except Phoebe.

Her heart lay heavy in her breast as she dressed in the indigo silk gown and sapphires that had been retrieved from Edith's things after the attempted robbery. Phoebe had wound her hair in a simple coil, then collected her reticule.

"Are you coming with us, Phoebe?" Maude called at the door.

"Go on ahead," she replied with what she hoped was a beaming smile. "Now that I have my own things back, I need to return some money to Mr. Cutter, then I've got to send a telegraph to my sister, warning her to be careful. Once I've done that, I'll join you outside the church."

It was clear from the way the women paused, their expressions growing concerned, that they didn't completely believe her blithe explanation.

Twila grasped her hand. "You don't have to marry Mr. Ballard, Phoebe."

Since the others were still waiting for an answer, Phoebe shook her head. "I know that you think I've fallen in love with Mr. Cutter, but I can assure you I haven't. I was merely...swept away...in the excitement of the journey."

Dodging their sad gazes, Phoebe stood stiffly while the other women filed from the passenger car. Then, summoning what emotional strength she could muster, she scooped her reticule from the seat and hurried outside.

One chore down; the hardest yet to come.

Pausing, Phoebe took a deep breath, her eyes darting from one end of the train to the other.

Find him. Find him quickly, then say your goodbyes.

The moment she caught sight of Gabe's lean, hardened frame, she felt a jolt in the region of her heart. Her body trembled, growing hot, then icy.

Would she ever feel true joy again? Would she ever look at Neil Ballard with even a hint of the same rush of passion?

Or would she forever wonder what could have happened if…

If…if…if…

Hadn't she already learned that such wishes were useless? The only thing that truly mattered was what a person made of life. One had to work with the cards he or she been dealt, not wish for the moon.

Stiffening her shoulders, Phoebe realized she had best finish her errands. If she didn't, Neil Ballard might come looking for her, and that would never do. She would not shame the man by confronting him with evidence of her infidelities. He would never have reason to fear that she would betray their vows.

Lifting her skirts free from the dust and rocks, Phoebe slowly made her way toward the front of the train. With each step she took, she rehearsed what she would say. Above all else, she must stay cool, calm and collected.

She wouldn't cry.

She wouldn't beg.

Phoebe was only yards away when Gabe looked up. In that moment she was consumed with emotion and sensation, so much so that she stopped, unable to continue any farther.

Please, please, don't let me lose control, she begged of herself.

Forcing herself to look at the man who stood at Gabe's side, Phoebe recognized Josiah Burton. Then Gabe excused himself and moved toward her.

Each step he took caused her heart a tangible twinge of pain. Within the hour, they would be parted for good.

Gabe came to a halt a few feet away from her. But she couldn't ignore the way he hungrily studied her form.

"You look beautiful," he murmured, his voice thick with awareness.

Phoebe smoothed a nervous hand over the dark blue silk. "Thank you."

An awkward silence followed, punctuated by the beating of her heart.

Could he hear her labored breathing?

Knowing that she must finish things now, before she lost her nerve, she blurted, "I need to return the money you loaned to me."

With trembling fingers, she reached into her reticule and withdrew the small bundle of money, which she had tied in a handkerchief.

"Keep it," Gabe said tightly.

She shook her head, saying firmly, "I will not be beholden to you."

Had he caught the trembling of her voice?

Gabe's lips tightened. "You aren't beholden to me. Call it your reward for a job well done."

Phoebe felt as if he'd slapped her. Was that what their relationship had been?

Gabe swore. "I didn't mean... Damn it, I was referring to the capture of the Overland Gang."

Knowing it would be foolish to try to speak, Phoebe

thrust the bundle into his hand. ''Goodbye, Gabe,'' she whispered through a throat tight with tears.

Lifting her skirts, she tried to run away, but she'd taken only a step when he grasped her elbow.

''Is that all you have to say to me, Phoebe? An airy goodbye and then...nothing?''

She stiffened, anger stirring in her breast. ''What more would you have me do? Kiss you? With my husband-to-be waiting at the church?'' She shook her head. ''I won't do it. I won't disappoint him that way. Nor will I trade a lifetime of security for a man haunted by grief and secrets.''

''And what about you, Louisa?'' he demanded, hauling her close. ''What secrets are you hiding?''

''I'm not hiding anything!'' The moment the words were spoken, she froze, realizing her error.

She had responded to the wrong name.

Whirling, she tried to break free, but Gabe held her fast, forcing her to turn and face him.

''Who are you?'' he whispered forcefully. ''I know for a fact that you've taken a name that isn't your own. Who are you trying to protect? Why would you live a lie?''

Chapter Nineteen

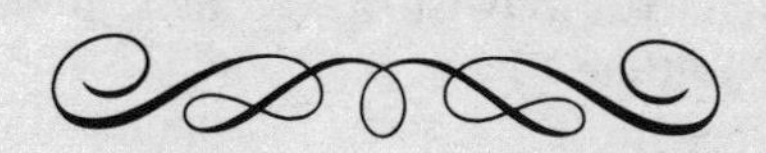

Why would you live a lie?

The words echoed in Phoebe's head, filling her with an unnamed sadness and fear.

Yes, she had lived a lie. She had assumed an identity not her own in order to escape a future she had considered to be nothing better than a prison. She had sworn she wouldn't tell anyone what she had done.

How had she revealed herself? Were there others who had uncovered her deceit? Had she endangered her sister's position through her own carelessness?

Sobbing, Phoebe searched for an avenue of escape, but could see none. Even if she managed to free herself from his grip, there was no place she could run where he wouldn't find her again.

"Please," she begged. "Please let me go."

"Damn it, Phoebe...Louisa..." He exhaled harshly. "I don't even know what to call you. I don't know who you are."

She swiped at a tear that plunged down her cheek. Misery twisted her stomach and threatened to break her fragile attempt at control.

Don't tell him anything. You promised to take the secret to your grave.

But when Phoebe looked up to find Gabe watching her with his own brand of sorrow, she couldn't remain silent. ''Sometimes I don't know myself.'' The words were torn from her mouth, frightening her with the anguish they revealed.

Again she tried to twist free of his grip, but he held her fast. ''Tell me.''

She bit her lip.

''Trust me!'' The words were little more than a whisper, but in an instant she was reminded of all she had given to this man—her body, her heart and her unconditional love.

''Louisa,'' she offered in a choked voice. The moment the word was spoken, she felt as if a great weight had lifted from her chest. No matter what her past had been, or how joyless it had seemed to her at the time, it was *her* past, *her* history. By denying her identity and her struggles, she had denied a part of herself.

''My name is Louisa Haversham. I am the only daughter of Oscar Haversham, Marquis of Dobbenshire....'' Her words trailed away. ''At least, I thought I was his only daughter.''

Gabe released her gradually, making sure that she wouldn't bolt.

''So Potter was right. You do have a sister.''

She shrugged. ''I have to believe him. He had no reason to lie. He knew he was dying.''

''Does your sister know yet?''

Phoebe shook her head. ''I've just sent a telegram warning her to be careful. But how could I explain anything more in the brevity of a telegram?'' She laced her hands together and stared at the wrinkles forming in the leather of her gloves. ''You must think I'm horrible to deny my birthright by switching places with my sister.''

''No. I don't think you're horrible.'' Reaching into the pocket of his shirt, Gabe retrieved a ring and held it out to her. Phoebe gasped when she realized that it was the signet ring she'd sold in New York.

''But how—''

''I went to visit with Adam after you'd sold him this. He'd been quite excited about the sale, so it cost me a pretty penny to get it back.''

She took the ring, wondering at the pure joy that flooded her system as she took its weight in her hand.

Why did she care so much? She'd hated her father. Why would such a link to her past prove anything but painful?

But as she slid the gold circlet over her largest finger and held it up to the light, she realized that she had been instilled with far more family pride than she had imagined. Distantly, she remembered that things hadn't always been so bad. Vaguely, she recalled a jovial grandfather with large jowls and a booming laugh who had drawn her onto his knee for peppermint drops and stories. Even the long succession of mothers had not been without advantages. The women had honestly tried to make her feel loved.

''Tell me how you came to be here, Louisa.''

Stifling a sense of loss, she slid the ring from her finger and held it out to him. ''Take this.''

''It's yours.''

She shook her head. ''No. You've bought and paid for it.''

''Consider it a loan. One day you'll pay me back.''

''I could never repay that kind of money.'' She

steeled herself against the little voice inside her head that urged her to accept his offer. ''I'm about to marry a simple farmer, remember? I'm sure our life will be far from extravagant. Any money we have won't be spent on fripperies.''

But when she pressed the ring on him, Gabe still refused to take it. Instead, he settled it in her palm and curled her fingers around it.

''I won't accept it, Louisa. I know more than anyone how important a person's name is to them. That ring is a part of your heritage, something you'll want to pass on to your children.''

The tears came harder then. Children. Only days before, she'd longed for a time when she could be a mother with a family of her own. Now she realized that she shouldn't have a family merely for a sense of ''belonging.'' She would be no better than her father if she didn't love her offspring in their own right rather than for what they could give her.

Gabe took a step toward her, wiping away her tears with his thumbs. ''Tell me. Tell me why you would deny who you really are.''

She shook her head. ''I can't. I made an oath not to tell anyone.''

''Surely you can tell me.''

''No. I can't tell a soul.''

''But why? What can it matter who you are or what you call yourself if you are thousands of miles away from anyone who might have once known you?''

She bit her lip, struggling to breathe against the tightness gripping her chest. ''Because a life depends on it,'' she whispered. ''A life that isn't my own. Until I know my sister is safe, her secret will remain with me.''

Stepping back, Phoebe swiped at the moisture staining her cheeks. Holding the ring tightly in her hand, she said, "Thank you for this, Gabriel Cutter." Her voice wavered, but she forced herself to continue. "Thank you for everything."

She bent to grasp her carpetbag.

Gabe's jaw tightened. "So that's how you want things to end? After everything we've been through, you're going to marry the man without so much as a second thought?"

"No. I have plenty of misgivings." Her chin tilted to a proud angle. "But what choice do I have?"

"You could tell Ballard the truth, that you've changed your mind and you love me!"

The words shivered in the air around them.

Love.

Yes, she loved him, more than she would have thought humanly possible. But as she waited, she realized that there would be no returning avowals of affection. Gabe cared for her, she was sure of that. But he hadn't laid the memory of his wife to rest, and it was clear that Phoebe would always be second best. As much as she loved Gabe for the man he was and all that he had been, as much as she was willing to share his heart with a woman he had married long ago, she would not be offered a miser's portion of his affection. He must come to her with the same devotion and commitment that he'd been willing to offer his first wife, or she would not take him at all.

"Goodbye, Gabe."

Without another word, she turned and walked through the station house toward the gaggle of women waiting eagerly for their prospective mates to find them in the sea of passengers milling about the front stoop.

But with each step she took, Phoebe mourned the fact that Gabe hadn't been hurt enough at the prospect of losing her to call her back.

"Phoebe?"

She stopped, looking for the source of the call, knowing in her heart that she was about to come face-to-face with Neil Ballard.

But when she searched for the slight man with the curly hair and receding hairline who had posed for a picture he'd sent with one of his letters, she came face to face with one of the largest men she had ever known. He was tall, towering over her like a giant, broad-shouldered and powerfully built. He made her feel small and insignificant in comparison.

"Yes?"

"I'm Neil Ballard."

In an instant, all her preconceived notions of the man scattered to the four winds.

This was Neil Ballard? This immense mountain of a man?

"Oh." It was the only sound she managed to push past her lips. "But I...that is, you don't..."

He had the grace to look sheepish. "I don't quite match up with the picture I sent. Truth be told, I mailed one of my business partner's photographs rather than my own. I was afraid I might scare you off."

When Phoebe continued to blink at him in surprise, he swept his hat from his head. "Welcome to California."

Then, without further warning, he swept her into his arms and bent his head for a hungry, passionate kiss.

* * *

Yards away, Gabe took an instinctive step forward, his hands balling into fists, but he stopped himself just in time.

No. She wasn't his. She belonged to that man.

As much as he tried to convince himself of that fact, the idea didn't sit well with him. Ballard was all wrong for her—big, impatient, insensitive. No doubt the burly farmer would have her married and bedded before darkness fell.

No. No!

But even as he strode toward them, Gabe knew that he had no place deciding what was right or wrong for Phoebe Gray—or Louisa Haversham. He had given up that option the moment he'd refused to tell her that he loved her.

Growling in disgust at his own jealousy, Gabe altered his course and retrieved his mount instead. Swinging into the saddle, he urged the gelding into a gallop, not knowing where he was riding—and not really caring. He merely wanted to exhaust himself so that he wouldn't think, wouldn't feel.

Damn the woman, anyway. She was no good for him. No good at all. She argued far too much. She was willful and stubborn and…

And beautiful and loving.

No. He mustn't think about that. She had her own life to live. One that didn't include him.

And who was to blame for that?

Pulling on the reins, Gabe took a deep shuddering breath.

She could have been yours. If only you'd told her you loved her.

Bit by bit, Gabe became aware of his surroundings.

He'd come to a stop on a hill overlooking the rail yard. Turning his mount, he was able to see the crowd gathered below. In an instant, he found Phoebe and the giant of the man who had come to fetch her. They were walking toward town, and clenching his jaw, Gabe noted they were heading in the direction of the church along with the other women.

So he was right. She would be married in a matter of minutes and he would be left…

Alone.

Completely and utterly alone.

No. He mustn't think about that. He had to remember that this was the best course of action for everyone involved. Phoebe would have the life she had chosen and he would have…

Nothing but regrets.

Damn it. Why couldn't he forget her? He'd known Phoebe for less than a fortnight. Surely his memory of her would fade as quickly as his passion for her had developed.

But as he watched the distant couple move closer and closer to the church, he was filled with a desperation unlike any he'd ever known.

Why? Why did he hesitate? Why didn't he ride into town and wrest Phoebe away from that giant? Why couldn't he see that his future was slipping from his grasp? He'd seen battle and confrontation, hate and savagery. What did he have to fear from admitting his love for a slip of a girl?

Gabe trembled, his hands clenching around the reins until he thought his bones would crack.

He loved this woman with the same depth and breadth of feeling that he'd had for his first wife. And therein lay the problem. When Emily and Nathaniel had died, he hadn't thought he could go on. He'd been wracked with a grief so profound that he'd longed for death himself and had courted it at every opportunity. He couldn't bear to go through such loss again. He would die a thousand times if anything happened to Phoebe.

But wasn't he losing her already? This time through choice rather than misfortune.

Panic bubbled within him, then frustration, then self-loathing. Damn it, hadn't he learned anything from his wife's passing? Hadn't he learned that life was precious and that love was not to be squandered? Was he ready to turn over his chance at happiness to a total stranger merely because he was too cowardly to risk the future?

No.

No!

Reaching up, he tore the chain from his neck. Closing his eyes, he offered a prayer of farewell to his wife. He would always love her. But, as Phoebe had once said, Emily would not want him to live a life of sadness.

Nor would she want him to remain alone.

Tucking the chain and Emily's wedding ring into his pocket, he dug his heels into the sides of his horse, urging it into a gallop.

He loved Phoebe. If he let her go, he would never forgive himself. If she would give him a chance, he would spend the rest of his life convincing her just how much he cared for her.

Dear sweet heaven, don't let him be too late.

Thundering into town, he raced down the dusty main road. Ahead, he could see the last of the women entering the church, Phoebe was nowhere to be seen.

Damn it, had the man rushed her inside before she could even get her bearings?

Giving no heed to the commotion he caused, Gabe rushed full speed toward the church. He was nearly there when he spied Phoebe and Neil talking in the garden next to the graveyard.

With the barest touch of his reins against his horse's neck, he changed course, riding toward the woman he loved.

She looked up at him in surprise, and in that moment, he couldn't deny how much he had hurt her. She had offered him her heart and he had failed to give her anything in return. At that moment, he vowed that this woman would want for nothing from him. She would have his love—given openly and honestly. He would give her the life she deserved, one with roots. By hell, he would build her a house with a white picket fence and hollyhocks growing under the windows if that was what she wanted. He would fill the rooms with children and love and laughter.

But first, he would have to convince her to give up her planned, predictable future for an unknown one with him.

Gabe knew the precise moment she realized that he was galloping toward her. Seemingly in slow motion, he saw her turn. He registered her shock and then the first flicker of hope.

Willing her to believe in him, he thundered toward her, uncaring of the attention he was attracting. He thought only of this woman and the future they would have together.

Miraculously, Phoebe must have read a portion of his thoughts. Gradually, he saw her wounded expression fade to uncertainty, and then to hope. He saw her turn to Ballard, could read the words *I'm sorry* crossing her lips.

When Gabe held out his hand, she didn't hesitate, but reached up to him so that he could scoop her from the ground and lift her into the saddle. Turning, he called to Ballard, "I'm sorry for the trouble you took in bringing her here, and I'll reimburse you for the expense. But she's mine and I won't be bringing her back."

Before Neil Ballard could offer an objection, Gabe urged his horse into a gallop, not stopping until he had reached the cool green shadows of the upper slopes.

Phoebe clung to Gabe as he headed toward a canyon just north of the station. Within minutes, they were swallowed up by the narrow rocky walls. Keeping to a narrow trail, Gabe expertly traversed the banks of the swift moving creek for several miles. As they traveled, climbing up the gentle slopes of what Gabe briefly identified as Burdock Mountain, the greenery around them grew more lush, the air perfumed with the tang of pine and the sweet smell of wildflowers.

With each mile, the tension that had gripped Gabe for days began to seep away, leaving him with a peace he hadn't known in some time. No matter what the future might bring, he knew that he'd made the right decision by stealing this woman away from Neil Ballard.

Nudging the horse to the right, Gabe spurred the animal toward an even fainter trail, climbing to the top of a pine-covered swell, then stopping at its summit and gesturing in front of him.

Phoebe's lips parted when she looked down into the magical valley below. Like a piece of jeweler's velvet, the green meadow, heavy with grasses and wildflowers, stretched for miles in either direction.

Needing a few minutes to gather his thoughts so he could properly express his love, Gabe said, "I own one hundred acres in that valley. I bought it two years ago when I couldn't think of anything else to do with my wages. I'd had a happy life with Emily, and I thought that someday I might return to working with the land again."

He frowned, wondering if he should have mentioned Emily at all. But when Phoebe waited patiently, he knew she hadn't minded the mention of his late wife.

"In the years since, I've discovered that I'm not much of a farmer." Was that a shadow that passed over her features? He was quick to allay her fears. "But I love ranching—cattle and horses, I'm thinking. I also thought we could plant an orchard. Apples should do well. And cherries."

He saw the way she caught her breath, as if fearing his use of "we" had been a slip of the tongue.

"We'll build a house there, on that little knoll. That way, you'll be able to see everything from your windows. There's limestone in the canyon that we can use, or timber. Or maybe you'd like a little of both." He drew her firmly against his chest, wrapping his arms around her body as he pointed. "The barn and stables can go there. There's fresh water that bubbles out of the rock close by. We'll build you a springhouse to keep your milk, butter and eggs cold if you've a mind."

He paused, knowing that the moment had come when she could crush his own hopes for the future.

"Could you live with me?" he asked, his voice full of unspoken need. "As my wife?"

He felt her shudder against him, and he hurriedly added, "I know that we haven't known each other for long and that I haven't given you a reason to trust me. But I love you, Phoebe...Louisa...whatever your name might be. Hell, we'll give you a new name if you want, as long as you'll hook it to mine. I've been a coward and a fool, but when I saw you walking away from me, intent on marrying another man, I knew that I couldn't live without you. It was hard losing Emily and my son. But I'm still alive and it's long past time for me to move on. I loved them, there's no denying it. But the feelings I have for you are just as real and sweet, and I can't deny them any longer."

He felt her trembling again and feared that she meant to refuse him. But she turned, wrapping her arms around his neck.

"I th-thought I'd lost you," she sobbed. "And suddenly my life wasn't worth living."

Then she was kissing him, her body straining against his, her hands sweeping around his thighs to the hollow of his back, where she gripped him tightly.

"So you'll marry me?"

"Yes," she cried against his neck. "Yes, yes, yes!"

"Today?"

"Yes."

"You're sure?"

"Yes, oh, yes."

Her answer was a sigh against his lips, a promise and a benediction. When they kissed again, it was with a tenderness that went beyond words. Their caress was at once seeking and reassuring, hungry and satisfied.

Gradually, their position on Gabe's mount proved a

hindrance, and he slid to the ground, lifting her, carrying her, until they reached the shade of an old oak.

"I love you," he whispered again as he lowered her to the ground, his body resting intimately over hers, his hands sweeping each curve and hollow, absorbing the slickness of the silk and the heat of her body.

No longer shy, Phoebe began her own intimate exploration, moving her hands from his chest to his shoulders and then returning. Eagerly, she released the buttons of his shirt, then his union suit, pushing the fabric away. He hissed with barely suppressed desire as her fingers trailed wantonly over his bare skin.

Not wishing to be outdone, Gabe reached for the buttons marching down the front of her indigo bodice. But within moments, he drew back, swearing.

"Good hell, almighty," he exclaimed, his voice raw with desire. "What kind of contraption are you wearing? There must be a hundred buttons."

She giggled, pulling away from him and kneeling. Then, one by one, she unfastened the round glass spheres, taunting him with a striptease more erotic than anything found in a burlesque house—or even the Golden Arms Hotel. Inch by inch, she revealed the pale, creamy skin, rounded breasts pushed high by the tight lacing of her stays, the globes barely contained by her corset cover. Finally, she shrugged out of her jacket, then stood. Releasing a single button at her waist, she revealed the elaborate concoction of batiste, boning, lace and silk ribbons that comprised the foundation garments of a gentlewoman.

Within seconds, she'd unbuckled her bustle and stepped from the cage of wire and twill. Tossing it aside, she unhooked her corset, the tie of her petticoat.

Gabe's heart pounded within his breast as she

slowly revealed the final layer of her underthings—delicate silk drawers dripping with lace as fine as a cobweb, elaborately clocked hose and a ruffled chemise held in place with little more than a pair of ribbons.

Unable to stand another moment outside of her arms, Gabe pulled her close, whispering, "If Ballard ever saw you this way, I would have killed him."

He felt her smile against his cheek. Then her lips chased soft butterfly kisses across his jaw. Twisting his head ever so slightly, Gabe covered her mouth with his.

At that point of contact, the passion flaring between them could no longer be contained. There would be time enough in the future for leisurely explorations. They had a lifetime ahead of them. But at this moment, they longed for the deepest expression of adoration, a melding of minds and bodies.

Gabe held back as long as he could, drawing the sensations out to their fullest extent, creating a dramatic sense of pleasure and pain. Eventually he allowed Phoebe to undress him completely. Then he settled over her carefully, skin sliding against skin in exquisite agony. Preparing her, gentling her, he finally plunged into her waiting body, watching her expression for each nuance of thought and sensation.

When she reached her moment of release, he felt a rush of pure joy. And then, as she continued to move against him, there was no time for coherent thought. Gabe abandoned himself to his own pleasure, reveling in the profound sense of gratification and freedom that he felt in her arms.

Gone was the nagging cloud of regret, the self-recrimination, the yearning for escape. This was where he belonged, with this woman, in this valley.

Together.

Man and woman.

Husband and wife.

It was much later before either of them found the ability to speak. They'd lain in each others arms, Phoebe's voluminous petticoats serving as their only covering.

"I could have lost you," Gabe whispered, still stunned at how much happiness he had nearly thrown away.

"I have a confession to make," she murmured after a moment of silence. The tip of her finger continued to trace idle circles on his chest.

"You've absconded with my pistol? You never did return it, you know."

She smiled against him. "I *had* forgotten about that. It's still hidden in my things."

He toyed with her hair, hair that had come undone during their lovemaking so that it spilled over his chest like an auburn waterfall.

"Then what have you decided to tell me?"

She paused a moment before responding. "When you came charging toward me on your horse, I had already explained to Neil Ballard that I wouldn't be marrying him."

Gabe grew still, knowing how much that refusal must have cost her pride.

"I couldn't go through with the marriage, no matter the cost. I told him I would pay him back with interest, but that I intended to use the last of my money from the sale of my ring to return East. I would go as far as my coins would take me, then find a way to earn my passage the rest of the way.''

''What changed your mind?'' Gabe breathed, knowing how close he'd come to disaster. If Phoebe had gone through with her plans, she could have boarded a train and disappeared, leaving him no clues to help him find her.

She rested her chin on his chest and met his gaze, her eyes growing dark with remembered anguish. ''I changed my mind when he kissed me,'' she admitted. ''Up to that point, I had convinced myself that I could be happy with Neil Ballard and that my emotions for you had developed through our close proximity during the journey.'' Her voice became rough with emotion. ''But when he kissed me, I felt nothing but regret. I knew then that it would be better to spend my life alone rather than involve another person in my misery.''

Gabe drew her to him, kissing her slowly, sweetly, his embrace a measure of thanksgiving and delight.

''You'll never leave me,'' he stated.

''Never.''

''And you'll never doubt how much I love you.''

''I'll never doubt you.''

Again they kissed, the sweetness of the moment becoming tinged with the heat of desire. Softly, slowly, they caressed and cuddled and loved until the passion could no longer be ignored. Then their leisurely enjoyment faded beneath a wave of passion.

As he took Phoebe into his arms, their bodies joining as one, Gabe offered a quick prayer to heaven for allowing him this moment, this woman, this promise of fulfillment. Never again would he take such emotions for granted. He would cherish Phoebe for the rest of their lives together.

Epilogue

A pink tinge was beginning to color the sky when Gabe and Louisa finally dressed and made their way toward town again.

"I don't plan on wasting a single minute," Gabe murmured in her ear as they rode. "The second we reach town, I'm taking you to the church."

Louisa smiled, her body deliciously relaxed and heavy. "You'll get no objections from me."

She felt his arm tighten around her waist. "I'll be resigning from the Pinkertons, but there should be a reward for apprehending the Overland Gang. We can use that to begin construction of the house and—"

He wasn't allowed to finish as she drew his head down for a hungry kiss.

The moment their lips met, the world around them disappeared. Louisa knew there would be time enough to make plans for the future. But none of that mattered as much as assuring herself that they had weathered the storms behind them. Ahead of them was a bright, shining future for the battle-scarred Pinkerton and his mail-order bride…or rather, another man's mail-order bride—

Suddenly, Gabe broke away. "What am I supposed to call you?"

She smiled, feeling very much like the cat that had stolen the cream. "Darling?" she offered softly.

"Besides that."

She thought a moment and said, "Louisa. Louisa Haversham. I'd better use my real name, since I intend for this marriage to be completely legal and binding."

Grinning, Gabe spurred the horse into a gallop, eloquently revealing his own impatience to have all of the formalities finished.

They arrived at the outskirts of town in time to see the other brides gathered on the church steps.

"There she is!" Betty shouted, grabbing the arm of the sandy-haired gentleman at her side.

Forgetting the men they had recently married, the brides surged forward to greet her. With all of them talking at once, it took a moment for Louisa to catch her breath.

"Where's Mr. Ballard?" Louisa asked at the first opportunity. She felt a touch of regret—not for abandoning him, but for all of the trouble he'd taken to secure a wife who would marry another.

"He's gone!" Twila exclaimed.

Louisa bit her lip. "Was he really that angry with me that he went stomping off?"

"You don't understand," Maude said excitedly. "He took the first train East."

Louisa gaped at them in surprise. "He did what?"

Betty clapped her hands, jumping up and down. "I hope you don't mind. He looked so forlorn that we..."

"That we decided he needed to know the truth," Maude interjected smoothly.

"The truth?"

"Ooo, we told him all the tantalizing details—about how you were a twin without even knowing it and how you'd switched places with your sister in New York," Maude continued.

"*I* was the one who mentioned Mr. Potter and his attempts to kill you," Doreen said.

"Yes, and we all pitched in about your uncle and how he had threatened to kill you and your sister," Twila said.

"Ja, ja!" Heidi and Greta said in unison.

"Then you'll never guess what he did!" Betty exclaimed.

Louisa stared at them, feeling completely befuddled. "What?"

"He gathered a rifle and some supplies from the store in town—"

"My *husband's* store," Doreen interrupted importantly, clinging to the arm of a gentleman who was at least fifteen years her senior.

"Yes, that's it. He took everything he'd bought, gathered his horse from the livery, then left."

"Left?" Louisa echoed weakly. "Left where?"

"For Boston!" the women exclaimed in unison.

"Boston?"

"Yes!" Twila exclaimed, her cheeks flushed with excitement. "He said that he'd come to the train to meet his bride-to-be, Miss Phoebe Gray. And if she wouldn't come to him, he would go to her."

Suddenly, Louisa understood what the women were trying to tell her. "Neil Ballard went after my *sister?*"

"He was very upset about the threat your uncle posed," Maude said hurriedly.

"Yes! He realized that there were no guarantees

that she wouldn't have married by the time he arrived, but he was willing to take that chance."

"And he intends to bring her back!"

"As his bride!"

"*Ja, ja!*"

If Gabe hadn't supported her, Louisa was sure she would have fallen.

"He's already gone?"

"He left nearly thirty minutes ago," Betty said. "He said to thank you kindly for preventing him from marrying the wrong woman."

"Evidently, he'd fallen in love with your sister through her letters," Maude added.

"So he's gone to claim her."

Louisa took a breath, then began to laugh, slowly at first, then with more heart. "He's gone to fetch her?" she asked again, still unable to believe what she'd been told.

"Yes!"

Turning to Gabe, she slid willingly into his arms. "Should we do something more to help her?"

Gabe thought a moment, then lifted her head so she met his gaze. "As much as I would like to send an army after him, I think that Ballard would have a much better chance to help your sister on his own. She'll be safest if no one knows she isn't the woman she claims to be."

Louisa bit her lip, wanting to do more, but knowing instinctively that Gabe was right.

"Is he a good man?" she asked the grooms, who waited a few feet away.

"The best you could find."

"Cream of the crop," another offered.

"He's got a temper," Doreen's husband began, before his new wife elbowed him in the stomach.

"She'll be fine, Louisa," Gabe said softly.

Knowing that there was nothing more she could do, she turned to him, hugging him close.

"Then I suppose we'd best get married before the preacher thinks he's seen the last of the mail-order brides."

Around them, the other women squealed in delight at the news.

Swinging Louisa into his arms, Gabe carried her into the church, his own eyes shining with a joy like none she had ever seen in his gaze before.

"Perhaps, after we're married, we can take a honeymoon to Boston," he added with a whisper.

In that moment, her heart swelled with limitless love. Instinctively, Gabe had sensed the one obstacle to her total happiness.

"I love you," she whispered as he carried her up the aisle toward a very startled pastor.

"And I intend to spend the rest of my life showing you just how much I love you, how much I've been in love with you since that moment I found you weeping on the ship and gave you my best handkerchief," he murmured.

Louisa gasped, staring at him in astonishment as memories of the gentle stranger swept through her mind.

Then, in front of the pastor and the newly married mail-order brides, he kissed her with the same white-hot passion that had blazed between them from the very beginning.

And in that instant, she knew what it really meant to belong, to be loved, to be cherished.

For now and for always.

The pastor cleared his throat. "If you would kindly surrender the bride for a moment, we'll take care of the formalities," he said wryly.

Laughing, Gabe allowed Louisa's feet to touch the floor. Clinging to his hand, she peered at him closely as they repeated their vows.

She couldn't help but note the difference between the woman who'd stood before a man of the cloth to be bound to her proxy husband, and the woman she was today. Her journey had been a long one—not just in miles, but in emotions as well. In barely a fortnight, she had lived through more pain, delight, dread and exhilaration than she would ever have thought possible. She had begun her trip as an impatient child longing for escape and a certain amount of revenge against her father. But somehow, in the intervening time, she had become a woman. She'd learned to appreciate the fragility of life and the importance of love.

But most of all, she'd found her soul mate.

This time, she was conscious of her vows, conscious of every word that was spoken. The ceremony was without flowers or music, and in the absence of a wedding band, her heavy family signet ring served as a substitute, but Louisa didn't care. All that mattered was Gabe.

Once the pastor had proclaimed them man and wife, Gabe bent for a passionate kiss, one that sealed the promises each of them had made. Then, swinging her into his arms once more, he strode down the aisle in the same manner he'd arrived.

"Don't you want to join us for dinner?" Betty called out.

''Not tonight, thanks all the same,'' Gabe answered without turning.

''Will you be staying at the hotel with the rest of us?''

The women smiled at them indulgently, and Louisa was grateful that they would live nearby. During their travels, they had all formed close relationships that would last the rest of their lives.

At the doorway, Gabe paused and turned. ''Sorry. Phoebe—*Louisa* and I already have a plot of land nearby begging for a house. Come tomorrow, we'll see what we can do to make us a home.''

Home.

The word resonated in her heart, filling her with joy.

Yes. In Gabe's arms, she was finally, finally home.

* * * * *

What happens when Neil Ballard
catches up with his ''real'' bride?
Be sure to watch for Phoebe's romance
in
THE OTHER GROOM
coming only to Harlequin Historicals
in October 2003.

For a sneak preview,
please turn the page.

Chapter One

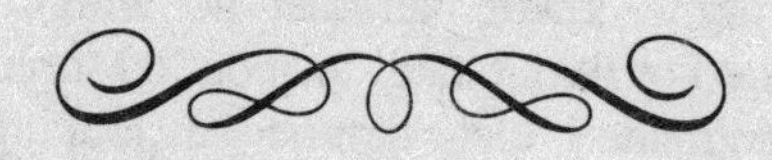

The moment was here.

So much planning and preparation had led up to this moment, Louisa realized. The real Louisa Haversham had long since donned the name Phoebe Gray and headed for the wild and woolly West, while Phoebe—or rather, *Louisa,* as she would be known for the rest of her life—had waited for her husband-by-proxy to show himself.

Not for the first time, Louisa felt a burst of pique. When she had agreed to assume the life and destiny of her friend, it had all seemed so simple. The real Louisa Haversham had been married by proxy to a wealthy American businessman, a Mr. Charles Winslow III. Weary of the life of a servant, the real Phoebe had impulsively agreed to marry Neil Ballard.

Dear, sweet Neil. They'd both been so young when last she'd seen him. How long had they proved to be an inseparable team at the orphanage? Two years? Three? Then, finally, his aunt had sent for him and he'd moved to America to become a farmer in Oregon. Yet even then their friendship had endured through years of correspondence. Indeed, Louisa would wager that they had each revealed more about themselves in their letters than they ever would have in person.

Shifting uncomfortably, she pushed away the wave of guilt that threatened to be her undoing. In hindsight, she realized that she never should have agreed to marry her old chum. The thought of living in the untamed wilderness of the American territories and becoming a farmer's wife had filled her with trepidation. She was tired of living hand-to-mouth. Moreover, Neil Ballard had made it clear that he was looking forward to having a woman to help "take care of his property."

Drat it all! By marrying him, she would have doomed herself to a life of servitude.

She pushed aside her misgivings about her cavalier treatment of an old friend as her attention was momentarily distracted by the blast of a whistle. Turning, she caught sight of a plume of smoke darkening the sky above the jumble of buildings in the distance.

He was here.

Her husband was finally here.

Convulsively, her gaze swung to the stranger who was standing next to her. She felt his presence in a way she'd never encountered with another human being. It was as if her body was attuned to him in an elemental way. As if she knew him...

Despite the huff of the approaching train, she studied the man more closely. Why, of all the passengers milling on the platform, was he the only one to capture her attention so completely? There was nothing about him that should have inspired such interest. He was dressed in rough buckskins, with his dark hair left long so that it tumbled across his collar. Indeed, there was something...heathenish about him.

No. That wasn't right. Not heathenish. Untamed. Elemental.

Unconsciously, she moistened her dry lips. The man looked as if he had recently arrived from the American wilderness. Undoubtedly, he lived the very life that she had shunned—one fraught with hardships.

So why did she find him so intriguing?

For a split second their eyes locked. Louisa was stunned by the flurry of sensation that tingled at her extremities and traveled inward to settle with a molten heat deep within her.

In that instant, she felt more feminine and beautiful than ever before.

The feeling ended when a loud bang split the noon-time air. Before Louisa could fathom what was happening, the giant in buckskins launched himself toward her.

In a rush, she saw the looming shape of his body, felt the impact of sheer muscle and bone. Then she was falling, falling, her body banging against the rough boards of the platform, the giant's frame protectively covering hers.

The world seemed to screech into slow motion, each sensation becoming sharp and distinct. Distantly, she heard the startled cries of the other passengers, the screams of fear. Tiny rocks bit into her back and arms.

But most of all, there was the heat, the strength, the power of the manly form that stretched over hers. A whiff of something like pine. The gentleness of his breath as he whispered, "Easy, easy." Even in the terror of the moment, her mind honed in on the weight pressing into her, the scent of soap and the inexplicable wave of possessiveness emanating from this man's body.

Then time seemed to stop completely. Dust motes hung suspended in the air, sound receded and there was only this moment, this stranger. Louisa became suddenly aware of the face that hung over hers, the angular jut of his chin and cheekbones, the chocolaty darkness of his eyes.

Those eyes.

Why was there a part of her that seemed to recognize them—as if she'd known him in another life? She felt as if she were melting into their depths. Instinctively, she gripped his arms. And when he began to close the distance between them, she did not resist....

The sudden shriek of a train whistle caused them both to start. In an instant, the noise shattered the intimacy that had twined around them like a spider's snare.

Horrified at her own reaction, Louisa became aware of the curious stares of the crowd, the horrified expression of her maid, the shriek of the oncoming train.

What had she done?

She mustn't allow herself to forget who she was. She was *Mrs.* Charles Winslow III, and she mustn't forget that fact.

COMING NEXT MONTH FROM

HARLEQUIN HISTORICALS®

• **THE NOTORIOUS MARRIAGE**
by **Nicola Cornick,** author of LADY ALLERTON'S WAGER
Eleanor Trevithick's hasty marriage to Kit, Lord Mostyn, was enough to have the gossips in an uproar. But then it was heard that her new husband had disappeared a day after the wedding, not to return for five months…and their marriage became the most notorious in town!

HH #659 ISBN# 29259-7 $5.25 U.S./$6.25 CAN.

• **SAVING SARAH**
by **Gail Ranstrom,** author of A WILD JUSTICE
Lady Sarah Hunter prowled London after dark to investigate the disappearance of her friend's children and unwittingly found herself engaging in a dangerous game of double identities with dishonored nobleman Ethan Travis. Now, would Ethan's love be enough to heal the wounds of Sarah's past?

HH #660 ISBN# 29260-0 $5.25 U.S./$6.25 CAN.

• **BLISSFUL, TEXAS**
by **Liz Ireland,** author of TROUBLE IN PARADISE
Prim and proper Lacy Calhoun's world was turned upside down when she returned to her hometown and discovered that her mother was running the local bordello! And even more surprising were Lacy's *im*proper thoughts about the infuriating and oh-so-handsome Lucas Burns!

HH #661 ISBN# 29261-9 $5.25 U.S./$6.25 CAN.

• **WINNING JENNA'S HEART**
by **Charlene Sands,** author of CHASE WHEELER'S WOMAN
Jenna Duncan was sure the handsome amnesiac found on her property was her longtime correspondent who had finally come to marry her. But when Jenna learned his true identity, would she be willing to risk her heart?

HH #662 ISBN# 29262-7 $5.25 U.S./$6.25 CAN.

KEEP AN EYE OUT FOR ALL FOUR OF THESE TERRIFIC NEW TITLES

HHCNM0503